WESTERN KNIGHT

JULIE G MURPHY

WESTERN KNIGHT
Copyright © 2020 by Julie G. Murphy

ISBN: 978-1-68046-975-2

Published by Satin Romance
An Imprint of Melange Books, LLC
White Bear Lake, MN 55110
www.satinromance.com

Published in the United States of America.

Cover Design by Caroline Andrus

Thanks to my kind-hearted friend Barbara Allen for reading and editing this book hot off my computer.

ACKNOWLEDGMENTS

Information about The Nez Perce Indian War was taken from a booklet titled, *Nez Perce Indian War and Original Stories,* printed in 1966 by the Idaho County Free Press, Grangeville, ID and written by Norman B. Adkison, a friend of my grandfather. Original names of some the settlers involved in the war are real, though their stories have been altered thus making the characters and situations fictional.

Cox and his friends are thanks to the Public Library of Cincinnati and Hamilton County's reserve section. They are historical figures, but they didn't, in their day, interact with the characters in this book. Lefcadio Hearn was a newspaper man in Cincinnati, and he did write *Beauty Undraped.* I couldn't resist using his name; what author could? The historical Lefacdio didn't go west with Mac and Maggie.

CHAPTER ONE

Kentucky, 1875

M agnolia Bathurst, Maggie to those who knew and loved her, watched her mother die. Blood poisoning. All the endless, probable last day, her mother had been lingering. With the priest droning the prayers to the Last Rites into the room as an unwavering single note, Maggie moved to the window. She almost wished the end would come, except then she would be alone.

"So alone," she whispered to the pane. Her breath misted the glass. She balled her hands into fists to stop the tears. She wouldn't cry, not with Sir Guy, her stepfather, and William the Weak and Pandering, her stepbrother, in the room. He's just nineteen, her mother used to say. Yes, nineteen unsuitable years of purposeless life, Maggie would retort. A lazy, pretty boy, blonde, white teeth. What consolation could two, practiced conmen bring her anyway? None. They had what they had come for, Garth Estates, in all but name and ancestry.

She looked up to the sky and thought, *with my last breath, I will make sure that they don't get my bloodline.* She promised that to her father, a man long dead to everyone but her.

"They're criminals. William is in Randolph McMillan's gang," Maggie had said countless times to her mother.

Even now Maggie could hear the reply in her mother's Kentucky-accented voice. "I don't believe it, darling. They're just rough around the edges. They haven't had the benefits in life you and I have had."

Maggie stretched the aching muscles in her back. Her mother had never believed her. Soon, according to the will, Guy was going to become her guardian.

She needed to wring out another cool cloth for her mother's forehead but didn't have the energy. Her stepfather's strong cologne irritated her. It reeked of false piety, and it was a reminder of her mother's stupidity. How embarrassing to have a mother so infatuated with this man. How could she not see that Sir Guy Didsbury had married her for money? Damn him. She'd said that to her mother too.

"He does have other traits," her mother had replied with a gleam in her eye.

If only she could live. If she just could live. A sob erupted from Maggie's throat.

The doctor had given the patient a palliative two hours before, so her mother, at the moment, neither lived nor died, but seemed to float between heaven and earth. She'd be pain free long enough for the priest to finish. Long enough for Grace Bathurst to reach God. Saint Grace. Maggie had heard the title so often.

"I'm no saint," Grace had said on a laugh. "I just always try to do the right thing, like anyone would do."

"Then you're foolish for letting a person of such repute into our house. Daddy would be shocked."

"I'm shocked that you are talking to your mother that way. Guy is setting everything right. You just have a plank in your eye when it comes to him. He's not as well-spoken as your Daddy was—"

"Well-spoken! No, he's not as well-spoken or as near a gentle-man. Guy's a rogue, a bacteria that infects our lives."

"You refuse to see the man as I do."

Tears filled Maggie's eyes now as they had then. She remembered running out of the room when her mother had told her to have more respect. More respect! For the devil? She heard Guy mumbling something about how he loved Grace, and Maggie thought of her mother's always-expectant look when Guy walked into the room. The thought made her angry again. Maybe there was room in avarice for love or whatever Guy felt for her lovely and loving mother, but avarice was Guy's first passion.

Oh God, will the priest never end? Daddy, I have become so hard.

It was all Guy's fault.

It was dark out except for a large, full moon to give the evening ample light. The fireflies would soon come. *I will miss them.*

Maggie's mouth went dry thinking that soon she'd be out in the evening shadows. The plan had been to leave earlier, in the daylight, but her mother had lingered, and the priest had arrived late.

At the window, leaning her forehead against the pane, she used its coolness to bring sanity back. She couldn't wait much longer. She needed her wits about her. The shadow-lit lawn gave her some hope of success. Gazing at it, she remembered visions of herself playing on the grass, croquet with her father. He used to put his arms around her, hold her hands curved over the mallet, and then would give the ball a great wallop, which had felt like a shot of vital strength traveling up her arms. Her father had promised her a knight. Seems like her mother had gotten one instead. Her dream, her promise had been upended.

Maggie wrapped her arms across her chest. The night was hushed, no wind, as if waiting for something, for Grace. Where would she find the energy to leave everything dear to her? She wouldn't think about it. It would be just a stroll to the stable, and then an evening ride.

Damn the will that would be read within the next few weeks.

She had to leave—now. She would never marry William. She would ride away. Surprise was her only ally. Keep ahead of Sir Guy and his plans.

She jumped as something scratched against the window. Ah, a breeze coming up. The branches of the magnolia tree—whose leaves died and fell throughout the long year, stiff, downed leaves that passed through rigor mortis before being raked and burned—swayed in the wind. She'd been named after that weed of a tree. Her mother's favorite, and Maggie hated it. *You and I, Mother, have never seen life in the same way.*

She turned. Father O'Grady prayed, sounding like he was the one dying. It was all taking too long. Months of preparing, soon all down to the final minutes, would he not finish! She wanted to put her hands over her ears as he continued to pray Latin into the shadows of the room lit by a single gas lamp by Grace's bed.

Crystal drops hanging from the lampshade reflected spots of radiance that danced on the priest's black coat as he anointed his patient's yellowed forehead. The crystal glint sprinkled over the dying woman and on her soft green spread—stilled brilliance.

Quiet yourself, Maggie thought, *or Guy will read you like a book.* She walked to the bedside, picked up a wet rag and squeezed it. Water fell through her fingers, chiming droplets as they cascaded back into the bowl. She pressed the cloth to her mother's cheeks and then took Grace's hot hand. Time seemed to have stopped. She breathed with her mother, in and out, in and out. No, the priest was doing it right for Grace. She must be grateful.

Father O'Grady closed his prayer book. The blessed vials of holy water and oils clanged together as he replaced them into a black leather case. Oh God, the time had come. She didn't want to go. How could she go and leave her mother dying on the bed, leave her home? She tried to swallow the catch in her throat.

"She is a good woman." Father kissed the stole around his neck and then folded it and put it on top of the glass bottles.

"That was very nice. Mother would be pleased. Will you have a cup of tea?" The time to go had been hours earlier, but to put out the priest without ceremony would seem inhospitable. It was getting so late, though. She would have to slip out while the priest was still here.

It was a four-hour ride to Cincinnati and a hotel room already booked there. She'd already sent her luggage ahead. She knew the road well. It had seemed a stroll in the park weeks ago when she had first started planning. Mitchell, the family lawyer, hadn't liked the idea of her riding out by herself. He had spent the entire two weeks plotting alternative scenarios, but she knew Guy would never guess her plans if she were alone.

Now at eight o'clock, the shuttering of the day, her courage, an echo of her confidence with Mitchell, was finding excuses— like tea with the priest.

"I'm going," William announced. "I can't stand this anymore."

How awful he is. But hadn't she said that until she was blue in the face? Even a single night in this house without Grace was unthinkable. She let go of her mother's cool, waxy hand. She'd settle the priest and then she'd be gone. Guy watched her with a long look that lasted until the door. She knew as she hustled Father O'Grady out that she was making a mistake. It was too fast, but her courage might fail.

As the door closed behind her, she heard William say, "No, I won't stay. I'm late already, and I've done enough. I've had enough of this death." She imagined Will's truculent study of the floor, his lip curled in a pout under his spotty mustache. He could never look Guy in the face, meet his eyes; his growth hadn't stretched to his father's height.

Guy was stuck. Good, she had been counting on it. Lady Luck was shifting to her side. She moved the priest faster. What a boon, William was helping her. He'd leave; he had that much strength, and then with the priest in the house—and a front to maintain, Guy would have to stay at the bedside. *Consider it a fee, Guy, for all you are about to control. So damn hard to leave Garth, daddy's study, the swing we*

5

sat on together hour upon hour, but until I am married, Guy is going to be my legal guardian. I'll be married to William by the end of a year. God, no, no, no. He wants my Garth blood to legitimize his presence here. I have to leave now, but I will be back.

She settled the priest into the drawing room in a floral chair by the window. Her father's portrait used to hang here, the last gentleman on earth. All she had ever wanted was what her father had promised: a knight who would love her as no other man could.

"I'll go out to the kitchen myself to ask for the tea. Everyone there will be waiting for some news. Please make yourself comfortable."

Maggie arrived to the adjacent building that housed the kitchen.

"How is she?" Millie the cook asked. The large black woman wiped her wet hands on a towel and then wiped her forehead.

"Not in any pain. Guy is there. Would you take him a large whiskey and take the bottle with you and leave it? I'll take the priest tea." Maggie watched Millie put on the kettle. A comforting, familiar gesture associated with better times. Tears flowed into her eyes. She turned to lay a tray.

"You look like you've been shot at and hit. Put that tray down and go up and rest yourself."

"But Father O'Grady?"

"I'll take care of him. I doubt it's a cup of tea he wants."

Millie reached for a bottle of tonic. She poured out a large measure. "Take this, no, no arguments. Nothing worse than grief and being sick in one body."

Maggie drank and then coughed and blew air up her windpipe to dispel the heat in her throat. "My God, what is that?"

"It settles the nerves. Another spoonful... no, take it... just one more. Now go rest for a little while. Don't worry. If you sleep, I'll wake you." She hugged Maggie, picked up both trays and said as she left, "I'll bring you a chocolate in a half hour."

As the warmth of the second spoonful spread through her, Maggie watched the cook leave, the woman's broad hips skimming the door jam on either side. Millie always said a kitchen was the center of any house—even if it was next door—and then she'd laugh. Food was the great healer. Maggie inhaled the herbal scent of the room. She exhaled. There was no rattling in her head now, no mental pain, just softness.

Maggie lifted heavy legs that seemed like someone else's. Her hand didn't shake, wasn't hers, as she opened the door to the courtyard.

What's in that tonic? Oh my Lord, it's good.

Her mind felt soft as she walked into the darkness without emotion. She stumbled at a snap of lightning and straightened with the subsequent thunder. It was her only misstep as she reached the threshold of the stable.

Good luck vindicated her. Confident fingertips reached up to a rail for parlor matches. She lifted the glass shade of a lantern, and then with a strong percussion of thunder, she dropped it— butterfingers. She struck a match; the wick caught. Next, bridle, and blanket, and saddle. *They won't be looking for you just yet. Be calm.*

The next clap of thunder rattled the wooden structure and disturbed the dust. Wind flung open the open and it smacked a wall. Maggie dropped the bridle on her foot. Her light gutted.

Her fingers seemed thicker as she struck another parlor match. At the same time that the match took, a lightning bolt struck just behind the stable. She dropped the burning end into a bed of hay. "Damn, damn, damn." She stamped on the flames like a devil's dance.

Oh my God, it's out. Thank God it's out.

Still, smoke thickened the air. The lightning was coming in quicker now, bolt after bolt. She leaned on a wall and rubbed at her temples. "Get the bridle...put it on Lady Fair." There was another close sizzle and a crack, like a hard slap to the face. The horses snorted and began pawing at their stalls. "Whoa," she called over and over as two animals tried to climb over their rails.

She closed her eyes and pressed her fingers into the pain in her forehead. It was all unraveling. Illumination from the bolts high-lighted the windows. What was she to do? Her mind wouldn't cooperate.

Think, girl, think before someone comes out.

A horse kicked through his door. Its eyes were white with fear. Her precious horses, she cooed and talked. Another sizzle of lightning, but farther away.

The storm is moving.

Through the open stable door, she peered at the sky. A bolt lit the courtyard, the stable, and her body at the open door. In the light, she noted Guy, at Grace's bedroom window—and he stared at her. Maggie's red blood cooled blue. The storm had him at the window, and now with the next bolt, he was not at the window.

He was coming for her.

She ran, across the long lawn and into the woods. Any brightness through the trees was periodic. Honeysuckle bushes ripped her skirt and bodice and scratched her arms and legs. Her feet seemed to trip over every root and rock. She picked herself up but was beginning to feel that it was easier to stay down. A picture of Guy in a tearing rage, bursting onto the courtyard, was the only clear thing in her mind. Her back itched with the thought of him.

Panting, she reached the western edge of the forest near an old logging road that cut through Garth land. She leaned against a tree to ease the pain in her side, and to breathe.

"If only I could catch my breath.

"You bitch!" She heard him yell. He was so close she could hear branches break as he fell. "Ouch...Jesus-H-Christ-son-of-a-bitch."

Maggie pushed off the trunk. He was so close he might see her move. She raced forward again, running without direction, like a panicked deer. She burst into the clearing, ran toward a road, and then fell headlong into the shallow ditch meant to drain it. Something soft broke her fall. Her arm hurt. Her hands stung.

"I hate you, Guy."

The storm had found a home above her head. She was sobbing as she pushed up. She had to keep going. She had to get to Cincinnati. Everything was ready there. It had all been so well planned.

The storm increased intensity. The air sang like the voice of a steel foil. A length of lightning stabbed through the thickening air, hitting the earth—slicing it. Decibels of sound exploded. The air smelled seared. It was then, in tucking her head, in trying to become smaller as the lightning struck earth around her, she saw the face. In the brightness of another lightning bolt, she saw the eyes, the dead, glazed eyes of the man under her in the ditch.

She back-clawed from the deceased body and the blank, sightless eyes that stared at nothing. A fraction of a moment later, the ground shook. The eyes animated and a vital, blue clarity saturated them.

When they looked at her, Maggie screamed.

CHAPTER TWO

England, 1375

A breeze brought in the smell of dead seaweed and rotting fish. James "Mac" MacArthur recognized the odor of decomposition that was Arundel Castle. He followed the line of the stone cliff to its peak and then farther to the high roofline of the edifice where the FitzAlan flag hung, wrapped around its pole as a stale dressing around a festering wound. He would have died here but for Elizabeth FitzAlan.

Mac shut down the memories of his five-year-old self, the son of a traitor to the crown, a child blackened with burns to his chest and groin. A deadened manhood that has never functioned but to release piss. A boy given by the crown to the house of the devil himself as a bounty paid on his father's defection.

He'd been given no medical help and learned to live with pain. As he grew, only Elizabeth helped him cut the scars to make them stretch. A year younger, still, she taught him courage, steadfastness, kindness. She had kept the darkness at bay. He always thought of her golden hair, dark eyes, and soft, white skin in contrast to his black curls, blue eyes, and tanned muscular body…as an angel sent from God. That's the only way her goodness within the FitzAlan family could be explained.

Anger rolled through Mac as he rowed. May a pox cough its foul breath on this place and on the dark heart of its owner.

Mac lurched sideways as his oar fell short of a deep-water cut and instead splashed his friend rowing behind. The small *currach* rocked.

"By all the saints, man, concentrate! Sure as you know, I drown in water this wet, and I don't want to die before we get there, in the very small chance that I don't die when we do. Not that there is—a chance," Padric of the Black Irish growled.

"Shush, or they'll have an arrow through us where we sit."

"Then looking like innocent fishermen is a ruse that will have no weight. If we make no sound won't they be just as suspicious?"

"If we make no sound, they may not see us at all."

"Sure, as isn't it also the Lord's truth that if we were not here, they would not see us. Didn't me sister see the crow, and then didn't she throw the runes on the ground as a precaution? The foretelling is against us. Even though me sister is the devil's spawn, the Holy Mother of God Herself would come to her for a reading. She saw the crow." Strained was Padric's voice as he tried to make his point as a soft sound.

"So I've heard, more times than the hairs on my head," Mac grumbled as he readied for another pull of the oar. "If you don't let it go, the crow will be the least of our problems."

"Pffit. The crow is the sign of the Morrigan, Goddess of War and Death. Death, be jaesus."

"And rebirth."

"Only if the Goddess takes a liking to you, and only after you're already dead. *Dead.*"

"It isn't your head the crow is perched over." Mac was glad Padric wasn't part of the prophecy. He hadn't wanted Padric to come at all, but he needed him, and Padric wouldn't remain behind anyway.

Mac thought of the visions of his own that had been poisoning his sleep for weeks, and lately their death-images had been leaking into his day as well as his night.

Rooted to the soil, as were the trees around him, with the wind high and the sky dark with rain, he holds his chest as blood drains from a wound in his heart.

He shook his head to clear it. No good going into battle with ideas of defeat.

"We don't need your sister's prophecy to tell us to take care at this place, and anyway there is no other way. Just thank God the weather's good, and you're not seasick." Mac let the sound of his voice ground him.

"God, is it? God is shaking his beard at us. We're a twicepair of idiots, so we are, like lambs to slaughter and without a bit of sense. Hell's damnation to the FitzAlans, that castle, and this freezing, leaky boat."

Padric liked to complain to ease his fears. With the sound of his friend behind him, Mac concentrated on the rhythmic movement of the oar in his hand to drain the taint of seers, oracles, and childhood memories from his mind. He wished again he hadn't had to bring Padric here, to this place. No choice, even if he could have gotten Padric to stay away. He arched his back to give some stretch to old scars that had contracted in the cold night air.

"This is the last time. This is the last one."

"Sure as I've heard that before. I'm getting too old for this kind of outing. Saving flocks of helpless women is trying on me sorely. They should all be brought up as bitches and save us the trouble."

"I've never seen you run from a gratuitous kiss."

"And be jaesus, ye never will, but *eistigi liom.*"

"I *am* listening."

"*Bi curamach.*"

"I *will* be careful."

"Ye won't be foolhardy from the love ye have for Elizabeth. Ye're too close to this, so ye are. Your thoughts are not as single minded as the task requires."

"Padric—"

"I know the story. She saved ye're rotten life, but not to have ye give it to her now."

Fillean meal ar an meallaire, Mac said.

"Put evil in retreat me arse!" Padric spat back. "Evil doesn't retreat. Evil is a sore loser, and it sticks to my legs like a parched leech. Me sister's rarely wrong."

"I wouldn't mind the rebirth part. I wouldn't, so." Mac finished with an Irish lilt, hoping for an easing of his friend's mood.

"It would be easier to kill the plague-spot Elizabeth's slated to wed. Done and done. No marriage, no need of our services."

"If you see him, be my guest. He's already here."

Closer in, Mac had been startled to see the Plague-spot's heraldic flag hanging from a lesser pole above the Castle. The groom had arrived early.

The edifice had grown as the skin-sided boat moved across the water. Mac straightened. He lifted his wooden paddle out of the mirror of dark water and let the boat slow. The light of the bright, full moon disappeared as the craft skimmed into a long and solid shadow cast by the cliff and by the castle walls that grew up from it.

Mac heard the sound of Padric's oar reappearing from and then disappearing into the surface mist of the sea as his friend eased the canoe to shore. The rhythm calmed his mind as he blocked all further thoughts triggered by the looming building in which the taunts of FitzAlan and his son seemed to penetrate every crevice. He had to do this, take her out of here.

That's all there is, the contest and the prize. That's all there's ever been.

When the bow of the boat touched rock, Mac thought, *I have returned.* He stepped into the water and held the craft. "Well, get out."

"Never hurry an Irishman," Padric whispered. As he climbed over the side, the boat rocked with light sucking sounds from the shallow disturbed water. "Jaesus, this water's as cold as my sister's smile."

"It'll keep you awake then."

"I think the water's colder here than at the other side."

Leaving Padric to hide the boat, Mac searched in the bramble for a small path. "It's here," he said when he heard the rustle of the forest floor and knew that Padric was at his back.

"Would you like to go first?"

"The Irish always go second."

"What's going second got to do with being Irish?"

"Don't ye know, all Irish learn from the cradle the generosity of not going first?" Padric wiped his wet hands on his coarse linen shirt. "Besides, the Irish are also very practiced at guarding their backs."

"That isn't just an Irish specialty. Not here anyway."

Mac didn't hear anything human beyond Padric's inhale and exhale. No animals sounded. He breathed air that was pregnant with water droplets not yet swollen enough to fall back to earth as rain. The humidity coated his skin with a film of water. In the silence, the beat of his heart pounded within his mortal ears.

As he climbed, his possible death seemed more and more a reality than a vision. This was a campaign that needed a kiss from a well-meaning miracle, and only a fool counted on the unknown. No, he wouldn't be sad to leave behind his scarred body that had kept him from marriage, from children, but he had three people to get safely home. Mac stared at the castle, concentrating on it and thereby moving his thoughts to a better place. He had to be success-ful. There was no other choice.

The path wrapped to the right side of the castle. Rock changed to tangled blackberry, fern and ivy. Thorns picked at his tunic. As the track wound farther right, bushes gave way to oak and poplar.

At the edge of the trees, he crouched low to pause and get his bearings. Mac hoped that Molly and Elizabeth were prepared for him. Elizabeth stood to his chest and could fit under his arm. He remembered her tiny form standing firm before her father and in front of Mac's beaten body, all five feet of her. She had stopped the man's cane with nothing but determination, and then she had untied Mac's wrists herself, never leaving his mangled form. He might find her beaten this time. His anger flashed like an extra beat of blood through his veins.

Her father had laughed with each stroke, a sound like the pitch of a grinding, metal cog, a sort of greaseless whine. It hurt his ears to even think of it. Mac could still feel her soft touch washing his back and the sweep of her velvety hair across his shoulder. He could smell her light scent of distilled roses.

Padric needed to worry. Mac would do anything for Elizabeth. He would even die.

As if he had been listening to Mac's thoughts, Padric made the sign of the cross while dropping to his knees in the dirt next to his friend.

Mac grunted. "You never warm a church bench and hate priests."

"Himself owes us," Padric whispered.

"The problem with invoking the gods is that their plans are never quite what we hope for."

"How much traipsing through the building will ye be doing?"

"Just along the west parapet and down some stairs. Molly should have put the rope over the wall and drugged the guards by now."

"With poison, I hope. And if you don't find the rope she *should* have put out? What then? Will you enter through the front door?

We are mad... two women down a sixty-foot wall on nothing but a bit of tied hemp." Padric crossed himself again.

"Yes, we are. Just keep crossing yourself." Mac moved forward toward a castle profoundly black in hue and profile. He had had to come here as a child. Mac saw in his mind the charred, pathetic boy that he had been, the damaged son of a traitor. His shame had been to live. He was back now to show them all they had not won.

The rope was there, and Mac shimmied up it with not even a breeze lifting the sweat off his back. He traveled down a circular stair and along a seemingly abandoned corridor. As Mac rapped at a chamber door, his hand clenched the hilt of his sword so hard his nails bit into the flesh of his palms. Getting in had been easy, thereby saving the worst, condensing it so if trouble came, it would come in spades. His back itched.

"Oh, so there ye are." Molly, Elizabeth's maid, opened the door. "About time. This night has finished the graying of my head. So it is just ye, and ye didn't bring some army to back us."

"What is it about the Irish and their backs?"

"What is it about the English and their fronts? Wouldn't turn my back to one."

"You got the rope out."

"You climbed it."

"And the guards?"

"Sleeping like old men with their mouths open and drooling." Elizabeth stepped forward and touched Mac's arm, his chest. She looked him up and down seemingly for wholeness, for certainty.

"I am here." He hugged her. She wasn't hurt. It had been a needless concern. Her father couldn't transfer damaged goods.

That would soon be the husband's prerogative.

"I see that you're both ready." He laughed at the women in men's togs. "Down to the gloves. Molly, you're a miracle. I think you could manage this escape by yourself."

"Go on with ye. You're a sight yourself, and I wish there were at least ten more of ye. I can't die tonight; I haven't seen the priest."

"Padric is with me."

"Padric, is it? The Blarney stone's been rubbed smooth by that mouth. Jesus, Mary, and Joseph, and my knee is giving me fits."

"It will be better in the boat," Mac said as he closed the door and the light from the bedroom extinguished. "I will take the rear. Molly, you fight off the front."

"I thought ye're here to take the front and the rear," she muttered as she walked toward the stairs.

Elizabeth said, "You are wonderful to come. We are in your debt." She wiped at tears.

"It is my honor and my turn. Go quickly, or Padric will come in looking for us."

From slits in the round wall, moonlight stretched long across the circular stairs in a regular ascending and descending pattern. As Mac waited for the women to climb, he watched their hands hold the security rope that was attached to and wound around the center stones of the stairs. It bounced.

He took hold of it himself. It scratched his palm. The smell of the burning tapers triggered a memory. At nine years of age he'd clung to this rope as FitzAlan's only son Malcome used his foot to try to shove Mac to his death. Mac remembered the repeated blows to his shoulder.

Glancing down, Mac recalled the feeling of endless air under his dangling feet and the vicious blows to his hands and head by Malcome's boot. Mac had managed to avoid one stroke and that action had Malcome kicking into the air. Set off balance, Malcome fell. He broke his arm and leg, not his neck, and continued to limp until the day Mac left. *And probably beyond*, Mac thought as he climbed.

With Malcome, Mac had learned there never was an inevitable outcome in anything. Life had taken on a new glow. Suddenly glad to be here, Mac dashed up the rest of the stairs with the rope in his firm fist. The castle had lost. It held no more power over him. As he climbed to the fresh night air, he knew what had begun when he was five was now finishing.

At the top of the stairs, Mac followed the ladies onto the walkway. The round globe of the moon arched over the top of the castle. It lit the entire cove in a dawn-like soft light. An increasing wind had blown away the low mist, and an incessant sound of black surf lapped at him.

In the slight distance, black clouds were annihilating the starry sky. Soundless bolts of light sparked. He grabbed an arm of each of the woman and pulled them down the parapet to the ladder. The rain swept over them too soon, falling laterally, pushed by an increasing gale. Water washed Mac's face. His wet clothes stuck to his skin. The worn wooden floor became slick. Soon water dripped from the end of his nose, and he knew they were in trouble. There was to be no miracle. Never an inevitable outcome, Mac reminded himself. He knew at this moment, Padric would disagree.

The women clung to each other like threatened children as Mac leaned over the wall and cursed at the rope ladder, which was dancing itself to death in the discordant music of the wind. Padric waved him down with emphasis. Mac turned back to the women, who looked like carved wood, a quiet scream on both faces.

He could leave them back in their room. The drugged guards could be explained, the rope dropped to the ground. There was nothing else unusual, but the plague-spot was here. There would be no other chance for Elizabeth. The sleeping guards would make them cautious. He shook Molly until her eyes refocused. "Look at me. You've got to go. You can do it. Your weight will hold the ladder down. Padric is at the bottom."

"My weight, is it?" The words were forced out between chattering teeth.

A response. Mac breathed easier. He took her arm and pressed her toward the wall. "Don't look down; only look up. Keep a good hold on the rungs. Padric will let you know when you're close. I've never known a woman as fearless as you." The strong wind blew her cap off. The gust sounded hollow in Mac's ears, like the sound of a seashell held close. "Just hang on for your bloody life," he yelled.

Molly stretched her body onto the ladder. "Fearless indeed," she yelled at him. "Suicide, that's what this is."

"It's freedom, Molly. It's the price of freedom."

Mac steadied her until she had moved past his grip. *If she falls, I will never forget watching her die.* After ten lifetimes of light to dark and dark to light, of mind-numbing thunder and cold rain, he saw her fall, but only the final rungs onto Padric. They both collapsed onto the ground, each rounding on the other. Thank God, she had made it, and with fight still left in her. Only one more prize: Elizabeth. She hadn't moved. Her feet seemed suctioned to the wet floor like a barnacle to a post in a foaming sea.

He thought of getting her out through the castle. She hadn't Molly's muscular strength. No, they were lucky they hadn't been intercepted up to now. At least no one would be out for an evening stroll.

Elizabeth's cap was also gone, and her lengthy hair whipped her face. He rubbed her forearms, trying to invigorate her. As an extension of himself, his arm around her shoulder, he moved her forward.

"I will do it."

"Of course you will. Molly has already gone down. She'll be there with Padric. So you see, it's easy." He pitched his voice as to a frightened animal.

The seconds stretched by with Elizabeth hesitating at the castle's edge. Mac sweated the time, feeling it move around him. He slapped her—once, twice, leaving marks on her cheeks. He couldn't pity her now. They would both die.

She had to mount the rope, no other choices. He felt the sting in his hand. Madness. He reached for her, but her eyes had gone flinty and hard. She evaded his hand. She slapped him back, with strength. Thank God and all the angels and saints. He would give more to the holy church.

"He'll hit you. Every day. You'll be his wife, and in his bed, and on your knees to him. Get on the ladder and save yourself. Now." She could be strong.

Her body shuddered, and then she elbowed away from him and climbed onto the parapet. She breathed in and took hold of the rope.

"You can do it."

After he couldn't reach her anymore, Mac doubled himself over the stone edge while holding what he could of the ladder, like trying to hold a snake. When her foot slid, and she hung by her arms, he thought of getting to her, but the ladder couldn't hold both weights.

Why hadn't the blaspheming craftsman made it stronger? Mac hadn't thought to to specify. She'd die from his stupidity. Her feet kicked the air. The wall and the wind inflicted bruises to her body. He'd killed her. With every body blow, he said, "Jesus, catch her."

Light to dark, dark to light, Mac could feel his over-pumped blood coursing through his neck. Her grasping legs caught a rung but slipped again. She called to him. Another near footfall and another, this one stuck.

"Holy God," Mac breathed out. Years later, it seemed, and Mac feeling as old as a white beard, she collapsed onto Padric.

Padric had agreed not to wait, but to get the women settled into the currah. Mac stepped onto the rope. Lightning flashed and then a drum roll to battle. The storm highlighted his descent in crescendo and in white color. His nightmare dreamscape swirled around him through the heavy gale. Mac touched ground and moved along the castle, close to its side.

He turned the corner to find Malcome and a band of knights coming forward. He ducked back by habit, but they had seen him. Malcome called his name. Here it was then, what he must face. A sort of resignation released Mac's shoulders and calmed his mind. He wanted it, to do battle with Malcome. He always had. Every day, every hour, he had been waiting to end the line of FitzAlan.

Mac couldn't run toward the bay. He about-faced and led the soldiers away from the top of the path, in the only open direction, back along the castle.

"You never pitied me." Mac spoke to the building as he moved along the hard stone. "I compared you against all else in the world and used the knowledge to be better; to save others, and in the last I have rescued Elizabeth when no one else would. You have lost her, and now you will lose Malcome. I promise you that." When the castle and the cliff became one sheer drop to a churning ocean and a nest of honed rocks, Mac turned his back to the chiseled stone. He was far from the bay, far from the *currach*. He knew Malcome would follow him, focus on him, and miss everything else. Malcome could not envision women climbing down a wall to their release. He wouldn't even look for them. *I am his prize. He also has something to finish.*

Mac laughed at fate, at its heavy-handedness and lack of conscience. It used people. The men following him were closer now. He leaned against the cold stone, absorbing Malcome's maleficent smile, a death grin, it seemed to Mac.

"I thought it might be you," Malcome shouted. "Hoped so. Trying to get in? No one to let you in the front door? No welcome home?"

"Pray, don't be other than yourself for me, Malcome."

"I asked myself when I saw you, who is that crawling on the wall like a loathsome, vile cockroach in this storm?" Malcome called over the cacophony.

The tempest clapped over the top of Mac, its reverberations echoing over the waiting men. As they shuffled behind Malcome's back, Mac knew the weather had raised the skin on their necks. In flashes of light, he saw uncertainty in their frozen masks. Bolt after bolt burned the heavenly ceiling above them all. Malcome didn't see the disquiet of his men. He didn't look to his back, never had.

Malcome thought himself invincible.

"Oh, savior knight." Malcome had to yell with his large lips.

Mac knew the men behind Malcome. They didn't want to kill him, but they would fight him for their lives. He readied when his nemesis signaled two soldiers. With a single swing of his blade to their nervous throats, Mac dispatched them to hell. Two more, just as frightened, came on their heels.

Mac wanted to last until Malcome had to challenge him with his own blade. He would have to wait. FitzAlan's son would throw everything in front of him first. The next two went down with a gash to the face and a stab through the belly, then three more, these most hesitant.

He had nearly bested them all, and then the castle, tired of the game, gave up its adopted own when, with Mac's back against hard stone, a lucky thrust cut through his heart. The storm had reached its zenith in sound, light, and severity, and with thunder booming in the falling man's ears, and with the last pounding efforts of his failing heart, before the soldier pulled the sword from Mac's chest; Mac hurled his knife at Malcome's laughing face.

Cradled in falling, as if caught by invisible, black wings, Mac's blood pumped through his fingers at his chest. His dark vision had come to fruition. Wet grass cushioned his cheek for only a moment. He lived long enough to hear Malcome's death yell and then the loud, harsh call of a crow. The Crow, the Morrigan, Goddess of death, destiny, and rebirth. Padric's sister had been right, as Mac had known she would be. His life given in sacrifice. He drew in his last breath and let the Goddess take him.

CHAPTER THREE

Within the black void of time that carried Mac, sensation started again. The phenomenon began with a fluttering in his chest and the feeling of warm blood reaching his toes one solid beat at a time. He felt the first intake of air. Breathing was restricted for a moment and then that passed. His face tingled with raindrops falling on his skin. He heard the storm whistling around his ears, distant and then much stronger, until it filled his mind with noise.

A life-taking pox on the infernal tempest. Hadn't he died be Christ!

Opening his eyelids, he saw, across two hand-lengths of space, a face. His eyes met hers. Elizabeth? No, she mustn't have come back for him. The face screamed in his ear. He could feel her weight lift off his body. Christ's blood! They have her.

Mac's mind wrestled with his legs in trying to stand.

"I'll shoot you as a dog. You'll not have Grace's daughter," a man's deep voice bellowed.

Malcome? Damn the man to Hades. And…who was Grace?

Mac rolled to his side and pushed up to his knees; Elizabeth couldn't protect him again. Rising, and then moving to stand in front of the woman, he reached at his hip for a broadsword that was not there. Neither was there a castle at his back or a pile of dead men at his feet.

The world moved, and his eyes went black for a second. When they cleared, Mac saw a man; it was dark, but he could swear the man was not Malcome. The woman was not Elizabeth.

The man pointed the thing in his hand at Mac's chest.

"He's going to shoot you," the woman yelled.

Before her words registered with Mac, she threw herself at him, her arms around his waist, and her full weight as momentum to take Mac down to the ground. He heard two sharp retorts of gunpowder.

Exploding powder; no wonder the man is so confident. Stupid though, firing into the darkness.

The next sound was a click, and then another, click...click, click, click. The woman shifted to the side. Mac made his legs spring forward. Like a battering ram, Mac hit the man's stomach. Mac knew himself to be weak. He expected a quick rebound from the man. Mac tensed for it, but the man's belly was soft, and he lay on the ground moaning. Mac broke the man's nose with his fist.

"Is he dead?" The woman approached Mac.

Mac, bent at the waist and breathing hard, shook his head. He closed his eyes and tried to slow his breathing, and then he unfolded. He felt like he'd been squeezed through a narrow opening, the juices pressed from him, and now he had been let out to fill again with water and blood.

"Are you alright?" the woman asked him.

He probably owed this woman his life. Another woman to whom he owed his life. Padric would be on his knees from laughter. Mac surveyed the milky darkness. The edge of a moon hemmed a cloud and lit it from within. The full moon was the same. He didn't recognize any large landmarks against the sky. The air didn't smell right. No brine. He felt for his sliced heart. It beat under his hand. *By all that is holy, how did he live?* Mac knew for certain that Padric was not here. He hoped that they had gotten away.

The woman startled as if a memory had come to her. "You

weren't dead. I thought you were. So strange." She stared at him and then shook her head. I…it was but a moment. She rubbed her eyes. "Nothing is right."

The woman gave one last perusal of his body. Giving up, she walked over and picked up the other man's weapon. She held it high over the man's head as if she meant to strike him. Instead, she pointed the weapon at the man's head and made it click. Mac had thought she'd forgotten him until she said, "If only you'd killed him. Maybe, with the grace of God, he is dead." She spat the words.

———

A woman's profanity muddied the air, and then she stopped, like she'd heard herself. A slight tremor shook her body. She pushed at the dirt in her hair.

Was she addled?

She drifted toward the man's feet and kicked the arch of one foot. From the stiffness of her body and the spitting tone of her voice, if it had been he, he wouldn't have kicked the man's foot, but run him through. She couldn't kill him. She was trying to, but she couldn't.

She waved the weapon in the man's face. "You're an idiot, Guy. Keep the damn gun loaded."

Her voice had the sound of weeping in it. He restrained his hand from touching her wet cheek. Padric called it his weakness…his fascination with women of dysfunctional grace.

She did have movement about her from a lively mind. Maybe from bravado, or the instant anger, or the quick thinking that had saved him, he would see her to safety. He would play out what was given him to do. At least it would be with an interesting woman.

"Are you in danger?" Ridiculous question. He thought of Padric laughing at his predicament. She might be, the Irishman would say, and then he would laugh and slap Mac on the back.

How, pray, will you escort the woman to safety if you didn't know where you are yourself? Mac had to think. That her clothes, and the man's clothes, were odd he disregarded; he'd traveled much. That he'd never seen the weapon was unique, but the Chinese had something similar. Her speech was odd, accented, but he could make sense of it, find in it words he recognized. Mac concentrated on the woman in front of him. She held the weapon in a volatile hand and now, again, she stood over the man, like a contradicted queen.

She knew the man, so she must know where she was. Mac ran his hand through his hair, too short from his shoulder-length black locks. He studied the landscape, hickory, maple, oak, but no smell of the ocean. The castle was nowhere. No turrets above the treetops.

The man groaned. Mac hit him again. They had to go somewhere, soon. The woman began walking toward the edge of trees. She didn't pause, or look back, but dived into the forest. She was a spirit, a fey. He had been carried off. No, this was not purgatory, nor fairies, he had felt the man as flesh. He had smelled the man's blood. He'd swear by it.

He followed and found her once more stopped and ripping her hem from the thorns of a gorse bush and swearing like an oarsman. She was a woman, moods and temper, subtle and sweet.

She was crying again. Women seemed to capitulate just at the wrong moments. They survived famine, scraping together food with the blood under their nails, and then fell to the ground at the catch of a gorse bush. Padric would say they all needed a kick up the backside, but Padric was still unmarried.

Guy, was that the man's name?

"Guy will be awaking soon." Mac's baited words moved her. She tore at her skirt, and then moved past him, hurrying forward, leaving him behind again and forgetting the weapon. She didn't seem to mind his coming with her, neither did she agree to it.

She has a dangerous idea of self-sufficiency. She is actually rubbish at it.

The gun at his feet, Mac picked it up. It resembled a French *pot de fer*, only much smaller than the French and English cannons. As minute as it was, he smelled the fired gunpowder. Was he across the water? He'd heard that such weapons were becoming common there. Froissart told him that Sir John Chandos had used them trying to regain Poitou.

Mac glanced around. It could be Scotland, a forgotten isle that he had been abandoned to, only it was too warm. Maybe somewhere in Africa where the English had been. He would find out. He shoved the weapon behind him in the waistband of his pants. With that action he put behind him that he was well, that he had no wound. For those, there was no explanation other than the sovereignty of Deity or a Goddess. He wouldn't question either.

He didn't want to lose the woman. No chance of that. He laughed to himself as he listened to her accost the limbs of brush and damn to Hades rocks and tree roots. At the moment, he knew only one thing, that he would have followed her even if she hadn't saved him, even if she wasn't hounded by fear.

With a break in the clouds, strong moonlight filtered through black leaves, faintly twinkling off the drops of water left by the rain. The foliage seemed to float; he felt a part of all places, a part of all consistent human action in them, and the woman as all women.

Mac lifted branches and parted briars as he followed her. It was good to feel better with each step, invigorated by the magic here. When he reached the forest's edge, he stopped, amazed by a large building. Highlighted windows the size of two men beckoned, such a large indefensible house on this lip of the forest, and not a soul about. It had no walls or city ringing it, only acres of clipped grass. He knew now for certain that Padric and Elizabeth and Molly were nowhere near at all.

His mind ached with a nightmare of images that needed sorting through, but if he stopped, he'd lose her. What was the other part of Padric's sister's prophecy? A woman?

She walked without caution toward a brick outbuilding. A stable from the smell of the place, and the odor seemed real enough. He watched the sweet sway of her dress and relaxed somewhat as she

27

had relaxed. She was familiar with the place. Her home. Must be so, and she was running—and Guy had followed, but he hadn't shot at her, just at him. Guy wanted her, but he wanted her alive.

Mac followed her inside and watched as she picked up a lantern. She knew just where it was, and then she reached precisely above her head for something to strike to light it. The stable took on a golden glow.

Mac turned to close the stable's door.

"My God," she gasped, "your shirt. It's blood. That's blood, it's everywhere."

He ripped the shirt open, buttons flying, and put his hand to his chest. Nothing, not so much as a cut.

She touched him just below his shoulder. "No, on the back."

"The back?" So many had fallen. The garment did stink of vital fluids, sweat, and mud, but he'd had his back to the castle.

"But there is nothing there. Strange. Perhaps you lay against a dead animal?"

A voice called from somewhere outside the building they were in, and then he heard a door shut. Metal clinked; she grabbed a bridle and then picked up a saddle. Mac selected another bridle.

She was hunted. He was lost. They would do well together.

He studied the horseflesh around him, all skinny things, except one, a muscled black mare. He stepped forward.

"She bites and kicks."

"Most women bite and kick." Holding the animal's gaze, he approached, footfall after footfall, one hand out in front, one hand with the bridle behind.

"It's your neck to break if she gets the better of you."

His fingers open, Mac let the mare inhale his scent. The smell of blood startled her. He let her toss her head. He watched her withers shake, and after talking to her, he put his hand on her head, stroking her, giving her courage through the steady heat of his touch. After waiting for her hooves to still, he petted her behind her ears as he held her eyes. She tossed her head and Mac laughed.

"That's it," he said in a silken voice. Down her back and the length of her flank, he stroked her until she shivered. With his hand on her neck, his calming whispers in her ear, Mac lifted the bit to her mouth. She took it.

"That's my girl," he said and then covered her long back with a blanket.

His hand blazed the path of the cinch belt, an intimate touch on her underside. He knew that the animal was too feisty to ride and probably a virgin to the saddle. With Mac standing close, breathing against her, his scent in her flaring nostrils, he pulled hard on the cinch. She bucked and tossed her head. He let her, liking her spirit.

Mac didn't want her to hurt herself, so he led her out of the stable and mounted her before she knew his intentions. She side-stepped and shimmied. The bridle jangled. She kicked up the smell of wet dirt. He hung on to her with his thighs strong against her flanks. She tried to throw him off. She had a determination that made her interesting. She scraped his leg along a wall of brick.

"Got your own that time," he said as she danced. He let her enjoy her moment, and that is all, a moment. Time pressed their departure. He looked to the woman, who had followed him into the courtyard—expecting her eyes, knowing that they would be there, and they were. He chuckled as she took in the settled horse.

He noticed the way her wet clothes hugged her curves, her hair glowed around her head in the moonlight like a crown. She was fairy, an enchantress.

And then she barked, "That horse is a traitor to all females everywhere."

"It's a skill."

"It's a vice."

"I suggest we go."

This one was a woman of spleen. She was like Padric and Elizabeth put together in this strange world, and she didn't seem to care that her dress was wet with rain and mud and sprinkled with twigs and leaves. She knew this place, these horses, and yet she was leaving without changing her dress—riding out without a cloak or food.

She stood by her horse, her head against its neck, and then as if her back became iron, she mounted without aid. He saw her glance up to a window. It was only for a moment, and then she turned the head of her horse to the road. What was left of her pinned hair released, and flew behind her, as the animal cantered down the lane. He realized that he still didn't know her name...maybe...

Rhyannon, nymph, pure maiden, fairy queen. Guy arrived to the edge of the lawn in time to yell at them as they cantered off. Mac turned his head towards the sound. Finally the sky had cleared, and a full, large moon gave light to the world. Mac saw the bloody ravaged face of the man, and also shock and finally recognition.

CHAPTER FOUR

Maggie welcomed the scratch of her horse's mane on her forehead. The road from her home to Cincinnati had never seemed so long or black. She was tired to the bone. Things had gone a little off track, but now she was on her set course and things would be fine. Her father was looking after her from heaven. She believed that. She had to because as the night deepened and the air got colder, her dress felt wetter. The first hour or so of the ride seemed never ending, and she knew the world was indifferent. Except for the man, trailing behind.

He had been singing strange songs with "ye" and "thee" in them. The chill and the aloneness seemed less desperate with his flat baritone just behind her. If Mitchell, the family lawyer, knew she was out, with a stranger, in the dark, he'd be so angry. She wasn't alone, but to the lawyer that condition might be worse. Maggie listened to a piece of a ditty about a jaunting horse. Still, the darkness did seem less dire with the man around, even if he couldn't carry a tune.

Mitchell had been right. "All the complications," he'd said over and over. She hadn't listened. God she was tired. Yet, if she had listened to Mitchell, she would still be at Garth. She strained to see if the sweeping bridge across the Ohio River was anywhere near, and then all she had to do was cross the river, ride the few blocks to the Saint Nicholas Hotel, and then drop into the deep feather bed that waited for her.

With the monotony of sitting in the saddle at night for hours, Maggie knew she was fighting sleep. Catching herself at the beginning of each slow slide toward the dirt road, she'd straightened and widened her eyes. If she could just close her eyes for a moment, just a moment of sleep, that's all she wanted. If she could just let her troublesome lids close. Her mother was gone. She'd never see her again. It would all be easier if she could escape into a syrupy slumber.

Later, Maggie woke from a deep sleep on the stranger's saddle, and in his arms. He must have shifted her over from her horse. Drowsy still, she snuggled into his warmth. Years fell from her mind. Childhood. She had ridden like this with her father, safe and coddled. Reality had too much bite to it, and she pressed her eyes shut to keep it out for a moment more. She was so tired, and the male arms that cocooned her were so secure.

His breath moved the hair at the top of her head. He smelled like inside a forest, not like Guy and his splashed-on scent. If she didn't open her eyes, she'd not make that transition from sleep. With the rocking of the horse, she'd let herself doze.

She heard a voice and wondered if it was a part of a dream.

"Jesus, it is, would you look at that. Is it you, Randy? Back from the dead, and up to your old tricks? By God, that is you. Are you risen from the dead? Bribe Saint Peter?" The speaker let out a shaky laugh. "Can't believe it," the voice continued. "The way you was on the ground, I thought you took those bullets hard. We wouldn't a left you otherwise. We wouldn't have, honest."

Maggie realized the words were real. The speaker was real. She had to open at least one eye. Standing beside tall honeysuckle bushes were two shadows of men in colorless clothes. The man in whose arms she lingered said nothing.

"You ain't sore? We thought you'd had it. Looked like you'd taken about three slugs. Kind a peculiar, ain't it? Half a gun load in the back and here you are." The speaker's partner made the sign of the cross.

Now they were all staring at the man with her.

When the barrels of two guns pointed at them, he slipped her down to the other side of the horse. "Forgive me, but I don't recall either of you."

"Har, har, har. You don't remember. That's a good one. You don't remember the sheriff chasing us out of the First National Bank in Bardstown, and your horse going lame and him shooting his gun empty at you?"

She could have laughed at Mitchell's "complications."

Maggie grabbed the reins of her horse and positioned herself to mount.

"Hold it, mam. I'm pretty sure that that's my horse. Damn sheriff rode us all to the ground. We lost him in the caves, but he got our horses. Step back, little lady."

Anger sliced though her. Her mouth opened to say over her dead body, but the man who had been in the ditch tapped her in the ribs with his foot. Lose her beloved horse! No, no, no, no, no! Not one more thing. She almost stomped her foot. *Where is that damn gun?*

God, she'd lost it. How stupid could she be?

"Do something," she seethed.

The first thief chuckled. "Nothing he can do but get down off that horse, real easy."

The two mange-infested dog-men were watching their ex-partner, never getting near him and calling out his every move. Maggie gave up the last present her father had given her.

"Now, don't take this too personal, McMillan, or, you know, whoever you are," they called. "It's just as you say, stupid just is, and there are only two horses. A two-way split is better than three. You don't need them anyway. Go to Daddy. Glad you made it, though."

She lowered her head, closed her eyes and listened to the cream of Garth stable canter down the road, the hooves of her horse clopping in a steady drumbeat to the thieves' underbred laughter. She hoped the green horse threw one of them off and trampled on his snotty face. Words exploded from her. Words from her core, from the year of her mother dying, from the emptiness of all the planning, from the place she had in her thoughts for Guy—from the hardness of her heart.

"You? You!" She spit the words at him. "You are Randolph McMillian? I saved Randolph McMillan! I've been riding alone with Randolph McMillan! Where's that damn gun." Then she remembered again that she had lost it. You owe me a damn horse! Two damn horses!"

She wanted to kick him, kick Guy. She thought of...of William's irritating, deprecating drawl every time he opened his smirking mouth. The great, rich, depraved Randolph McMillan, here in front of her in an open, un-bloody shirt from her stable man. "For God's sake, button that thing up."

He wasn't moved by any of it. He was like a stone, letting her pace, letting her rant.

"The buttons are gone," he said.

Tears. She backhanded them. She wouldn't cry. She inhaled a sob. Some weight crushed her inward; the events of the days, weeks, months were turning her to jelly, and she couldn't support the world on her shoulders any longer.

"I am *not* Randolph McMillan," he said as he found a single button that had survived and stuck it in a hole.

"Who else could you be?" She shook her head and sniffed in. "Damn you." Walking up the road, she still talked. "You will have to kill me to stop me, I-Am-Not-Randolph-McMillan."

She strode away but burned to look back. He might be where he stood, or he might be just behind her with a weapon. She listened for his footsteps on the gravel on the road. She'd heard that he could break the windpipe of a person with just one hand. Her back itched, wondering if he was behind her.

Cursing him in her mind, she swept around. He hadn't shifted an inch. He was a tall man of simple masculine proportions, and he was just waiting there, with his shirt still haphazard with one button, the only button, buttoned. In his long-reaching look, she remembered his arms, the comfort there, and then she remembered that her horse was gone. That's how it started with people like Guy and Randolph; they made you feel safe.

"You conned a man out of his life savings last month, and then he shot himself, "she yelled across the distance. "You have more illegitimate children than a sunflower has seeds," she called over the hard dirt road. "You let them have my horses!"

"They had us both."

She was wet, tired, hungry, and homesick. She had snuggled against him. It was the most stupid thing she had done all night. She picked up clods of dirt and threw them at him. "Guy put you up to this."

"I don't know Guy. We had no weapons." He lifted his hands, as if to prove to her they were empty.

"You are unbelievable," she spat out. A chunk of dirt hit his forehead. Such a good feeling. He was becoming a better target as he moved closer to her. She picked up a rock.

He caught her arm like the tongue of a frog to its fly. So surprised at his grasp, his face so close, she froze. His eyes were narrow. "Stop," he said.

"You——"

He shook her arm until she dropped the rock and then he stepped backwards and let her go. "I am not McMillan."

Damn him and his "I am not McMillan" basic English he'd been using since she stumbled onto him. Damn him for acting so likable. Damn him for…everything.

"My name is Mac."

"Hah," she said as she watched him brush the dirt she had thrown off his shirt. "Oh, that's so very different." Maggie walked on. Her legs felt like lead, but her mind was racing. Glancing around, she figured she had at least four miles to Cincinnati and her hotel and her clothes. *Oh, my God, four miles!* Behind her Randolph was lagging and singing again. "He is demented," she muttered.

Half a mile later, in the wet, her shoes had shrunk, and her big toe seemed to be boring a fresh hole in the leather. She tripped and tasted dirt. Maggie rolled over and remained where she fell.

Mac paused at the foot of her aching feet.

"Comfortable?"

"Very." Damn him. He'd been strolling behind her for forever, his songs droning into her ear like the constant tap of a hammer on metal. And all the thee's and thou's and ye's... for pity's sake, he sounded like a character from a play.

Fake, that was Randolph McMillan, or Mac or whatever he called himself. She remembered stepping from the stable and seeing Guy looking at her, angry as he could be. She had dashed for cover. Not planned. But still, of all people in the ditch, *faking* his death, smeared with blood, it had to be Randolph McMillan.

Guy would never have hatched a plan that included two hard smacks to his jaw, though. And, he had shot with real bullets. But he'd missed. Guy was a decent shot. Maybe the crack in the jaw was Randolph extemporizing.

Those horrid men had thought "Mac" dead though. *They* had been with him. *They* had seen him shot. What time had it been? Had it been dark? Or maybe they were part of the con, too.

Randolph had been in the ditch and was now walking and singing odd songs through the night. All these inconveniences seemed too taxing for a man like Randolph, for his work ethic. Dear Lord, lying on the road seemed easier than figuring it all out, easier than walking one inch further. Her breaking point had come. How disappointing.

"We are in our wandering, Blithesome and squandering, Tara, tantara, teino!"

He was not going to leave her, it seemed.

A thought bubbled to the surface. Guy knew and was afraid of McMillan, of that Maggie had no doubt. Maybe she could use Randy

"Mac" McMillan. If she could control him, she could employ him. She congratulated herself on the idea. He had both power and a certain cache. She flattered herself that she might manage him for her own gain.

"Craft's in the bone of us, Fear tis unknown of us; Tara, tantara, teino!"

Then again, maybe Randolph McMillan had gone insane.

"I need to figure out how to use this." Mac took out the gun and pointed it toward the horizon.

"You had that all along?" she sputtered.

"A weapon is useless if you don't know how to work it. It's heavy enough to have done damage to one of their heads, but I wasn't close enough, and remember there's nothing inside it."

"You could have faked it."

"Ah, that might have worked." He studied the gun in his hand. "I'm not used to having the thing. Wouldn't they have used their weapons against me as I reached for it?"

It was a con man's line from a world gone mad. She couldn't understand what this was about from any angle.

Maggie stopped caring. After her burst of energy, fatigue was blowing a milky fog into her brain. With stones on the road pressing into the flesh of her head and back, she closed her eyes.

"This place is awash with horses," Mac said

Such a simple truth. She lifted her eyelids, raised up on an elbow, and gazed around herself. She regarded Randy-Mac. He had the most masculine face profile, with black, curly hair, blue eyes, and a faint growth of black beard.

"Work your McMillan magic then," she said. "You have the ability to steal, bargain, good Lord, even to buy on credit. Any one of them is a talent of yours. Seduce the man's daughter."

"A bit in the still of night for that." He flexed his muscles and stretched his back.

"The best time." She lay down and closed her eyes again.

"Methinks it would be a good idea for you to get up and hide while I am gone. After you rode from the house like the hounds of hell were after you, in a last look around, I saw an outline at an upper window. A man, I think, his hand holding the curtain. He watched you and me with a steady regard, as did Guy, who had just arrived back, the worst for wear"

His English is improving. It's a hard fake to keep up with.

"You noticed that but missed the men who waylaid us?"

"They were hiding and still. Your home had no fortifications. It seems safer in this land."

"And yet I had to save you from being shot. Excellent job," she muttered to the night air as she heard him leave. She let him go and wondered if he would come back. Why wouldn't he? He'd come this far. Why would he? What did he gain? She picked herself up and began walking, but off the road. He'd never come back. Still, she was back up and walking. The song had gone mercifully quiet, but now she was looking over her shoulder, no one at her back.

After one more half-mile of slogging down the road, she heard him calling her name from the back of a flea-bitten mule that trotted under him with a bone-crushing gate. Maggie laughed. She had to. Dignity had left the man, what with the mule not picking up its feet, all the stumbling and snorting.

"You have a beautiful smile. It flashes in the moonlight," he said to her when he arrived.

She hadn't meant to smile. She hadn't meant to warm when she saw him. She sobered herself. "Big spender, you."

"I didn't want to steal a good animal."

"For pity's sake stop it. So this animal is for me?"

"It can do for both, and I am already sitting on it."

"Both of us on one mule, with you and the animal smelling the same."

"You may continue walking if you wish. You're not smelling all that great yourself."

The bantering was too comfortable, too endearing. She looked away, baffled by the camaraderie—too much like her mother and Guy. No, she'd never be that stupid.

"I'll ride behind you," she said, remembering waking to his front. She had intended to sit straight with her hands at his waist, but as the wee hours of the morning grew longer, she rested her head on the back of his shoulder. That was all, though, and just until the bridge. It must be close now.

The sound of the mule's hooves on the planking of the suspension bridge that soared over the Ohio River brought Maggie from her half slumber. Oh God, she was here, she had made it. The buildings of Cincinnati reflected pink in the sunrise. The city seemed a blessing.

She should kneel and thank providence, and she would later, but right now, she wanted a bath. She'd pray from the tub. She kicked the mule. The animal only tossed his head and shimmied and shied. No wonder. Randy-Mac had been reining in the old thing at the same time as she had been kicking it forward, and then he jumped off the nag's back.

His feet on the floor of the bridge, Randolph McMillan, himself, gaped, his mouth open, as he walked to the edge of the structure. He rubbed his hand on the steel bands of the suspension bridge. He looked long over the side and down the length of it.

"Oh, for pity sake, now what is he doing?"

His gaze followed the bridge as it rose up from the banks of the water from mud and gray stone to sleek steel that rose upward like reaching silver fingers. Between the fingers, steel bands draped in the webbed shape of a duck's foot.

Maggie eyed him. She couldn't understand the behavior at all. There was no point. They both knew he had seen this bridge before. As he leaned over the railing she called, "Fall into the river, go ahead. I am not waiting any longer for this nonsense. Whatever you're up to, you're now up to it by yourself." She kicked the animal's sides.

All the way across the bridge, and until after crossing a trolley rail, she thought about not needing Randolph anymore. She didn't want him. She refused to stretch her ears to listen for strains of his jaunting songs.

She saw the twin pinnacles of the St. Nicholas Hotel pierce the new-morning skyline. The flags on top seemed to be waving at her. She had arrived, tra, la, la. She absorbed the solid brick structure; its arching twinkling windows, its Greek columns, its green canopies. She had arrived against all odds.

She swept off the donkey and through the door as a queen.

Maggie inhaled the flowery perfume of the well-appointed lobby. Letting its elegance wrap around her, she strode across an oriental carpet of vibrant hues and felt it cushion her steps.

At dawn, the building slumbered. The night clerk quick-walked toward her. They have been worried, she thought. *I was supposed to be here yesterday evening.* The skinny man with his hair a shell of pomade took her by the elbow and about-faced her. With his same pace, he pulled her back to the front door.

"No prostitutes."

Maggie tripped on her tongue as if she'd tripped on the hem of her still damp gown. It wasn't until he had her by the exit that she shook him loose. Words formed, "Prostitute!" Her open hand hauled back and was caught...by Randolph.

"She can't come in here," the small, suited man held his ground. "Sorry, but not even for you, Mr. McMillan."

She pulled her wrist from one man and her elbow from the other. "I have a reservation," she spat, "and I am not with him."

"Of course you have," he said, fake smile and all, "but in any case, you can't come in the front door."

"It's dawn, for heaven's sake. If I were a prostitute, I would be leaving, not arriving, you stupid man, and I wouldn't be in black silk."

Another clerk joined them and now stood on her other side. She noticed the two exchange glances that people traded when they felt superior.

"Can I be of help, Mr. McMillan?" the new idiot asked.

"You two milk-livered imbeciles, I've had a long night, and I'm tired. I'm hungry, and I have a room here, reserved since yesterday. My name—"

"I'm afraid that my companion has had a fall, a bad fall, and needs a room to lie down." Randolph pointed to his head. "We've been in an accident. She may faint at any time, here on your floor."

Randolph McMillan had the stage presence of those who live large and unbound. The clerks surrounded Maggie and hustled her back into the heart of the hotel.

"I am not with—"

"Of course, sir," Clerk One said.

"I said—" Maggie tried louder.

"And two hot baths and a change of clothes," Randolph continued, taking her arm himself and moving her ahead.

Maggie heard the word "bath" and then noted that the idiots were moving. Randolph picked a twig from her hair and gave it to her.

"You've been leaving bits of nature on the man's floor," he whispered. "I don't believe any other of the guests come in after swimming in a ditch and lying on a dirt road."

"How about you? You have one button."

"Now, if you'd just sign in for me." The little man was in a hurry and pushed papers forward. Dawn was advancing. The clerk clearly wanted McMillan and his filthy female friend to move to a more private part of the hotel.

Maggie glanced around. Her arrival couldn't have been any worse. She would be gossip fodder. Grace's daughter with that awful man and covered in mud. Fine. So she was with Randolph McMillan.

She took the book from the clerks and signed her name, pressing hard on the paper and on the nib of the pen. Her name. Yes, she was here, and she had reservations. She had survived to get here. Damn it, and after a good hot bath and a meal, and some sleep, she'd be leaving. She had her train tickets. Nothing would stop her now. She wouldn't see any of these people again for years and years, and she didn't want to.

"I have luggage here already," she said in an unforgiving voice as she gave away the pen.

With satisfaction, she watched the clerk's eyes widen in horror as he upside-down read her name.

"Of course, Miss Bathurst." He glanced up at her.

Maggie took her key. As the clerk pushed the registration book to Randolph, she side-glanced toward McMillan. It was a wasted smugness, as he was staring at the registration book like she had signed it in the blood on his old shirt. The pen in his hand, hung over the paper waiting for the puppeteer's string to loosen.

One glance at his face showed beads of sweat on his brow that had not been there before. She watched him shake his head as if to clear it. She almost touched the sudden white-pale of his face. He was ill. Maybe his heart wasn't strong. Those men had said that he'd been hurt.

He had ceased to move. Even the clerks glanced at one another. Maggie studied the sheet. The date headed a list of names, as usual. The guests identified line by line didn't bring any recognition to her, but maybe to him. Someone he had cheated. Hard to believe that would bother him. Just after the clerk stammered, "Are you all right, sir?" Randolph dipped the pen into the ink. Maggie watched him scrawl an indecipherable signature.

Giving the pen back to the clerk, who dropped it, Randolph walked away with his key without once looking back at her.

Maggie watched him leave her as if he'd forgotten she existed. Just what she wanted, she told herself, only she couldn't stop herself from staring. Something was wrong with the man. Oh for God's sake, what did she care? But she climbed the stairs after him, perturbed and angry with herself for feeling slighted.

CHAPTER FIVE

That there was something strange with Mac's present existence, he could no longer ignore. There'd been the man with the gun. Mac hardly stood and someone was trying to kill him. And then the woman, following her, but now he was alone. The huge wrongness that he had been suppressing now raced through his mind and made his ears buzz.

He weaved, unsteady on his feet, as he climbed the stairs. Never, not even walking into Arundel castle for the first time, not even in battle had he been so unsettled. In those things he had had control, a certain understanding. He didn't understand this at all. Not at all, and he didn't like it and wanted to pull back on the strings that had put him here. He wasn't full of ale, or dreaming, or demented from opium.

He walked a connecting hallway all the way to its end, passing all the dark oak doors while thinking of past chronological events. He tried to collect the chaos in his mind. He had been stabbed. Christ's blood, he did remember that. He felt a nonexistent sword in his hand and remembered the men coming at him, one after another, tiring him and beating him down. Blood spatters in his eyes. The smell of men dying. Yes, he remembered. The grimace of pain and surprise in each of the men's faces as they had been cut down.

Mac looked at his sword hand, now only a key in it. A key that didn't look like the keys he was used to. It was small and dainty. This key couldn't lock out anyone. He had been noticing since he had opened his eyes that there was a grave lack of secure holdings in this new place.

He stared at the diminutive key. And then there was the ledger. He recalled the black on white letters and what he had read, the date —eighteen hundred and seventy-five. Five hundred years. Five hundred years in the future. His fingertips braced against his forehead as if trying to collect the tension there. He was five hundred and thirty years old. He'd been stabbed in the chest, a mortal wound and now he was five hundred and thirty years old. The weight of the idea on his consciousness staggered Mac. The shirt that he had sweated through was cold.

"Christ's blood," he said out loud this time and with strength. His mouth, in contrast to his body, was dry. The slightness of the key between his fingers was like air. Looking at it, dread moved through his blood like poison. Mac stared at its gleaming metal with horror. Such a little thing to cause such fear. It represented what he didn't understand, like a date on a piece of paper. All the other small things washed over Mac. The dress, the bridge, the crisp edges of brick in the tall city buildings. It wasn't possible. He must have been unconscious for a very long time. Maybe he had been put on a ship.

The world had many places.

He was being duped. He wondered how Miss Bathurst fit into the deception. He didn't want to think of her as lying. The thought hurt him. "Ah," he said, thinking of her. "So the blade strikes both ways." But the deception was so complete as to be impossible.

He turned over his free hand and inspected the back of it.

He had aged well.

"Hey, you there, you all right, buddy?" another patron slurred. "Need...you need some help? You know...find your room?"

Mac realized then that even to a drunken man, he was acting daft. "Like the divil has your ears," Padric would say. The thought eased Mac. Padric at his back. Holding the key tighter, he stood straighter, and then turned toward a door, then to a second and back down the hallway until the number on the door matched his key. He put the key in the lock. It clicked open. That the thing worked pleased Mac. He slid inside his room.

In the dark space, he exhaled like he'd been holding his breath. His heart was still pounding against his chest. Christ, his chest! He needed more light. He couldn't figure out what to use for illumination. No fire in a grate to use to light the tapers.

Someone knocked at the door.

Christ's blood.

The knocking wouldn't end. He angrily opened the door. "What!"

A woman took a step backwards. Frowning, she said, "That sort of treatment will cost you extra. Here's your fresh clothes."

She brushed past him. "It's dark in here."

She said it as if he didn't know, which made Mac laugh.

"What's so hilarious?" she asked as she walked about touching things that clicked and then sprang to life with a yellow luminescence. She turned and sashayed closer to him. Her face wrinkled in distaste.

He thought of the burn scars on his face. Most women reacted like that.

"How about that bath first?" She walked to another door and left it open behind her. All sorts of strange noises then. Clanking, a roaring noise like water falling.

His smell, that's what she meant. Just when he thought he'd gotten used to his looks, a woman looking at him so closely reminded him that he hadn't.

She put her painted face around the jam. "What are you waiting for, an engraved invitation?" She laughed at her own joke and her displayed chest jiggled about under a garnish of not-quite white lace. "Better get in here. It's cooling fast."

45

Mac followed her lead. She had pushed her sleeves up to her elbow, and her delicate hands and wrists were wet. The tops of her creamy, well-formed breasts shone with moisture. Her waist was trim in a blue gown that fit her well. Her eyes needed no makeup. She pushed back a lock of brown hair with the back of her arm. No joy in the tilt of her head, just impatience. He leaned against the door frame, his arms crossed over his chest.

She was not the lady of the house come to make him welcome.

"I didn't hire you."

Her eyes narrowed. "You're not skunking me. I was told to come and draw the bath and bring clothes, and for your regular if you wanted it, and here I am."

His regular! He looked her up and down. This wasn't the woman he wanted.

She watched him with a look of incredulity mixed with suspicion.

"I don't have any money."

"Is that a joke? 'Cause I'm not laughing."

"Thanks for the clean clothes. Ask them for some money at the entrance."

Mac shut the door to her back. Alone again, and finally in the bright light, he pulled his shirt over his head. He ran his hand over his bared chest. Nothing! Just pink healthy flesh. No wound, and what's more, no scarring. Like a man possessed, he clawed at the "buttons" that held the material together over his crotch. He ripped through the things and dropped his pants to his ankles.

Holy sweet Jesus in his cradle. Mac almost dropped to his knees. All the burned skin...gone. Perfection. He'd never seen himself like this, and he couldn't stop looking. Blessed miracle. His hand shook as he probed the healthy flesh. He couldn't believe it. An animal-like cry released from his throat. He pulled off his boots and kicked off his trousers. He danced around the room in a joyful dance to his own music.

A Padric-voice in his head said, "Ye've died, sure as the sun in the morning, and ye've come out of it with a working stick. God bless the virgin and all her handmaids."

Mac laughed at himself. "You should be here yourself," he said to the ceiling. "The time we'd have."

Mac saw that he was dirty. He wanted this perfect self to be clean. He strutted back into the room with the bath and saw the toilet... a toilet with water in it. He pushed down the handle and watched an eruption of water. Christ. He held his brand-new toy and peed into the bowl. Not that he couldn't do *that* before, but... With joy that it worked so far, he watched the toilet flush again and then, sighing, he eased into the bath water. He scrubbed his fresh, pink skin until it squeaked. He washed his too-short hair.

He should sleep but wondered if he'd be able to. Stretching out on the bed seemed luxurious. Like the towels. He dried his back and then played a bit with the water taps.

She had left the clean clothes in a chair, but he ignored them. Naked as his exit from the womb, he figured out how to empty the tub and kicked his dirty pants and shirt into a corner. He felt along his jaw and across his cheek. It was rough with old whiskers. How had he not noticed that? He'd never been able to grow whiskers. That his face had also healed occurred to Mac.

With hope strangling the beat of his heart like the ribbon on a wrapped package, he searched for a looking glass, and strode to one in a corner. It was four feet and as shiny as cut glass. He could see part of the room in it... perfectly reflected. Perfectly. He stepped in front of it. He saw something he didn't expect: someone else.

He jumped, glancing here and there. No one, no one at all, except maybe a specter. He didn't have much faith in ghosts, but there had been another man. He slowly redirected his gaze back to the image, with more purpose this time, and there in the smooth surface... the same man. Mac held the man's eyes. They looked hard at each other. Neither moved. They both only breathed.

Then Mac widened his stare. The bed reflected behind him was exactly as it stood, as was a painting of purple mountains above it.

Then something so cold and unnatural came to him that his blood seemed to end its flow through his veins, and his temples began pounding. He tore his eyes away and then rounded the room like a trapped lion. The glass was oval and long and in a stand. Nothing behind it, thin, the bed still in its glossy front. He grabbed it on both sides and turned it to him. Again not recognizing the man there, Mac carefully again looked right and then left, as did the person in the reflection.

Horrified, he watched himself. When he reached out to touch the cool surface, so did the stranger—their hands met. Mac held his hand there while looking into the face. He moved his arm and touched his cheek and felt and saw the stroke of his thumb on his beard. He gazed at himself as his index finger followed the line of an unfamiliar nose. He felt his own fingertip on his lips and saw that they were wider, more pronounced. Not that he had seen much of himself back then, but this was not the same visage. "Jesus," he said, and then the ghost of Padric's voice finished: "Sure as ye wouldn't 'a wanted to keep the old body."

Fascinated by his control of another's hand, he watched it flex and shut, flex and shut. He turned his head right and left, studying it, the short black hair, thick and curled, the broad forehead, the solid jaw. The nose had been broken at least once, but the eyes were stable and clear.

Mac gazed into eyes that looked back at him. The eyes were a rich blue like a deep, overcast lake. His own eyes, same color, same hue, and the same expression in them that linked to his thoughts, sense of humor, and personality. *The eyes are mine; they are me.* This relieved him—this fact that he could see his own thoughts reflected to him through his own color of lens.

He didn't want to look anymore. He turned the mirror to the wall. Wasn't there always something? The new manhood had come with a new face. Randolph McMillan's face, it seemed. The men in the road's words came back to Mac, 'Is it you, Randy... back from the dead?'

Mac needed a drink. Something wicked strong. Randolph McMillan had died in a ditch, and James MacArthur had died his back to a wall. He didn't know if they had died at the same time, or one just before the other, the time circular and wrapping over onto itself. He thought of the Morrigan's prophesy, life and rebirth. "If the deity takes to you," Padric had said.

Mac leaned on the window, watching the movement of the city, and thought of Elizabeth, now long dead. He wondered if they had gotten away. Had she lived her life as a beaten woman or had things had gone better for her? Padric had died, too.

"He's a great man. You had better of moved him along as well." Mac addressed the air and hopefully the Morrigan in it.

Mac sat on the bed and thought of his first meeting with his old friend, in an alehouse in London.

"Ye Englanders cannot hold your ale, satisfy your women, and you're all ugly as bog mutton, so ye are. That one," Padric pointed to Mac, "would take the balls out of yer eyes." And then Padric smiled.

Mac laughed as he remembered the drinking contest and his sore head the next morning. He woke under the table, his head next to Padric's. "How I will miss you." A friend was better than ale.

Would he sit in this room alone, as another, and mourn? "No, we are both alive. I know it." A very big drink was the order of the day, and many of them. Mac had no idea where to go, but he'd find somewhere. He couldn't be in this small room with himself any longer. He grabbed the clean clothes that were left for him and dressed quickly. As he left, he lifted the mirror from behind it, where his reflection could not be seen, and put it out the door.

Moving with purpose, and moving toward people, Mac could forget the other man and feel more himself, maybe even better than himself. He walked the hallway while inspecting his clean clothes. Not bad. Nicely sewn. Fit like a second skin. Rich. More richly made than he'd ever worn.

Suddenly, what he really wanted was to see the woman for whom he'd made the trip. He wanted to inhale her scent and touch her soft skin. He was growing, his tailored pants bulging. He laughed. He'd never even imagined the feeling. He could live with that miracle. Mac inhaled deeply and walked with long steps, glad, at least, that this body worked so well. Human noises clamored up from somewhere at the bottom of the stairs. He wondered more keenly about the woman he'd traveled over time for, and why he was here. She must be in trouble for such drastic action. Of course she was.

"There's a looking-glass in the hall beside my door. Would you get rid of it?" he asked as he passed the clerk, who jerked to attention.

"Yes, sir. Yes, sir."

Fear there, Mac noted. Always fear with people and McMillan.

Walking from the hotel into the smoky city that was Cincinnati, Mac planned to imbibe enough to rout the sight of an unfamiliar nose. In the end though, The Drink, as the Irish called it, wouldn't change the shape of his face. The battle was living tomorrow and the next day and the next with the modifications. Just who the hell was Randolph McMillan, that's what he wanted to know.

The face of the man wasn't weathered. It was a sheltered face that had been kept indoors for most of its life. A soft countenance. That was easily fixed. Mac had noticed its regular features. Probably a face that was agreeable to women. Mac's vanity warmed. He'd never been comely for women, with his scars and his big ears from his dear mother.

Randolph probably had had his pick of females. The woman knew that. It was there in her expressive eyes. That's where she wore all her emotions, and there were plenty of them. She had an extreme honesty that got her into trouble. *I don't know her name*, he thought.

He'd meant to read her name as she signed it, before that awful date at the top of the page had engaged the whole of his attention. Suddenly he wondered what he'd written for himself. If he had written his own name, no one had commented. More than likely, he could do anything as Randolph and be believed.

Mac followed the straight line of the lit lamps down the street.

On the corner a sign read Vine and Third; he smelled ale.

Thank God.

He turned down Vine. Loiterers, men of all colors, all with hats, some with long flowing beards, stood in the arched doorways of establishments that littered the streets with signs. The scent was getting stronger. He picked up his step.

'A wienerwurst with each drink,' Mac read. 'K and L cigars and tobacco.' The smells of stale ale and sausage wafted through an open door. Male voices hung on the wind. Around Mac were universal odors and sounds. He rubbed his hands together. A good ale—a welcome thought, very welcome. His mouth watered. He threaded his way to a high counter, very glad that drinking with your mates was still the order of the day.

He had been so looking forward to wetting his upper lip, that he forgot that he had no money. A ripple of attention met him as he passed deeper inside the tavern. *I'm Randolph McMillan,* he thought. Funny, he didn't feel other than himself. The outline of the other man's skin housed him perfectly. Mac moved a finger, the finger moved. No thoughts other than his own. He didn't have any of the other man's memories. He was like a freshly stuffed hide.

The tavern owner recognized him, Mac knew, because he came over immediately. Gave up his conversation in the middle of a word and was moving toward Mac, smiling. Mac had to say something. He stood at the long high counter and glanced at what the other men were drinking. It looked like ale, golden in color as fair maiden's hair. It looked grand.

"Mr. McMillan."

"I have a dry pocket and a dry mouth."

The publican didn't even blink. "Bad day at the cards?" The man grabbed a glass. "There's a game at the back," the bartender said as he slid a full mug to Mac. "Maybe your luck will change." Not just a little pleased, Mac went to sit down. The beer felt good in his hands and tasted wonderful on his lips. The malt was a little lighter, but he liked it. He settled into a chair and let the drink ease through him. He thought of Padric. In normal times, that black Irishman would be next to him, singing songs and gulping ale and delighted at the free drink. Solitude seeped into Mac with each fresh glass. Still, the day had been interesting, and the ale was dulling his pain.

About Mac's third tankard, a doll-like man sat next to him in the only empty seat in the place. Other men had eyed the chair at Mac's table but had left it alone. The man placed a whiskey and an ale on the table. Moisture immediately gathered in a ring around the base of the mug, and both glasses jumped slightly when he threw down a heavy sheath of papers. The stranger's body odor flattened every- thing around him. After sitting, the little person picked up his news- paper and tucked his narrow face behind it. Mac read the title of the top sheet on the table. *Beauty Undraped* by Lefcadio Hearn.

An Irishman. O happy meeting. Mac shifted his chair in closer. Mac read more. It was a story about a nude female. "You write about naked women?" His opening line as he welcomed the man, his nationality, conversation, information, a bit of home.

Lefcadio lowered his paper. He raised his very thick but red eyebrows as he glanced at his addressor. His eyes, full of cynicism, like a man with a gut-full of the world, flicked to the top sheet on the table and back to Mac. "I would say that I don't write at all," he countered with a self-deprecating glimmer of a grin. He stared at Mac until a slight smirk moved his lips. "A bit like you don't work."

Mac sipped his ale and absorbed the Irish accent. "You're from Ireland?"

"The place of saints and sinners. You'd be welcome there."

"Once upon a time I was," Mac replied.

"And if ye're going to ask me why I'm here. I have no idea why I'm in Germanland in the state of Ohio. The weather isn't any better."

Mac wanted to ask if that was a long way from Ireland, but he was beginning to understand that a question like that would sound daft, and anyway Mac knew he was far away from everything he knew and from things he understood.

"But," Lefacdio continued, there are at least one hundred and seventy-five drinking establishments on this road alone, so there you are. And faro, and that's a great draw. And then there are the other carry-ons like strawberry festivals and a lovely opera house with circus animals in its basement. The poor and hungry are here as well. Sure as I'm here to look after them. The divil take them all as he will." Hearn indicated the papers. "I write for this piece of shite."

The brogue sounded so good to Mac. It soothed his loneliness. "You happen to know an Irishman named Padric?"

"I have known many a Padric. To whom would ye be referring?"

"No, I don't think you'd know him."

The Irishman started a song and was promptly told to shut-up by the barman. "Indeed, I am under-appreciated here in German town." Lefacdio winked at Randolph. "Another drink then? I hear you can afford it."

"I'm guessing you think you know who I am, then?"

"Only as a pretty face and a string of headlines. As you're asking, I'd say that I know you're fecking mad. Having it all, all that money, and throwing your life over for a bit of danger. Or, be jaesus, you must be as fecking bored as a constipated man languishing in an outhouse."

The Irish never change.

"What headlines?" Mac asked.

"Sure as ye knows, yourself." Hearn studied Mac. He was looking for something. He seemed satisfied. "I did enjoy early on in your career when you'd dress as the clergy to... well... to reassure your female victims, as it were. The clergy are mostly all on the take anyway. But I was just as annoyed as the last man when you made railway tunnels as feared as God himself after the Thomas Underwood murder—the poor man battered in the dark and then thrown from the Cincinnati-Chicago, the Twelve-Fifteen, just after the

Hammond tunnel, and all for his gold watch and chain, and his gold rimmed glasses. For shame, to be sure."

Mac indicated for two more beers and two more of whatever was in the small glass Hearn was tossing back. "All for things I already have," Mac assumed, from their earlier conversation when the full glasses arrived.

Hearn made an appreciative sound as he drank a slug of beer.

"In spades," he said, backhanding the foam from his mouth.

"Gratuitous thievery. Are ye thinking of having a conversion then?"

"Something like that."

"With a newspaper man? Be jaesus, the scoop would be like the second coming."

"How far and wide am I known?"

It seemed that the Irish in Hearn liked the game. "You're like, for criminals, a trend setter. You lead rather than follow. Far as I know, old Tom is the only man thrown from a train in your personal life of crime, but the copycats. By her mother's holy womb, the tunnels haven't been safe since... and the clergy, they're going to start wearing blue, so they are."

Mac couldn't help laughing while Hearn quickly drank.

"Laugh, will you?" Hearn blustered.

Mac drank from the small glass like Hearn's that the bartender brought. His lips went numb. With five more, his words were getting sloppy, sounding more old English-y

Hearn, now equally without the full command of his tongue or his mind said, "There is a bit of the adventurer to you. I'm surprised you haven't the clap from the ladies you own on the wharf. Maybe you do. No one more deserving. Jaesus, what a sorry place that is. You want to know what I write, is it? I tell the sad stories about those poor, poor ladies, and stories about madhouses, opium smoking, suicides, leeches that call themselves doctors, and slaughterhouses. People who aren't happy with themselves and can't make a go of life. People like you."

Hearn could barely get his mug to his mouth. He put the mug down with a thump. "More's the pity that I've done all the talking and you haven't told me a thing. It's not meself with a story after all. You are the sly one." He tapped the end of his nose twice and pointed to Mac. "To the drink," he shouted. Hearn sloppily lifted his small glass in a toast and then tossed it back. He began singing.

"Damn Irish," a patron yelled from one corner. "Quiet, you. We don't want any of that war mongering stuff here." Hearn turned it up a notch.

The Irish are always stirring the pot, Mac thought.

The man was still yelling at Hearn. The little man suddenly stood up with his hands fisted in front of his face. He walked surprising straight toward his heckler and swung a punch. He hit his perse-cutor in the jaw with the accuracy of a man used to fighting, drunk or sober. The man was out cold. Mac was impressed. Hearn straightened, his knuckles out to draw anyone into the arena. He danced in a circle.

"By all that's holy—" Mac spat out. To Mac, the fight had been won and to ask for more was incompetent and useless.

He meant to grab the Irishman by the neck of his shirt and take him out when the friends of the unconscious man jumped. Swearing at Hearn, Mac kicked the man closest to him in the back of the legs. He clocked the side of the man's head as the man went down.

Like rabid dogs, at least six men attacked Mac. He could feel the hate for McMillan in every punch. They were safe from rebuttal in numbers. Back to back, the Irishman and Mac battled until they were both breathing hard.

Mac took a kick to the groin that had him fighting twice as hard. *God, not there!* His eye, his jaw, his back, his chest, and Hearn egging them on the whole time. Randolph McMillan's body was in very good shape, but Mac figured that he and Hearn were going to go down anyway. He'd have to defend his crotch as best he could. Suddenly, they both fell out the door and onto the sidewalk. The battle stopped at the door, although Hearn sprang to his feet—still calling out. Mac tripped him. Hearn landed face first in a puddle. The cold water seemed to bring some sense to him.

"Relentless," Mac said, still breathing hard. He knew that he'd stand in battle with this man anytime. Hearn started singing again. Mac shook his head. Hand over the other man's shoulder, he drunkenly strolled with Hearn back towards the Saint Nicholas. Mac sang his own song. He knew that his face would be unrecognizable by morning. That thought pleased him.

Mac noticed himself weaving in and out of the straight path set by the upright and newly lit lamps that illuminated his way home. He liked the lights in the darkness. His head sloshed with memories as his stomach sloshed with ale. Hearn sang all the way back, more quietly, but still singing. All the while the Irishman sang into his ear, and the rain sprinkled down. The sidewalk glistened wherever a bit of light hit it from the lampposts, windows or doorways. Shadows shifted as the milling groups in the open doors of the bars moved.

A crew of young boys and young men climbed ladders with rods in their hands, lighting the lamps. He watched as one rested his ladder against the post, scampered up and turned a screw valve. The lamp then exploded unto life. The glass case twinkled in the pink of the sunset.

Mac thought as he lumbered along that Hearn hadn't been right. McMillan hadn't been a bastard because of boredom. Mac had met many like Randolph, men mean from birth.

If McMillan's father was king of the pigs in German Cincinnati, The Hog King, as Lefcadio had said, then Randolph had been the prince of Porkopolis. What the father had built impressed Mac. Speaking of pigs, a worker was herding about fifty pigs down the street in front of Mac. To the butcher, no doubt. The smell. Randolph didn't have the honest smell of pigs about him.

It appeared that no one would miss the man. Somehow that set Mac's heart to rest. The original owner had had to give way. He'd made a mess of things. Mac's turn, but he'd have to leave.

Go far away. He'd miss the free ale.

Back at the Saint Nicholas, he paused to look at the facade. The place was like a castle. She was in there—the most insufferable woman in all of Cincinnati. He was glad that this time he didn't have to scale the side of the building to get to her.

He was Randolph McMillan, the bad guy. He could just walk in the front door. No wonder she was trying to shake him like a bad omen. He remembered her on the road as he'd gone for the mule. She thought she could use him. He knew just when that thought had occurred to her. He chuckled. He liked that she thought she could take on a man like McMillan. Stupid thought of course, but so full of hope.

Mac checked Lefcadio Hearn into a room and arranged with the clerk for a bath, and for God's sake a decent breakfast in the morning, compliments of Randolph McMillan, and then he went to bed. He liked Hearn. He could stay here except he'd have to be McMillan every day. He could reform the man, but there were too many enemies that were unknown to Mac. Staying would be too dangerous. He would have to always watch his back. He would have to leave, and Randolph needed to die in some accident. How, Mac had no idea.

He hadn't slept since the thirteen hundreds. One thing, he wasn't going to fight any more of Randolph's wars. Mac sunk into the mattress and sighed. He slept like the dead with a dead man's dreams.

CHAPTER SIX

As Mac strolled from the Saint Nicholas and onto the sidewalk, he thought about how good it was to be alive. Everything worked, everything! A barber had appeared at his door with a hot towel to shave him. The man had heated a towel by his fireplace.

Mac's battered face felt better for it.

In front of the hotel, he watched the movement of the city. He let the new words—new things flow around him. His more relaxed mind absorbed them. He'd always been good with languages, any of them English, Gaelic…French. A "trolley" moved up the street and then another moved down it. The noise of metal on metal was loud and when the trolleys stopped, they disgorged large numbers of people who then hurried on their ways. He could see that a certain peace had settled into this world. People need fewer walls to hide behind. The root of all things here had begun in his time, fountains…stone buildings. They were just better. He assumed tools had improved. Guns had.

He'd had a headache and queer stomach this morning, but another knock at the door had produced some tonic drink that had made him feel better. He'd slept in, and now was stepping out into the light of a new day.

He wondered how Randolph might look to people as a gawker in his own city. Mad, probably. Finally over the bend, no doubt, but Mac couldn't help but laugh at "bicycles" weaving in between the traffic of horses, carriages, and trams. Two wheels! On Third Street, he passed the umbrella makers and their ringing bells. He watched hawkers of oysters who blew horns. The noise level, the smells were something more like home only with oddly dressed characters.

He still noticed a constant flick of the eye his way from the locals. They weren't glowering now...more gloating...and Mac thought about why until he remembered his face. With no mirror in his room, he hadn't examined the damage. He knew he had been bruised. His teeth felt slightly shifted in his mouth.

His search for a moneylender ended when he spied her, his fairy. She was better than any other curiosity he'd seen, trimmed out in fresh black and with her auburn hair washed and loosely arranged. It swung with the easy sway of her hips. He'd never seen her clean. Her hair must smell wonderful.

She carried herself more smugly with a bath—sweet, with self-satisfaction. She hid behind it. He would breach the wall. She didn't feel safe with him, and she wasn't.

He rubbed his hands together.

Time for breakfast. Suddenly he was ravenous. She might not even recognize him. That would be fine. The more she forgot about McMillan, the better.

He met her at the corner, took her elbow, and maneuvered her toward the hotel.

"Have you eaten?"

"Good lord...your face."

"Just a little dust up. Believe it or not, I didn't start it. I was helping out a combative Irishman."

"Sure, the halo over your head is out-shining the sun. You look awful. Truly."

Looking at her, her creamy oval face, her suspicious stormy eyes, her generous mouth, the thickness of her heavy hair, the last of his uneasy emotions about being McMillan blew away. He felt indifferent to his strange environment and newly shaped face. The body would do. The place was fine.

"Where have you been?" he pestered her.

"None of your business."

Sleep hadn't improved her disposition. "Will you join me for breakfast?"

"Breakfast? Lazy man's brunch."

He had watched her react to his touch at her elbow. Her eyes had darkened even more as her spine stiffened. He had startled her, had penetrated her reserve. She hadn't winced or even pulled away. She was as unflappable as they came, except she wouldn't meet his look. That was too personal.

God, he was hungry.

Back in the Saint Nicholas where he had credit, and after he had guided her to the dining room, she stood beside her chair, waiting.

"Aren't you going to sit?" he asked.

"When you pull out my chair. I'm sure this is how you treat all women and most of humanity, but not me."

Mac walked around to shift her seat, and then left her to sit herself. She glared at him as she scooted her chair closer to the table. Her prudery had returned tenfold. Her lips narrowed and her nose turned up.

"I thought your walking off to your room without so much as an until-later signaled a more permanent parting of ways," she said as her eyes flashed feminine tantrum.

So she did care. Mac chuckled inwardly. A hot temper was often passion in reverse. "Let's eat something," he said. "What's good here?"

"Anything."

Not exactly what Mac wanted to hear as he glanced at the strange menu, but then again, food was food.

A waitress twittered while Mac called out the names of things he recognized—ham, eggs, bread. The waitress automatically poured him coffee.

"Coffee for me too," Miss Bathurst said.

"How's your room?"

"That's right; you walked off, so you don't know."

"You needed help to find your room?"

"Not needed. Not expected either, really, as I think about it."

"Are you running from something?"

Her temper unleashed into her eyes like a summer storm. "You know, you are insufferable. One minute you're all attention... are you running from something... are you in danger... the next you're walking off. I can't depend on that. I can't depend on you. Of course I can't...you're a liar and a thief. Just look at you. I leave you alone one night, and you look like a horse kicked you. I would be foolish to view you as anything else than bad, and I am not a fool. I've decided that maybe you can't help me after all." A few tears dropped to her cheeks, and she pushed back her chair to stand.

"Quiet," he said like a sudden thunderclap. She froze. "Quit the histrionics. They won't be helpful."

"Go to blazes, if that place will even take you."

"Apparently, it won't."

Her gaze was hard and full of hurt, but she didn't run off. He'd expected her to, was planning for it. When she didn't, a beginning of pride for her flickered through him. He was, after all, McMillan with a busted-up face. She must be in some trouble to need a man like him so much. He put his hand on her white and bloodless fingers that pressed on the edge of the table linen.

"No one should be alone. It's dangerous."

"Damn you," she said again, so distantly it seemed she had spoken to someone else.

"I've already been to hell and back, remember?"

"However did you get the release?" she said, sinking down into her seat. "Hell is, after all, home to your kind and permanent."

"We are both rowing through fresh waters here. Let's say that I'm not myself."

His hands still covered her fingers. He rubbed the edge of one with his thumb. She pulled her hand away. "Amazing, you seem yourself."

Mac had noticed all the silverware. He wished she had ordered something, just so he could see how she used them. He recognized a spoon and the knife. When the waitress returned with his food, he broke off a piece of bread and dipped it into the yolk. He could barely get it into his sore mouth and then he had to swallow it nearly whole. It must have bulged the length of his neck before hitting his stomach. He swallowed hard. His suffering must have loosened some sympathy from her firm grasp, because when he said, "Let's start with your name," she answered, "My mother died yesterday." She did not look at him.

"I'm sorry." He didn't think he would get any more. Like all women, she only talked when she wanted to. God, she was more tightly wrapped than an infant in a swaddling cloth.

"Two nights ago, Mr. Mitchell, my solicitor, told me to stay well away from the likes of you. He said your sort is not the help a lady should look for or consider. He warned me because your type is from whom this sort of help is most often offered. He said that I should have a woman companion with me." She was looking straight at him now. Measuring him. "But what good is an elderly female going to do for me if Guy has his dog-meat friends after me? I must counter dog-meat with dog-meat."

She picked up her cup. "That damn waitress didn't fill it." She glanced around.

"I don't think they heard you." Mac tossed his head at the other patrons.

"Well, the waitress did. Whatever. I'm not hungry anyway."

The cup clattered back into its saucer. "Your fee will be mitigated by the fact that you already lost our horses."

"Tell me about Guy." Mac had heard enough about himself.

"My mother married someone like you, handsome, unscrupulous, glib. He didn't fool me. You don't fool me."

Mac was out of bread. He had to study the room again. The men sat upright with napkins on their legs and only forks in their hands.

"He did one thing for her, though. He protected her from other dishonest men. She was taken, so to speak. Hands off. The difference here is that I know all about you. I cannot be influenced by your methods. I will pay you more than Guy has offered. Are you even listening to me?"

She made to stand. Mac reached over and clamped down on her forearm to hold her in place. "Sit down," he said with a growl in his voice.

Startled, she sank back into her chair.

"And I'll get you that coffee."

She watched as he waved to the waitress and then picked up his fork and held it in his fist. He stuck it into the middle of the ham and lifted the entire slab at once. He glanced around again, and then shook it off the fork. He then picked up his knife and used it to cut the meat that slid from his plate onto the tablecloth. He mumbled gruffly to himself. "How do they work together?"

"Hold it with the fork. I can't believe I'm sitting here with Randolph McMillan, who dines every night with crystal, telling him how to cut meat with a fork and knife. It is all too much. What is it you are after? What have you and Guy possibly thought of?"

Food, Mac thought to himself. He was sweating and salivating.

Each bite was an effort. Finally, he had enough in his mouth to sit back and chew.

"I had planned to offer you some sort of financial arrangement for your defection and protection. You are the most unexpected and safest person for me to be with," she said as Mac ate through his plate and down to the table.

The waitress leaned her hip against his shoulder as she poured him more coffee. "Need anything else, honey?"

"With milk," his dining companion added in a, *Damn it, I'm a Bathurst* sort of way as she lifted her cup.

The girl jumped, gave his dining companion the look competitive women give each other, lifted the chin under her compressed mouth, filled the cup with a cascade of coffee, and stalked off.

"I should report her."

"Are you running from Guy?"

"Did you hear me?"

"You should report her?"

"I want to employ you."

"Ah, hired out as a mercenary to the queen," he mumbled.

"First I need to know your name."

She looked at him as if she was the longest suffering of people. He'd lost their horses; he'd... well, he didn't know what else he'd done. Seemingly he was just Randolph McMillan. He didn't need to do anything.

The room was muffled. He couldn't believe how quietly people ate here, with the stealth of moles. The long, tasseled, brocade curtains drowned sound, and the table linen, and the carpeting. He could almost hear people chewing.

She kept glancing around, like she could feel them watching. He didn't get as much as another askance. If he was waiting for her to confide in him further, he'd be waiting a long time.

"I'm not sure if you and Guy are partners or not. But it's not beyond your character to double-cross him for money. Do we have a deal?" she asked.

"Name? And how much money?" Mac smiled. She kept her eyes hard and her smile brittle. She wanted him to know that she would never, ever dance with him.

"Maggie Bathurst," she said as she stood. "Are you with me now?"

"Yes, Miss Maggie Bathurst, I am."

"Then meet me at the train station at six o'clock, ready for a long journey."

Mac watched her flounce away. Padric's voice came to him:

"What do you want to take on a spoiled girl like that?" The coffee was good so he let the waitress pour him another cup. Mac thought back to that moment when he had opened his eyes. She had been the first thing he'd seen and felt in this new world, her body on his. Yes, Maggie had a deal, but not the one she thought.

He had six hours until the train. He still needed money. Plenty of time. As he walked down Third Street, women bumped against him on the sidewalk. Dressed in poor or rich skirts, they batted their eyelashes and blushed and giggled as they passed. The lively interest startled Mac. He began laughing.

More comfortable, he began to notice familiar smells, like manure in the streets. Also, the sweat of men and horses.

On a street named Walnut, he had to stop and study a fountain. A very tall piece of granite, Mac figured, and some bronze. The fountain was a woman with robes over her body and the water flowing from her hands. He took a drink from the conduits that lead off the fountain for public consumption.

At a place called Price Hill, he rode an amazing passenger elevator up the Hill's inclined plane. At the top he gazed down at the city. He saw the bridge and the river with its cookie-cutter paddle-boats. He heard wheezy music, an instrument with bellows. Padric had played a bagpipe. With the expanse of the city frontward from Mac, he thought of Padric's sister, of how she would have liked to know that her prophecy had come true. She had known he was about to leave them, and she had cried.

His heart heavier, he descended the hill and walked on. Slowly becoming familiar with the newness of everything, he rode a streetcar and found it like a large open carriage. He saw an advertisement for a zoo with elephants and tigers, and he jumped off the moving trolley.

At the entrance was a stuffed donkey and a dead, equally stuffed lion. Someone had positioned them against each other, as if in mortal combat.

"Why in God's name?" Mac asked himself and a man within earshot answered.

"That lioness," the man pointed, "had escaped from her cage, and she attacked that donkey. The donkey, not to be outdone, kicked the lioness to death, but the donkey had his own wounds and died as well."

Mac must have looked amused, because the man added, "A tribute to the brave donkey."

"But they're both dead," Mac said. "Anyway, my experience with asses is that they are bad-tempered, all of them." Mac pondered the animals and thought of Malcome. He wondered if he had killed the pus-rot with that last knife throw. God, he hoped so. It worried him that he might have left the job undone. Left Padric, Elizabeth, and Molly all to pick up the threads of the mess he had begun.

Mac left the zoo feeling sorry for the sick-looking, caged elephant. This new world had taken the simple things of his previous life and made them so much more complex. Once, at a market place, he'd seen a lion in a cage, and now here was a whole zoo. He felt no better about the caged animals then than now.

His money problem reoccurred to him. Time was closing in now, and he didn't know how to ask where McMillan kept his stash without sounding ridiculous. Mac retraced his steps back to the marketplace. He wandered in the foodstuffs. Randolph surely never came here and wouldn't be known. He asked where the nearest moneylender was. He asked a woman, hoping she would take pity on him.

"A bank?" she harshly declared. Mac forgot that a woman in business was not one given to chat with non-paying persons, especially while scaling and gutting fish. "On Walnut." She hadn't even glanced up at him. Two fish had been beheaded during the conversation.

The bank was like plundering the castle of a rich man, except the money was, on a small technicality of facial recognition, his. He had to close his mouth when smiling tellers handed mountains of it to him with happy smiles. Too bad he had to leave Cincinnati. His "father" would have enough power within the town to get Maggie out of her predicament. Randolph could be "saved." Too much of a lie, though. Who would believe in a reformed Randolph? Maggie didn't. Besides, how would he explain a deficit of Randolph's memories? He wouldn't be able to recognize his own mother. He'd have to suffer from a head injury to cover for the fact that he didn't know an aunt's name or an uncle's profession.

He didn't know if he had a sister or brother.

He assumed, based on Maggie's reaction to him, that Randolph had many enemies in hiding. It's impossible to fight an adversary you don't know. Killing Randolph was the only solution, and Mac had no ideas about how to do that without producing a body.

He thought of Maggie. That she was leaving was perfect for him. He suspected her problems didn't need such a drastic solution. He wondered why she'd chosen to sever ties. Maybe she didn't know herself. He'd make her forget about McMillan, and he would forget, too. He was looking forward to it. Maggie, she was cavalier now, but leaving her home was going to be hard on her. She was going to hate every minute of it, and she was going to take it out on him, but she'd also have to depend on him. Mac felt the rising in his pants. "Tara, tantara, teino!" He rubbed his hands together.

CHAPTER SEVEN

As a screen to her travels, Maggie had bought third-class tickets on the b-train to Chicago and then in the same class, the coach from Chicago to Kelton, Utah.

The train waited by the platform, all seven hundred feet of it. It boasted three Silver Palace cars of about six feet each behind the engine. Its brass shined and the tenders burst with coal. In longing, Maggie ran her hand along the metal, shining sides of the Palace cars. She thought of stewards with hushed voices and of the beds there, three and a half feet wide with a hair mattress on springs, oh, the linen sheets and soft blankets, the silver lamps hanging from the roof. She pouted that she would be missing the silence of soft Axminster carpets and green and red striped velvet curtains.

She stared at her third-class ticket and then stumbled as she kept walking to the back of the train, past the smoking car to the second of five passenger cars. It was going to be a full train by the looks of it. She watched the press inside and turned away.

She felt like the two stubborn mares that were resisting being loaded into a baggage car. The horses tossed their heads and kicked out behind them. They were fine horses being shipped against their wills to somewhere not of their choosing. To add salt to her wounded thoughts, she noticed McMillan arriving just beyond the horses, to trumpets, it seemed, as the crowd parted before his very footsteps.

Wait until they watch him get on at third class.

He sauntered straight to the engine.

Here we go again, she thought as he stared at its steaming metal sides. He seemed to want to memorize every bolt, all the dizzying glint of metal, the rush of stream from the idle wheels. He even stopped to touch its side and then to peer behind a wheel. He moved closer to her. When he got close enough that she inhaled his scent of soap and musk and saw the blue of his eyes alight with... God... curiosity, she said between her gritted teeth,

"You made it."

He startled and then turned his head.

"Isn't it marvelous? Its wheels run on the track beneath it?" he asked.

Maggie stared at him and shook her head. "Oh, for the love of God," she muttered as she took her first step onto the step of the train and away from her home with McMillan at her elbow. How could she properly mourn her leaving everything dear to her with the heat of this man's hand warm on her arm as she made her way to a seat? *Sit down*, she wanted to yell at the other passengers leaping from their seats to make space or remove themselves from his proximity. They were all thinking of train tunnels.

The whistle blew. The carriage jerked as it engaged with the rest of the train. Metal on metal screamed. Released steam hissed, and the train gained speed with a chugging sound.

"It's very noisy." Mac peered out the window. "Like thousands of crows. How fast will it go?"

"It will get up to thirty-five miles per hour. The trains that go west, they get up to seventy miles per hour." A boy turned and knelt on the bench of his seat to talk to Mac. "It's got superheated steam turbines."

"Superheated steam turbines in the world. Are you going west?"

"Naw, just to Chicago. But I will someday."

"Yes, you will."

She intended to ignore him with the steadiness of the pendulum of a clock that first train to Chicago, but Mac and the boy stared out the window and chatted. The ride was as boring and relentless as that tick-tock.

Should she ask him if he wanted to accompany her to the dining car? She gazed at him.

Does he know the train has one?

She was hungry, and she didn't want to eat alone.

Finally, about to leave Chicago for Kelton, Maggie was sorry she hadn't booked first class. "If anyone is looking for me, they will never look in third class," she had told Mitchell, stupid girl. She had never traveled third class. The condition of the coach was a shock. She'd turned and returned to the station.

"I'd like to trade these tickets for first class."

"Sorry, lady, but that's all full."

"I can't believe it. Full," she steamed as she walked back to the train with Mac behind her. "I won't make it four days. A total lack of judgement, Magnolia," she continued to berate herself. "Just how did you think you'd survive this?"

Smoke seeping in the open windows as well as the acidic smell of baby urine mixed with the richer picnic smells of hard sausage and pickled eggs and chewing tobacco spit had her numb. She didn't feel the seat under her. The unceasing, high-pitched voices of children had become like the sounds of badly-played violins. The staccato of the Chinese language hammered her brain. The unending blades of pale prairie grass had been framed for countless miles in the train's dirty windows. By the end of the second day of travel, around Nebraska, her interest in the landscape of the plains and in her fellow passengers had waned to absolute nothing. Mitchell had said she hadn't been raised for this. *Oh pish-posh*, she had said.

Maggie waved the thought away as if it was a bug meant to bite her. She had no patience with the introspection. Still, all she wanted to do was rip off the coarse wool of her skirt that scratched through her undergarments, and then shake Randolph McMillan next to her. But lethargy trapped her, and anger. Not a peep out of him about the smell or the lack of space, or the children. Randy-Mac sat in third class as if he were meant to be there.

She glared at him with the purpose of rearranging the pleasant countenance of his face. If she weren't so dispirited, she'd think harder about him, about it all. Probably as an outlaw, he had stayed in some bad places. She was too hot from the press of perspiration-soaked bodies to think any more about it. Her fan arm hurt, and it was irritating her that the other women in the train car, with their sausage greasy lips, were either keeping their children from him, or gazing at him like they wanted to eat him for dessert.

"You're encouraging them," she snapped, when she wanted to kick him instead. It annoyed her that she was irritated. She began fanning herself faster and when he glanced to her, she gave him her profile.

He *was* a good mama's nightmare. An exceedingly nice package over a very dark soul. What a waste. She envisioned him as he might have been, as an upstanding part of society, at a ball for instance...in black tails. His waist was trim with his black hair slicked back from his face. As they waltzed, his blue eyes would absorb her. He would be loath to return her to her friends. Maybe she'd let him dance her outside, and they'd walk. He'd catch her at the waist as she tripped in the falsely-lit darkness, and then deliver a light kiss on the lips. She'd be in a dusty purple gown with... *oh, my God.* She shook her head.

The train lurched and a young woman who just happened to be walking in the aisle fell across his seat and onto Randolph's lap.

She giggled and swept her fingers through his dark hair.

Trollop. Maggie turned away to the dirty window. What did she care? Let them all compress him into a lump of coal. She closed her eyes and dreamed of a well-stocked bathroom. The room shined, as did the bottles of rose-scented liquid bubbles. She was in a white fluffy towel, and warm. With her hand, she upset the calm surface of the tub of water, steaming water that curled her hair. She dropped her towel and slipped into the warmth, like wet satin. Soapy hands massaged her shoulders, deeper until the creases in her forehead lifted. She let her head drop back to the lip of the tub and gazed up at the person whose hands were such a delight. Randolph.

Maggie's eyes flew open. She'd fallen asleep. Barely awake and still a part of the dream, she tucked her arms close against the sides of her body. She slid her feet in, like a turtle that had been touched. Protection was survival.

The train lurched. The steel wheels screamed from the pressure of the brakes. She, along with the frankfurter-eating populace around her, put aside their dreams, embroidery, and hampers to gaze outside.

The train stopped within the face of the open countryside.

Maggie tried to wipe the window, but the dirt was on the outside. A conductor appeared in their compartment calling, "Buffalo herd to the right side of the train." Every last passenger stood and brushed their clothes of crumbs to exit the train into that sea of flat landscape. Randolph too. The air in the compartment freshened with the exit door opening and closing.

A strong wind blew the hat feathers on the women's heads as they bobbed along outside the windows. With the children on their shoulders, the men were pointing to something. Randolph, staring with them all, had that silly look on his face that he'd had on the bridge.

Maggie couldn't help but look into the distance. If any of these people had any sense, they'd be back on the train. There were Indians around somewhere. She rubbed at the gray dirt on the window. "Well, I never." She lifted her skirts to avoid the debris on the floor and walked outside.

With her hand shading her eyes, she had just pinpointed a huge, matted animal with a humped back, when a gunshot from overhead took the animal to its knees, and then another gunshot and another animal, until the ground trembled from the firing of weapons and from the herd of animals that stampeded in all directions. Within moments, hundreds of animals lay dead and bleeding where they fell, and with the human babies bleating into the bosoms of their mothers, the conductor called through the crowd, "All aboard."

Maggie had never been so stunned at anything.

"How? How—" she faltered, "—can that be allowed?" As she turned her head from the acres of grass that had just become a killing field, she swallowed bile back down to her stomach. Even with her head hung and her eyes averted, she could see the mound of the animals' pelts as they lay dead on their sides.

The sound of firing still rang in her ears. The side of the train, hot and substantial as it was, seemed to sway. She knocked into some passengers whose faces were grotesque in their broad-grinned laughter. Maggie staggered, bumping shoulders, trying to get her footing. She held her stomach. Her nose recalled past smells... the mixed odor of urine, caged bodies, sausage, and warm beer.

Randolph was at her elbow then, making a hole in the crowd for her. His voice was mild and was developing, as he was becoming more fluent, into a sort of British lilt. The manufactured accent had been exasperating her in its fakeness, but not now. Now it sounded reassuring as he guided her tripping feet to the opposing side of the train.

"They're just going to rot there," she said through the handkerchief at her mouth. She leaned against Randolph's shoulder as she tried to swallow the contents of her stomach. He was her companion in all this and anyway, the look on his face seemed appropriate enough that she could forget the crowd, the cautious stares her way, and the conductor's whistle.

"I've seen men taken out like that."

The timbre of his voice sounded like he had. She inhaled as if breath would calm her stomach and her mind. She knew she was going to forever link death to the scent of sausage.

Back on the train, Maggie retired into mourning; there had been no time for it before. She gave herself to it, let it squeeze her mind dry and make her arms limp. She shut her eyes more tightly when a man began to smoke. Not that he'd listen if she'd said anything, or maybe he would have, but it didn't matter, not with gray soot belching from the train's stack like a forest fire.

She listened to Randolph talk to some people about English-Scottish wars. Something about an English mother and a Scottish father and about living close to the border. She let the cadence of his voice and its lilt calm her to sleep. It was good to have him here. As she listened and dozed, in the dreamy space of being both asleep and awake, Maggie thought that's why with a name like MacArthur he sounds more British than Scottish.

She slept fitfully. Sometime in the night she heard rain slick over the train. When she woke finally with dawn the wet had dried and had stuck the soot to the windows, dousing the morning light. As the sun rose and heated, it dried the covering into a hard-bitten crust of dirty ash.

By day three, Maggie didn't want to lift her head from against the window. The children had lost the energy to do anything but whine. There was a new odor, sour breaths. The babies were still wetting their diapers, and Randolph had disappeared.

When he finally returned and leaned down and scavenged through their food basket, she ignored him. Taking out two apples, he handed one to Maggie, saying, "Eat this and talk to me, by God. Tell me about your mother if it will help."

She looked over to him slowly, calmly, as if peering at him from a long distance.

"I was thinking of my father." Her voice was whispery.

"What about him?"

She smiled a sad little smile at his insistence, how he was trying to make the words penetrate the fog. "How unlucky he was." She didn't go on.

"And?" Mac demanded. He lifted her hand, opened the fingers, and put the apple into it.

"And then he died so young." Maggie closed her eyes. The apple like a still life painting on her lap.

————

Battle fatigue. Mac had seen it often, especially after big campaigns or in very young men. That's what Maggie had. He watched her sigh. He'd welcome back the shrew, some light in her full eyes, or especially the potential for a wide smile that he rarely saw on her generous mouth. Considering her, he shined the apple on his jacket and bit into it. Her hand lay gracefully on her lap, the oval fingernails a light pink against her black skirt. He traced the line of her profile with his gaze lingering slightly on her lips and neck. Her bosom was quiet, hardly rising or falling. Mac's eyes narrowed as he meditated on the woman before him who had become sinew "less." She needed to talk. Mac kicked her shin and watched, satisfied, as her eyes flew open.

"*And?*" he said.

"What?"

"Your father."

"Nothing."

"Aaaannnnd?"

"He left me." A sob stuttered out as she tried to inhale it.

"Who helped you and your mother?"

"Mr. Mitchell. He must have sheltered things for Mother, invested. He loved my mother."

"And then Guy married your mother."

"He mesmerized her," Maggie spit out and then startled as if the tone had surprised her. She settled into her anger. "Sir Guy Didsbury of Tallyrand, for God's sake. He's from somewhere in England. That's his name. Inherited no doubt, a penniless title because he arrived to Garth bankrupt. Hah! *The* gallant Sir Didsbury. Chivalry, he squashes the word like a butterfly under his thumb."

As did most of the knights Mac knew. He brushed at his pants and cleared his throat. Here, finally, was a conversation he knew about. An ideal that he'd never guessed had lived five hundred more years. The reality of knighthood had been on its way out as he had lived.

"Guy knows nothing of chivalry, of love, of even basic kindness," she continued. "As far as that goes, you don't have a courteous thought in your head. Courage, honor, service, have either of the two of you, Randolph McMillan, Sir Guy Didsbury even heard of such things, duty to countrymen? How about protection of the weak and poor?" Maggie scoffed and waved him off with her hand.

Mac laughed outright then. The sound startled Maggie. She looked at him the way a woman looked when she was being made fun of. She watched him and Mac knew that she was measuring his open face, the leftover sounds of his mirth. She was thinking of how to best him. Good. The calculating Maggie was better than Maggie as a lost soul.

"My father said he would find me a knight," she said in a lofty voice as she looked straight at Mac. "A man who was both gentle and gracious to a lady."

Mac could let it go at that. He could let her have the last word about something she knew precious little about. He could let her sit back in the tight fit of her smugness and then slip again into some fantasy world her father had spun for her, but instead he said, "The knights I knew were too busy with the spoils of war to worry about women."

Ice could have formed along the length of her stare. "You have no damn idea. You are as far removed from it as a person can be." She turned her knees, her upper body, and her face from him.

Mac had been worried about her state of mind. He had been missing her mercurial moods, as they had passed the hours in the soot and train noise. Emotions moved through her face like relentless ocean waves. She was at one time sad and seemed that nothing in the world could brighten her again and in the next moment a small smile played at her face, and her eyes glowed briefly with humor. Now he had the thread of a topic to keep her going. Mac's skin itched to start. "What do you know of knights beyond the word itself?"

"My father read Froissart."

The jolt Mac felt, the eagerness when he heard that name, surprised him. He leaned forward. "John Froissart?" Jesus, it was as if she'd reached into his past and physically pulled forth a piece of it and dumped in onto his lap. "*Sir* John Froissart?"

"What do you know of him?" Her voice dripped with suspicion, but she let it go. Tipping into her bag at her feet, she rummaged and said at the same time, "My father's favorite. My English grandfather sent my father and mother and myself to England just at the Civil War. Grandpa told my father that he could do more for the Confederacy from there, supplies and such. That he was not allowed to fight affected my father deeply. He loved Froissart's description of honor. My father was a dreamer, a cavalier, a gentleman."

AH, the qualities of a fine man Mac smiled and wanted to chuckle.

Mac had known Froissart as a good man, a devoted knight, and a lover of women. Whenever the man saw Mac, he would tisk, tisk at Mac's groin injuries as a more profound injury than the amputation of a limb. They'd get very drunk together. A great Frenchman.

"I have the book Froissart wrote. I always carry it."

She pulled the small volume out of her purse and held it before him as a woman holds forth her affections. She glanced at him over the spine of the book with a superior eye and a bunched mouth that indicated she thought the thing too precious for the likes of him. Its burgundy leather had faded. Its new-bound smell was long gone. Undoubtedly opened daily by Maggie over the years since her father's death, the book bended at the spine.

"You wouldn't understand its motto—"

"For God and ladies?"

Maggie juggled the book, almost dropping it to the ale-sticky floor. He had to keep from laughing at the surprise in her face.

He'd recited the exact words she had been about to read to him.

She pressed the pages to her bosom.

"By God, you do have it." Mac reached over to move her little finger and read, "*The Chronicles of England, France, and Spain.*

Which volume?" Mac moved her thumb. "Volume One. How did you come by it?" With his hand out, he said, "Please, may I have a look? A knave such as I could only benefit from it." He couldn't tell if she would part with it, smashed as it was between her breasts, lucky book.

"Just for a moment."

Her arms loosened forward and Mac tugged the volume from her tight grip. He sat back with it, turning pages and stopping to look long at the picture of Sir John Froissart, whose photogravure was stern, with an unsmiling face under a chiseled nose and heavy brows. Mac recognized the man's floppy hat and the heavy, square, carved chair in which Froissart sat. As he paged further, he found the names Sir Reginald Lord Cobham, Sir Walter Manny of Hainault—his friends, so alive when Mac had last seen them, last read their names by the fire in Froissart's home, now appeared so dead in black print on a white page.

Maggie grabbed the book back. "Let me tell you of my favorite knight, a man like my father. He respects woman, does not use them. He improves the world, does not abuse it. If you want to learn," her tone sounded doubtful, "this is the man to learn from." She flipped through the pages and then settled into some text and read the favored-above-all knight's name, Sir James MacArthur.

She might have read more, but the man to whom she was reading broke out in laughter again, this time to the point of tears. Mac couldn't help it. This woman was that earnest, to the point of single-minded obsession, and the Morrigan had answered her prayers. So the goddess had shoved him through time to this woman who was promised a knight, her favorite knight. Mac reduced his hilarity to some bass chuckles as he watched her freeze, her eyes the last to go hard.

"I'm sorry. I know the name. He never thought of himself as a saint." Mac leaned forward and put his hand on her knee. "Please read."

"You do not know him. I will not—"

"What's the story about?" A little girl appeared beside Maggie. She had pulled her thumb out of her mouth to ask. She had protruding teeth and too-widely set colorless eyes. "I like stories," she finished as she leaned in to glance at the book. She scooted next to Maggie and waited, her thumb back in her mouth.

As Maggie let the girl snuggle closer, Mac leaned his head against the seat and his eyes closed, ready to listen. Froissart had never liked Padric. Mac's friend had not made it into the book.

Maggie's voice was a disembodied background to the musings of a life Mac had been living only a fortnight ago. He knew the stories better than Froissart had, and his mind filled in the gaps. He opened his eyes when he finally felt a hand on his knee. He looked up to her eyes looking keenly at his.

"You have been sleeping." It seemed like a triumphant accusation.

"Not for a single minute."

"What?" she asked. "What could this book possibly have for you?"

He saw in her eyes, in the tone of her voice, in the uprightness of her person that what it had for him she would forever underestimate and never believe. Mac remembered that moment in the stable when she had seen the blood on his shirt before his exterior identity had been revealed. She had gazed at him with an inspection that was both tender and concerned. Her hand had been small and light on his back. He had wanted to turn and cover it with his own.

As she sat on a train going west, he measured the sadness he had seen in her against the person of action that she was. He loved the broken heart that still beat against her chest. Her dead father may have had a role in bringing him here, but Mac knew then that the Morrigan hadn't brought him here just for Maggie's sake. Padric's sister would be impressed with herself. Froissart, the writer of courtly love, would be ecstatic.

He could see as he asked for the book, in her profound hesitation in giving it to him, that the moment of sharing his story was a long time off, if ever. Maggie wasn't ready to hear who he was, or how he had gotten here, something which he didn't understand himself. He'd wait until her touch was less tentative, the love in her eyes full, and then they'd explore the impossible together. Only, for all that, the Morrigan would need to bring forth Froissart as a mediator.

Promising on God's everlasting life that he would not harm the volume, and that she could watch while he held it, he eased book one from her grasp. Her look measured the worth of the book against the man, and Mac knew he was losing.

CHAPTER EIGHT

M aggie hadn't missed how quiet, even insular Randy-Mac's face had become as he listened to her read. She knew he had forgotten the train, the malodorous breath, and the greasy sausages. For a moment, she had been jealous of his escape.

She gave him the book. Now she envied the heavy interest Mac had in its pages. She watched him read, and then flip pages, rereading some. When she saw him settle into its entirety, heartburn churned in her stomach. Contemplating his happy face, she felt like she had drunk too much tea. She touched her knees to his but got no reaction. Why would Randolph McMillan be so affected by a book on chivalry? The man was an artist in misdirection. He should be on the stage.

When he read for hours, never even glancing up once, she turned her face to the window again. She leaned against it and wished for sleep. McMillan had bested her; she just didn't get it.

Maybe Guy had, too.

Like an animal that hibernates in winter, she wanted to close her eyes and pass the time until spring in happy oblivion. But her dreams gave her no peace. Maggie was half awake and in the drama of her mind, she was watching Guy and her mother sashay across a buffed ballroom floor, looking at each other.

Later, at each turn, each revolution, her mother's partner was not Guy, but Randolph. Randolph and then Guy and then Randolph again in a dizzy dance. On the floor, a fog moved with her mother's dress. The vapor rose higher and got denser until there was nothing but a wall of opaque froth, and then a knight on a silver-gray charger galloped out of the spindrift. The horse was snorting and tossing its head.

The knight, his woolen tunic moist and imprinted from the links of chainmail, jumped from the horse to lift Maggie up, and walked with her up winding stairs. The fabric of her thin shift, molded to her breasts, shaped the roundness there and the hardness of her nipples.

She waited for his face, the visor hiding it. She begged to glimpse it, her mouth pouting, the strength of his arms against her back and legs. Instead of lifting his hands to the strap of his helmet, he placed her on a silken bed and slid his hands under her flowing skirts. His skilled hands slipped up her thigh and into her under-garments, lightly grazing a place there, a touch that was warming like hot tea to a cold breath. He traced a ring around it over and over with the tip of his finger, now and then pressing through the middle. She heard herself cry out. The cry woke her. The sensations from the dream remained between her legs and in her mind and heart.

Across from her, in the dawn light, Randolph still read her book. His face was relaxed, unshaven, his dark hair tousled.

He is more than just the combination of his well-drawn features. Without any hardness from anger or discontent, he is in total command of himself.

Her mind was still dream heavy. With just-awakened-from sleep clarity, Maggie felt her body needing him. Uneasy, she closed her legs more tightly and withdrew her knees from his.

I am not my mother. I am not my mother.

She didn't like him and didn't need him. Only her mother needed men, bad men.

As she watched him, Randolph rested the book on his thigh and closed his eyes. If his eyes had been open, she would never have reached over to ease the book from under his hand. That hand, the hand in the dream. Those fingers, as a whisper on the length of her leg, she growled at her thoughts and slid the book away from him.

In a quick-time reflex, Randolph came to life. He put his hand over hers.

"A knight, is that what you want? You want a knight to save you? From what?"

She snatched her hand from his. "I don't need saving. Men, men need saving. Not a chivalrous one in the male race."

He put his hand on her knee. "Women always save men."

Maggie paused and let his hand remain on her knee—the hand that held promise and warmth.

No! She was not her mother.

She worked not to flinch as she stared him down. She could let his hand touch her without emotion.

"Men live life from a point of view from which they will always need saving." His finger stroked the back of her hand.

"Like you and Guy."

"Not me. I'm in Froissart. I don't need saving, either."

Maggie did grab the book then, closed it with a snap and smoothed the cover. "Chivalry, love, valor, loyalty, generosity—"

"'A love of independence and a decided inclination to court danger wherever it might be found—the love of danger, not perhaps for its own sake, but for the glory of surmounting it,'" Mac added to the quote from Froissart.

She gaped at the words, perfectly said. Beautiful words. Like he knew them intimately, from his heart. She hated them coming from this man's lips. She felt bruised.

"Glory! How can you, a man from an extraordinary birthright who throws it all away in daily debaucheries like you do, speak of glory? You grew up in a house with forty-three rooms, twelve bathrooms, and an atrium with volcanic rock to create some kind of tropical climate. You chose to degrade yourself. Is that your excuse, the glory of rejecting a rich and noble past?" The snap in her voice whipped about his ears.

"I really have no idea, but if I were guessing, I'd say that it may have been a rich past, but not a noble one."

"Noble, who knows? There is money, lots of it. Wealth is not usually gotten through noble methods. So you resort to death and mayhem, and your excuse is that your family wasn't noble. Couldn't you find the basics of life another way?"

"A knight, a real knight of the realm, was always in the company of thieves. He loved independence and danger."

"Is that the deepest thought you have?"

"At the moment." He leaned forward and beckoned her toward him with the movement of his index finger. Into her ear he said, "You had some very unladylike moans in your sleep that made me blush—a sweet blush like the one on your cheeks now."

Maggie's crushing retort was lost in the jostling by a very large woman from across the aisle who stood above Maggie to lift down a suitcase.

"Opposites attract," he said just before leaning back.

"No, they don't really. Not in a healthy way." Maggie pulled her skirts from under the bag that now rested in the vacant seat next to her. She smoothed her dress, fussed with her cuffs, and tucked her hair back. The actions were meant to make her feel more in control, but she was aware of Randolph watching her. Under his scrutiny, she was more aware of the line of her arm to her slight wrist, of the rise and fall of her breast, of the sound of blood in the curve of her ear. She noticed her every feminine movement. Nothing was too slight, even the modest lowering of her eyes and her lashes on her cheek. Her escape had become absurd. She had escaped from one dishonest man and had ended up in the hands of another.

Somewhere in all these thoughts, her inner voice was vaguely repeating what Mitchell had said: "It is too big an undertaking, too many things to go wrong." With the little girl gone, the woman and the luggage left, Randolph sat down next to Maggie.

He picked up her hand and held it loosely, his thumb gently rubbing her palm. The direct touch without the sheath of her glove felt magnified. With a sound of resignation, she adjusted her body away from his into the space he left her. What was in a hand anyway, if he wanted it that badly? It was just a hand.

She let the comfort of his presence warm her. She'd been so cold for so long. So cold. She wanted the sun. Soon she'd have to send him packing, and she'd be very lonely, but she wouldn't think of that now.

By early evening, she saw that civilization was gratefully arriving. The beginning dregs of Kelton, Utah were passing outside the train window. Soon she and the rest of the travel-worn humanity swarmed onto the wooden platform beside the locomotive and then moved into a dirt-shrouded station house.

A woman with five children slapped the tops of their heads to get them to stand together in an orderly fashion. The father of the children shook Randolph's hand after he helped them all disembark. Randolph had gone back and forth with them for all their bags and bits. They'd offered to put him up for the night if he needed it. Maggie wasn't sure if that included her.

He addressed them all by name. In the three days, she hadn't introduced herself to anyone. Well, she was in mourning. Her hair flipped as she turned away, but her feet dragged through the clapboard station. Before Guy, before all this, she had been nicer. How absurd, she thought in an unhappy humor, that she was feeling low in comparison to Randolph McMillan, who was either not being himself or being himself to perfection. Damn the man.

Maggie's legs needed airing after sitting so long. She paid a baggage man to deliver her trunks to the best hotel in the place. A setting sun was the only color in the infinite, flat topography of brown, not a tree or flower. Thank God for the sound of voices, many voices. Without them, she was likely to get back on the train. She pulled gloves over her moist palms. As she stepped down the stairs, her knees buckled, and she caught herself on the railing. Her head was light with the thought of a bed, of being stretched out. This adventure had had a sorry lack of beds in it.

She gathered her skirts to step from the station. She paused. If she walked out of this, well, train station, she wasn't sure that he would follow. Of course he would. He was on a mission, and she was the center of it. Only she couldn't figure that out. She hadn't been good company. *Look at him over there, like they're all the best of friends.*

You've been miserable, like a sodden cat. Who wouldn't be under the circumstances? My mother just died, and I'm all alone in the middle of nowhere.

She was alone. Only he'd been at her back, singing, from the beginning. She couldn't have survived that train without him. Randolph McMillan. First, she looked out at where she was heading. *Dear God, this town.* She glanced over at him to catch his eye. His lifted straight to hers like he'd known where she stood all along. It was relief, she told herself that tickled her heart.

The rough planked-wood structures of the town of Kelton, Utah needed to stand and shake dust off them like a dog shakes water from its fur. Once she had visited her father when he had been camping on the Red River. She couldn't understand why he'd want to live even for a few days under a canvas held up by poles when Garth Mansion was only a few miles away.

Her father had had a look of desperation to him, in his shirt-sleeves and with his unshaven face. It had scared her. It was the same with this town of toothpick buildings and mud and brown, not a hint of shade and no fragrance except of dust and horses. The air she breathed in was dry and brown. She began to fight to inhale. She began sobbing.

A man came up from behind. Randolph, of course. He linked with her arm and said, "Giddiyap."

The short walk to the town kicked up dust along the hem of her black skirt. She'd lived in the small mourning dress for five days. She arrived at Caldwell's Hotel in the same state that she'd arrived at the Saint Nickolas. This time she smelled worse. Here, the clerk didn't bat an eyelash. Randolph climbed the stairs with her. At the top, she turned right.

"Go get a bath. I'm going to. We both stink of sausage. I'm going to the bank then. There must be a laundry here somewhere for the clothes you have on?" she said before parting with him.

"A liberal drinking establishment to drown the dust in my throat is a better idea."

"You're under my employ."

He waved goodbye backwards over the top of his head.

Men!

Her room was clean, the bed without bugs. It had four walls and a picture, but no bathroom. Maggie poured water into a bowl and bathed her face. It was more blotched than the hide of a cow. Drying her face, she knew she'd feel better when she checked that her money was here, sent by wire. She'd be fine when she bought her ranch and had the house fashioned to her needs. She combed her hair and changed into a new garment. It was wrinkled, but fresher. The hotel clerk hadn't cared about dust or the smells of sausage, but she wasn't sure about bank managers.

The Utah Bank and Thrift was the only brick building on the main street. Its name had been engraved on its large glass windows. Two men opened doors for her. They swept their hats from their heads. Maggie held her head a little higher and used her hips to swish her skirts. She arranged her face and smile. Randolph McMillan wasn't the only one who could attract attention.

Impressed with how solid the bank appeared to be, Maggie walked with more bounce to her step. Compared to the rest of the town, its brick looked impregnable. The building took away some of her doubt about the cash Mitchell was to send. Surely it had arrived and was ready and waiting. Mitchell had been in charge. Dear, kind Mitchell. She couldn't remember a time when he hadn't been there for her. That's the sort of man she should have, or her mother. Instead, her mother married a debauched man like Guy and began the events that landed her daughter in a damnable town like Kelton. Maggie felt the now all too familiar sting behind her eyes.

She was dabbing tears when the bank manager finally came out, putting on his jacket as he walked toward her. She noted his exaggerated open face and wide eyes didn't suggest the large deposit he had on hand for her.

"Miss Bathurst?"

"Yes."

"I'm so sorry." He took her elbow and guided her to a chair.

"A glass of water, Miss Smith. I see you know."

"Know what?"

The sweating man shoved a telegram at her face. "I do apologize. There seems to have been a mix-up at your end."

When she opened her eyes again, she found herself on a brown sofa in a plain room. With a coverlet up to her neck, she lay with her gaze on the ceiling, like the ceiling was all that mattered, but even that didn't matter. What of it? She had fainted on the polished marble floor of the bank, the air squeezed from her lungs before the fall. No one cared that she lay on a sofa that had a blood stain just by her head and smelled of camphor and horse liniment. Bad names for Guy welled up with her tears. The day was dark even with the relentless desert sun spotlighting her from a cheery window.

The door opened. She closed her eyes again. If she could only go back into that black place. She heard the door close and then footfalls, but nothing else. She had expected a voice... *how are you feeling...* or some such question. She tried to breathe as if she still slept. Her wrist tingled with the anticipation of a doctor's touch to take her pulse. She tried not to squirm.

Quit watching me, damn it.

"Oh." And then she knew who was standing there. Growling, she let her lids fly open. Randolph waited next to her, not a bit of a sympathetic look in his face for a sick patient. He didn't speak. The silence became unbearable.

"What do you want?" She curled up and turned away from him a little. "There is no money."

A chair scraped across the room. Close to her he said, "I read the paper."

"The telegram, for God's sake," she corrected, shaking her head and wanting him to quit pretending. "Mitchell promised me it would be here." She was crying. She could taste the salt in her mouth. "He promised." She noted the lack of inflection in her voice. Her arms felt heavy, and her legs. Exhaustion and despair had all but stilled her heart. Was it still beating? She raised her weighty arm to cover her eyes from the bright sun. She let the sofa support her, like it would support her forever. The last man she ever thought would have failed her—had.

"Don't think of any campaign as winning or losing. It's more about strategy."

"Damn you. Strategy! From the moment I stepped out my door nothing has gone right."

"You are here."

"I hated that train ride here, third class, every minute of it, every second of every minute. I can't do this. In all of this, I didn't think there wouldn't be any money."

"Many people live without money."

"That's very rich coming from you. Damn it, I don't understand what happened. Mitchell has never, ever failed me."

"The doctor says you're fine. Overtired, so the sleep was good, but fine. Time to get out of bed."

"How did you find me?"

"Where anyone starts a journey. Where the funds are."

Maggie popped up to a sitting position. She listened to the muffled tramping of boots on the boarded walkway outside her window, people calling to each other, children playing. She rejected it and lay back down. She only had enough money to pay for another few nights at the hotel, and then there was Randolph, now planted in a chair and judging her.

"Damn it," she said quietly in her thought of going home.

"If you get up we'll have something to eat, and I'll tell you my plan."

There it was. They all had her where they wanted her. Briefly she wondered if Mitchell was dead. That's the only way he would have failed to get the money to her. She couldn't conceive of how they'd done it, of how they knew, of how they'd commanded the wind, rain, and thunder. She even suspected Cook.

CHAPTER NINE

Sir Guy Didsbury sat in his library. He was alone in the fire-less room in a cold, quiet house. The velvet curtains remained drawn, smothering the spring air and healthy sun. He slumped in a wide chair, drinking. Grace had died. He had started drinking and he hadn't stopped. Around him, glasses, like breeding bric-a-brac, had damaged furniture with rings of water. The wake had ended, the servants had fled, and the room smelled of sour booze. He scratched at his unshaven face and could hear the bristles. Everyone had asked about Maggie.

He had hated the endless people coming and going with their sorrowful faces and their cliché words. It was unusual that he had despised such a day, as he normally craved the place of honor, from where he excelled in the games he loved. The weight of the funeral and subsequent debauchery was evident in his fleshy face.

Guy felt old, and he drank in pain from McMillan's blow.

He had lost her to Randolph McMillan. The thought amazed him still, and that worried him. He thought he had known her well. He sipped pensively at his brandy his hands cold around the glass. Guy was amazed he was still alive. He had shot at Randolph McMillan and lived. No sense to the world.

A Tiffany lamp illuminated his desk in broken colors. A minia-ture of Grace smiled at him. He reached for her and missed slightly. Hell. He got it the second time. She had been a beautiful thing. He traced the line of her face and her mouth with his thumb. He could smell the phantom of her flowery perfume, and he imagined her fine brown hair sifting through his fingers. She had had a lovely laugh, and she moaned gently when they made love. She had been everything.

Maggie, damn her, was like her mother unfettered. She wasn't as beautiful in the classical sense, but the girl had more passion than her mother. Her eyes were more memorable because of it. Guy threw his glass across the room. Where was his damn son? That Guy had done all for this room, for this leather chair, for the bankroll that bulged in his pocket seemed little enough, suddenly. He stum-bled to a table to pour another brandy. Greed made for a lonely life, and after a slug of booze he again didn't give a damn.

He looked up as footsteps punctuated by the tap of a cane on marble in the hallway. "What do you want, Montague?" he called through the open door in an annoyed and sobering voice.

A man appeared at the frame with his cane planted in front of him. Long gray hair carefully combed and lacquered off a large face told Guy he'd been right. Linden Montague sniffed the room and pulled out a handkerchief.

"What do you want?"

"Be gone your temper," Montague said with a wave of the linen in ringed fingers. "Have you bathed lately?" He moved hesitantly into the room, sitting on only the front half of a Chesterfield chair. "I have news for you, but I won't give it to you in that temper. Give me some of that brandy before you drink it all." He accepted the drink while adding, "It's awful in here. Why isn't the fire lit?"

"The servants have all gone."

"I know that. Everyone knows that. Still, you are quite capable of lighting it yourself, or are you weakened?"

"Damn, why do you always have to be so absurd?"

"That's it. I'm leaving. And my news is so very worthwhile to you."

Guy turned away from the man, sat heavily in his still warm chair and never glanced at his guest as he said, "Spit it out. You know you're dying to."

Guy heard the man stand.

"Not at all, really."

"For God's sake, Linden, sit down."

"For God's sake, maybe. Your son is gone?"

"You know he is. He's no use to me now."

Guy watched with growing anger as Linden shrugged his delicate shoulders. This crook was easy to hate with his affectations and allergies and beady eyes, but he was not easy to dismiss. The eyes of hawks are small, yet they penetrate the soul of a mouse from one hundred feet. Linden knew the makeup of Guy's being better than anybody, and the effeminate would wring out every last drop of Guy's fluid of life with his finely honed hands.

"You're the topic of the hour in all drawing room chatter. You're aware of that, I assume...Maggie gone...not even here for her mother's funeral, and after you've worked so hard to become respectable."

"Shut up."

Linden smiled and meandered to a sideboard, poured himself another drink and let his presence, his smirk, his condescension tap against the floor of the room like the insistent drip of water from a worn tap. Guy hated the man.

"Such rudeness," Linden said as he sat again.

"Either spit out what you've come to tell me or leave. Whatever information you have, I'm sure I can find on my own, because you are an idiot."

"But it will take you precious days. Soon your reputation will be sinking like a keel-holed vessel. Not only that, with Maggie gone, you have no chance of staying on here. You are her appointed guardian with nothing to guard. They'll bring in blood, a cousin or uncle."

"You have a terrible habit of asking things you already know."

"They won't let you keep Garth. They still don't know why Grace married you. Maggie, Grace, they keep you gentrified."

Guy raised a gun from the desktop and aimed it at the frill on Linden's chest. "No one will miss you either. Get to your point, if you have one, or get out."

"You won't shoot me, old boy."

"I'm in the mood to."

"Ha, ha, this has all been such fun. I think I'll just tell you anyway so I can stand back and watch the fireworks. For my compassion, you're about to give me a bottle of very old Scotch, and anyway, you shouldn't drink anymore." With the gun still pointed at him, but loosely so as he walked, Linden took the bottle and readied his exit. "The Saint Nicolas. She arrived looking the devil, I might add, with Randolph McMillan. What's that young man up to now, I asked myself? They left together."

"I know about McMillan, you reprobate. Unless you have anything else, leave the bottle."

If Linden was nonplused, he didn't show it. "She's gone west. As far as Utah. Now there, I've given information worth a fifteen-year-old bottle of Glenmorangie, and don't worry about thanking me. It was my pleasure. I know how much you need her back." Linden left laughing. The door shutting behind him cut off the sound.

Alone again, Guy picked up Grace's will at his fingertips on the desk. He reached over to the only light in the room and pulled it closer to him and read, carefully. He had no other purpose now but to find Maggie, no other need but to see her back here or dead. He still didn't inherit, but he'd see to that, too. His alcohol-infused blood began to clear with purpose. He didn't need his son, either. Maybe it was better if Maggie died. He'd marry the next person beyond Maggie to inherit. Grace's sister. That was better anyway. That such thinking was the product of Scotch, gin, and/or brandy, he recognized. He still tingled from forward thinking. It aroused him. Hate had always done that.

She'd been seen with McMillan—so much the better. She had also missed her mother's funeral. It would be easy to brand her insane. A fusion of electricity passed through him. Nothing would be left of her anyway after McMillan had had his way.

Everything had gone wrong. Bloody bitch. Guy stood and with a single arm swept everything off the dusty top of his desk. It all landed with little noise onto the carpeted floor. Nothing had broken, not the lamp, Grace's picture, the will, his worn-out crystal tumbler, or a picture of William, his goddamn, absent son. Wanting to smash something, he upended the desk and threw the chair, and then he grabbed the servant's bell-cord and rang it like a madman. Kicking the legs out from under a small table, he burst through the door that Linden had last used.

In the hallway, he wiped at his face with his hands, feeling the stubble there. The quiet of the room, the house surrounded him. It helped soothe his breathing and reconnect his brain. He had let his guard down too far. He had allowed himself to be taken in by a woman with a kind heart and a good smile. She had died.

Left him.

Oh, Grace.

He knocked a vase off a hall table. It had all been a ruse, a play day for the Fates. Well, it was his turn to play now. He cleaned up and then pushed his hat low over his burning eyes and went to the stables to saddle a horse.

Guy rode straight through the gates. He looked at nothing for miles, never pressing the horse, but never letting it stray from his single-minded road to the office of Jules Mitchell, Garth's solicitor. Standing in front of Mitchell's desk, Guy's hard gaze nearly pierced a hole in the center of the lawyer's round head. Guy held himself rigid, trying not to kill the man.

"She's gone to Utah."

Mitchell was a poker-playing man. He didn't flinch.

"With McMillan. I have no choice but to have all the Garth accounts frozen."

"That's preposterous. He's got plenty of money."

"Doesn't matter. He clearly needs more. I must protect her inheritance from herself. You have to do it, and then I will send detectives after her. Is that clear? By a court of law, you will be summoned to tell me all you know, or you will be in jail. Is that clear? Let's not make this ugly. Nobody knows about McMillan but me and you. Is she staying in Utah, or is she going somewhere else? Where else?"

Mitchell didn't budge.

"She is about to lose everything on the grounds of either kidnapping or grief-produced insanity. She ran off into a storm the night her mother lay dying and she hasn't been heard of since except in the company of Randolph McMillan. She missed her mother's funeral. Either way, as her guardian, I am concerned for her."

"No one will believe that."

Guy moved forward slowly, with relish. He'd let the attorney enjoy his victory for just a moment more. Let it grow in the room. Guy delighted in finally saying, "I will make them believe me. God, when they hear my first-hand account of how she left, my concern will be quite believable. After that, she will have to testify to her sanity herself, here, in court. And then she will have to be watched, her money and Garth looked after. Who would marry a crazy woman? Let her know, will you? After you close all accounts."

"You're a bastard, Guy. If I have to freeze the accounts, I will be very sure that they are frozen to everyone. No payouts to anyone. What has she ever done to you?"

"What hasn't she done to me?"

"She will return married. By then no one will remember."

"Oh, is that her plan? Who will marry her after McMillan has had her in knots?"

"How do you know he is with her?"

"I tried to shoot him. She saved his worthless life. It's the real truth. Can you believe that, lawyer? She saved his life. Maybe she really has gone mad."

Mitchell frowned. He'd given the game away. Stupid besotted man. He'd also been sucking off the Garth tit.

Guy was gratified to hear the strain in the lawyer's voice. His plan with Maggie had gone wrong. So McMillan had never been a part of it. Fate? What did McMillan stand to gain?

Maggie married and back to claim Garth. I'll see her dead first.

Mitchell's whiskered lips had been so pressed together that they had gone bloodless. Guy laughed at the lawyer all the way down Fourth Street. He hummed as he entered the Ohio National Bank on Third. Power, the bald use of it, stretched him taut as a bowstring that hummed in a strong breeze. It thrummed through him now like a powerful lyric. He'd already stashed money for a rainy day, and it was pouring.

Business didn't take long. Back outside and with the Saint Nicolas in view, he stopped and leaned against a brick wall. He took a cigar from his jacket, lit it, and smoked deeply while watching the hotel through slits between narrow eyelids. The cigar eased and centered him.

He reviewed the semantics of his next sequence of events. His next victim would not roll as easily as the lawyer had. This man would not lose the debate so witlessly, but then again, Guy had the only card that meant anything to Randolph McMillan's father. McMillan Senior would be having lunch at the hotel, as he did every Thursday at twelve o'clock.

When it was time, Guy retraced what he knew of Maggie's steps across the oriental carpet and into the dining room. Guy had not always been comfortable with linen and lines of silver spoons. But he didn't think it all above him even if he wasn't a knighted landowner in England as he'd lead people to believe. Comfort with society was a matter of habit, daily practice, acknowledgement of skill, like learning to stab through a heart at the point of a saber.

He smiled inside himself, knowing what he knew, what he was going to tell the man he was meeting. He liked visceral, hard-muscled moments like this. He walked slowly, living the emotion bit by bit, moment by moment, feeding the hook phrase through his mind over and over, and basking in the mental kill. He almost drooled in anticipation, but his lips were stuck too tightly together as he controlled his face.

At the back of the room was the Hog King, Edmond McMillan. He didn't smell of hogs or look of them. McMillan sat at a table wearing a dark suit with a red flower staining its lapel, a white linen shirt, and gold cufflinks. The Hog King's face was firm and closed. He didn't look up at Guy's arrival but continued reading the menu. Guy sat comfortably in an opposing chair. Guy understood power, how it shifted.

After the waiter had taken McMillan's order and Guy had waved him away, the Hog King had to look at Guy across from him. The table was small and to look anywhere else was pointless. Guy was ready.

"Well, man, what is it?" The Hog King raised a large whiskey to his mouth.

McMillan may not have looked like the animals he slaughtered, but he talked like them.

"Come on, man."

The time had come. *Too bad,* Guy thought. Too damn bad. He'd have liked to be on good terms with the man, powerful as he was in this town.

"Magnolia Bathurst, daughter of Grace Bathurst, has been abducted by your son."

"The boy's good looking. He has a way with women."

"She was taken the night her mother lay dying. Magnolia deeply loved her mother. They were very close. You can ask anyone who knows them."

Guy didn't see a flicker of emotion in the man—and he watched him with directness so pure that blinking had ceased—and then the Hog King exploded like a wet wick finally drying out and then incinerating. The King ripped the napkin from his collar and threw it down—a gauntlet between them.

"And you've come to me. Who's seen this abduction? When you can prove to me she's in chains by bringing back the links, then we'll talk."

"She'll be ruined by then."

"By then...by now or by never. If you're taking me to a court of law, you'd better have your facts straight. On the other hand, if you want me to square them, fine, I'll square them. I tell you this, if anyone needs recompense for being carried off by my son, it wouldn't be you. Now get out so I can eat."

Guy walked out into the blazing sun. The air was heating up. He could smell McMillan's pigs, their muddy, crass, putrid stench. He swore on everything that's holy into the fetid air. His win with Mitchell was fading. He swore again and wanted a drink. He wanted it so badly his mouth parched, and his tongue swelled. Whiskey stilled the voices, eased his mind—numbed it to clarity. Got the smell of hogs out of his nostrils. He hated being small with big people over him. He'd take God's place if he could manage to swindle the deity.

He needed to think about what he had and what he didn't have as a result of his talk with Mitchell. But the drink first—double whiskey.

"Jesus H Christ." He had miscalculated with Maggie.

Guy started walking to Dead Man's corner, to George Burnside Cox's saloon—a place where anything could be bought, and nothing was paid for—to a glass of strengthening rye with an old crony. The one problem of freezing Garth assets was that he now had to be a little more careful. His bribes would be less plentiful.

He'd have his own man watch the lawyer, make sure funds weren't slipping through to Maggie. Mitchell would either have to come up with her whereabouts or freeze her out. Guy had plenty of reasons to require money to hire a Pinkerton man of his own. Find one, find the other. Guy liked his thoughts. He knew one thing: he could make a deal with almost any patron drinking at Cox's—a deal for anyone's life.

CHAPTER TEN

Mac let the front legs of his chair drop to the floor. It was time to rouse the fair maiden from her sleeping couch. She'd had a shock, but she would survive. As Maggie's red-blooded opponent, Randolph was something for her to measure and weigh, someone to keep her mind strategizing. "Who's going to tighten this corset?" he said, holding it up in front of her.

"Not you," she said as she continued to recline on the sofa.

Mac leaned the chair back again. The money was gone, but if he let her wallow in the sequence of events, she would be further hardened.

"Give me that, you ill-bred exploiter of mankind."

"You shrew of a woman, put it on."

He laughed when her eyes got wide, and then narrowed.

That's it, my love. Keep plotting my overthrow. Get up.

And when he handed her Guy's weapon, she glanced from it to him and back again. She took it and then flipped open the chamber and saw it was still empty.

"How does that work?" he asked.

With a long sigh like she was trying to deflate her lungs.

Maggie sat up and moved her feet to the floor. "Don't start that with me. My God, any person with any intelligence could figure that out by trial and error. You put the bullets in here, plink, plink, and plink. You close it. You point it. You pull the trigger." She aimed it at him and pulled the trigger. They stared at each other while the grandfather clock in the hall ticked five pendulum swings.

"Very good to know," Mac said, holding her gaze. "It's not something to play with, I would think."

"I've shot you, and you didn't die."

She broke eye contact with him and turned the corset. "Why do these miseries tie in the back?"

The chair legs thumped the floor again. Mac leaned in close. "I can help."

"Never, ever you. Call for someone else."

Her hair was tousled, and her eyes sparked from their debate. He liked her that way, though better without the stiffness and self-righteous anger. Her mouth taunted him, and he would kiss it thoroughly if he could just get closer.

"You will never touch these strings."

"Then who?"

"The doctor, anyone else."

Boots pounded to the doctor's door, and it crashed open. Some other voice, a male voice, called throughout the house for the physician. The same man kicked open the door of the parlor. It swung past Mac, and he felt the air move. The door smacked the wall. The man carried a child into the room, only he stopped short when he saw Maggie. Still carrying the little girl, he backed out the door, and called for the doctor again.

"Doctor's busy." Mac shut the door with his foot. "I can do it while standing five paces away."

"God forsaken. I am God forsaken," she muttered.

Mac watched her loosened hair swing as she prepared to stand by gathering the blanket around her. Her hair had had a hard time of it, staying up, that is.

"Well, turn around, and stay around. I'm going to be watching, and I'll let you know when you can turn, and then five feet away."

When she called him to help, Mac delighted in noting that he'd have to move her hair to get to the laces. He lifted the length of it. Soft, heavy. With one hand on the corset and blanket, Maggie jerked the bulk of her hair away from him with her other hand. She placed it over her shoulder. He brushed the curve of her neck with his fingers as he eased a few more strands forward.

"Just the laces."

Mac pulled so hard air expelled from her lungs. "Good?"

"You're an unadulterated ass," she squeaked out.

He laughed and let the corset loosen. Her mane forward left her neck vulnerable. Mac tied the strings off and then leaned down to kiss just at the curve of her shoulder. He knew he'd pay for it.

She turned and slapped him.

"I knew it," she said.

"That you did. So what's next?"

A knock at the window, and a face peered in. Maggie squealed and gathered her blanket closer. "Are ye there? Anyone home? Randolph McMillan? I haven't lost ye, have I? I had a dreadful thirst getting off that bleeding train."

Lefcadio Hearn, as Mac walked and lived.

"Ye will not be going without me? Fine bastard that ye are."

As Maggie sank back down onto her sofa wrestling with her shirtwaist, Mac left toward the front porch. She was dressed by the time he returned with a skinny Irishman wearing an everyday face and spiky reddish hair.

"Damn me trousers, didn't I say to myself the next morning after that beautiful breakfast you stood me that there's your next story: the sainting of Randolph McMillan. I'm sorry, me boyo, but I had to come."

From the blank expression in her eyes, Mac figured Maggie had forgotten about money for the moment.

"This is a lady who wishes to be called Maggie, and that's her real name. I wish to be called Mac and that is my real name. Maggie, this is a newspaperman, so he calls himself, whom I met in Cincinnati. His real name is... I'm not joking, and he doesn't mind you using it, Lefcadio Hearn. He is originally from Ireland, as you probably guessed."

"That she did, and I'm a terrible man altogether for coming, but I will forever be a scoundrel."

"Then I'm surrounded," Maggie said with a slight smile.

"She's the heart of the virgin herself, so she is."

"So she is," said Mac. "Lefcadio, we are off to homestead. Are you to join us?"

"Jaesus, homesteading is it? As dreary as all that? What about a Turkish Bath?"

"I can't see Maggie making that much soap."

The Irishman laughed and explained how he'd traveled, while Mac watched the corners of Maggie's lovely mouth slide upward as she reached over her back and loose-braided her mane. The pink was coming back to her cheeks. Such was the Irishman's effect on her when he said, "Your beautiful face was worth the long days."

"I like you. You're a friend of Randolph's? Would you lend me your elbow? I'm starving," Maggie said as she put her hand on his arm and walked with him to the door. "Let's at least find something to eat."

"I'm a bit peckish meself."

"I'll just pay the doctor then, will I?" Mac said.

————

Even though every piece of timber, from the chairs to the planks on the wall, was right-angled and raw, Mac noticed Maggie didn't sniff at the rough dining room as if she were eating in an oversized water closet. The waitress had a disdainful look, and the woman wore an apron that looked as if it had been touched by everything in the kitchen but soap. The aroma of roast in the air was wonderful. Maggie ate like a soldier.

Hearn's gift of gab never failed him as he shoveled in mountains of food. Maggie had never been as fluid as she talked in kind, even though Hearn smelled like week-old underwear. Her face only half-puckered as she drank cheap wine. In Hearn she had a shield. She was going to make the best of it.

When the waitress returned with Mac's plate and stayed with her breasts in his ear, Maggie "accidentally" knocked over her full cup of coffee, which dripped over the edge of the table and through the spaces in the slats in the floor.

"I'm very sorry, really so sorry," she said to the waitress' dour look.

The woman looked Maggie up and down, no doubt taking in the cut of Maggie's dress, the soft braid of her hair, and the stylish hat that perched on it. When she found Maggie's face again, Maggie grinned—a smile that had no friendliness under her direct eyes. *Move on, ye wee bitch.* That was the look. Mac finished eating.

Interesting times.

"When did you come up with homesteading?" Maggie asked when she finally leaned away from Hearn.

He thought she'd have more fight in her about it, but she needed Randolph right now. She knew he had money, and now she had Hearn as chaperone. As Mac had been watching her, he figured she didn't, as yet, so much want him, as she was loath to give him to someone else. Or maybe that was wishful thinking, he told himself. No bigger fool than James MacArthur over women. Padric had pointed that out, time and time again. *Face it, boyo, she has nowhere else to go—except home.*

Mac was amused that Lefcadio had followed along. He'd perceived something about the Irishman. Hearn was going to be useful with Maggie, and better yet, the Irishman could help him kill Randolph, by newsprint.

Mac leaned back in his chair. Thanks to the lilt of the Irishman's voice, Mac craved his old pipe and the acid smell of a wood fire. His mind ached for a sword in his hand, and the mental stimulus of an opponent. At the sound of Hearn, he could almost smell his own breath from the inside of his visor mixed with the sweat of his face and the odor of wet steel, while battling back to back with Padric, his friend singing all the while.

"Why do you lean back in your chair so often? You look like a cowboy and you're going to fall over." As if Maggie wasn't going to stay in Kelton, Utah one more minute, she stood.

Hearn, half standing over the table, drank the rest of his coffee in large wet gulps. "Not half like her mother."

"The potential is there."

"The potential is there in all of us. Sure as it's not always realized."

"That's why I'm here." As Mac followed her lead to the livery, he thought of the fragility of the village. No sturdy castle or city wall for it to huddle against, only false-fronted, hastily built stores. He wondered if this town had no enemies to invade it. Then again, the people living here almost all wore guns.

At the livery, the wagon merchant was as basic a thirteenth century market shyster as Mac had ever met. He strolled around the wagons just behind Maggie, hanging on her every syllable. Paying attention to everything, he agreed with whatever she said. Mac gave her imperial mood room. She needed to feel back in control. He liked to watch her with her head up and her nose higher.

She acted like she knew everything and missed nothing, acting with divine right and feeling comfortable at the raised height. She must feel too much air under her feet as she walked. She was a beautiful woman. She inspected wagons with an air of naïve conviction. Her world had been ordered; she'd never suffered failure. Failure made a person more cautious.

He left her to herself until she stopped in front of a wagon with rusted wheels. "Maggie." When she turned her head, he motioned to her with an index finger. He squatted next to the wheel and peered under. "With your experience in wagons, I'm surprised you didn't see this hairline split in the rear axle. This wagon won't last ten miles before it blows apart."

Her hot, rosy face turned redder and then it closed. She stood abruptly and turned on her heels. "Fine, you choose one then. Do you think I can handle the supplies?" She stiff-walked across the street to the mercantile. Mac let her go with a shrug. Then again, sometimes he got damn tired of all the dramatics, all the dust raised from the woman's skirt.

The merchant rocked on his heels next to Mac, pulling on his greasy beard and observing him from under his stained hat. He spat out the side of his mouth and waited with the patience of a man who had the whole of the hot, sunny afternoon to sell a wagon.

Mac knew the man had noted the silk of Maggie's dress. It was going to be a hard-made deal.

"That one's cheap, if you want cheap. You could replace the wheel or are you in a hurry?" the wagon seller spat again.

Mac wasn't sure enough yet of the value of the money in his pocket. He wasn't near a Cincinnati bank and so all the purchases had to count. So far, he'd been literally handing amounts to shopkeepers to have them pick through to find what they needed. He was getting better, but lacked a certain edge, and so he asked in rapid succession the cost of ten wagons, in all degrees of repair, trying not giving the man room to think. His goal was to compare the spontaneous prices and then offer half.

"Sarvin wheels on that one," the merchant said. "Makes things a lot easier if you can take out the spoke without taking off the tire, and it's got an iron hub. With regular wheels, prices go up with each mile traveled."

"We could take public transport."

"All you'll be doing is breathing dirt from the air and eating dirt from the lard mixed in the biscuits at the home stations. Add in the pricey canned butter and double the price for condensed milk for coffee. One buck each for a slice of bacon, and for desserts, leather-like, lard-soaked crust with a veneer of apples. Don't forget the bedbugs or maybe you just want to sleep upright in the stage—eight in a coach."

"You have a number of wagons. Surely you want to get rid of one of them." Mac started haggling on a middling wagon and made it clear he wanted the package to include two mules and a horse, and a canvas roof.

"It never rains in the desert," the seller grumbled as he dumped a load of fabric into the wagon.

At the mercantile he found Maggie reading from a book. He took it from her and read the title, *The Prairie Traveler*.

"I was told that anyone going west had to have this." She grabbed it back and used her index finger to help her read a list: "Forty pounds of bacon, one hundred pounds of flour, and make sure it's packed in stout double canvas sacks well sewed as Mr. Marcy suggests, thoroughly boiled butter in soldered canisters, twenty-five pounds of sugar in India rubber sacks. Desiccated vegetables and potatoes, a set of dishes and pots... four blankets, two pillows, and a mattress."

Mac winced at hearing the word mattress and said into her ear, "I thought you were broke?"

"But you're not. Your idea, your expense."

She held herself with her hip cocked. She had to tip her head back to face him, but she was comfortable in her shoes, her clothes, her book, and her new plan to spend McMillan money.

"And your very best scotch for bug bites."

"Two bottles," Mac held up two fingers. "How much have you ordered on top of the bed?"

"I'm going, and I insist on being comfortable."

"I could march an army a thousand miles on what you're buying."

The proprietor stood and waited for more directions while his wife moved back and forth to fill the order. A few other customers leaned on barrels of rice and potatoes on which the earth they had come from continued to cling. Maggie stood like she had two corsets on. Defiance under long lashes raked him from head to toe.

Hearn had just gained the store and was at the door looking in. Mac made a sweeping gesture with his arm, one that started at his head and swung in an arch to his feet. "Yes, milady, and just where are you going?" When she didn't answer, he turned to the proprietor. "I've heard a few at the bar talking about black soil for farming and ranching in Idaho. Going that direction, how far until the next town?"

"About three hundred and fifty miles."

"Water?"

"The Snake River about halfway. They're having trouble with the Nez Perce Indians in up there, you know."

"Indians," Maggie exclaimed.

"Won't join the reservation. That's north Idaho. The Bannock, Shoshoni, and Sheepeaters around Boise and Caldwell are settled. The good farming land is up to the north, though."

"That's what I heard," Mac said.

"Sheepeaters?" Maggie repeated.

"Better than people eaters," Mac replied.

"Boise has about two thousand people now. Real settled."

Mac sifted through the growing piles on the counter. "If it's only three hundred miles, we'll take about half of this."

"Mr. Marcy suggests—"

"Mr. Marcy must have been going to the Holy Land and back three times. We don't need any more weight for the mules than necessary." Mac picked up a folded cloth item.

"That's your gutta, percha poncho and four colored silk hand-kerchiefs."

"Does the book specify color? Will it be raining much in May around here?" Mac asked the storekeeper.

"April-May is the rainy season, such as it is. Desert from here to there, but good grass for the animals this time of the year with the hills greening a bit."

"We need bullets for this." Guy's gun was back in the sunlight that shown without brightness on the countertop through a dirty window.

"I'd also like to look at one of those with the longer barrel," Mac said.

"A rifle?"

"Oh, and soap." Maggie added. "A comforter and sheets and a pillow."

Maggie cocked her head and kept her gaze on Mac, daring him to say anything about sheets and a pillow. *Half*, he mouthed again to the proprietor as he retreated out the door to wait for the total with Hearn at his shoulder.

"What's her story, then?"

"You'll learn it soon enough."

The same waitress from lunch, a dozing, blowzy girl, approached Mac. She had a come-hither expression that Mac wasn't used to as a way of life. She carried a basket Mac had ordered. He took the weight of it from her.

"Why thank you. You're so sweet. I told Mary you were so sweet. Leaving soon? Anything I can do to convince you to stay...here...with me?"

A man from the restaurant yelled out.

The young woman rolled her eyes. "One of his wives is sick, and he takes it out on me."

"He's got more than one?"

"Oh yes, and they're all bossy. Where are you from?"

"England."

"Hm." She laughed—a lovely and lilting laugh that didn't fit her plain face. "You are leaving, aren't you? Pity. This is for her, isn't it, this picnic? She's so lucky. If anything happens, come back." The waitress flashed a smile.

Hearn regarded Mac, and he shook his head. "It's all beyond the understanding of mortals." He slapped Mac on the back. "And that's why I'm here. Me editor is wiring me money. I've got to stay until the gold is in the palm of me hand."

"We might as well get started. The wagon will move slowly enough that you'll find us. If we don't stay on the main road, we may get lost anyway. I was told that the homesteads are being taken quickly. I need some money soon myself. Can it be sent here?"

"Said as if from the soul of a saint. You have been blessed with the most innocent of faces. Of course it can, me boyo, of course it can. I will bring it if you vouchsafe my person with the bankers. Of course, your father will know where you have been then."

"What will he do with the knowledge?"

"I suspect he'll be glad you're out of town."

The newly purchased wagon and its two horses stood in front of the general goods store, and Maggie wagged her index finger at Mac. At her beck-and-call, was it? Mac couldn't help but laugh in his heart. She didn't know yet that Hearn would be delayed.

CHAPTER ELEVEN

A t sunup Mac watched Maggie climb without speech onto the wagon bench. She looked back to see each semi-solid building fall behind them and become smaller as the sounds of civilization silenced and the day lightened. The town hadn't been much, but as he felt the jolt of each rut in the road, he knew it represented to her a sort of security. The wagon path itself became the only sign that any single person had traveled within the endless landscape. She sat without as much as a breath of movement even with a direct wind on her face, until he sang...

"I can sport as fine a trotting horse as any swell in town.

To trot you fourteen miles an hour, I'll bet you fifty crown. He is such a one to bend his knees and tuck his haunches in, and throw the dust in people's faces and think it not a sin.

For to ride away, trot away

Ri fa lar la and e—"

"You aren't going to sing all the way, are you?"

"So my singing brings you to life. I brought some sweet bread from the restaurant."

Mac reached into the wagon and handed her some.

Maggie took it but, didn't bite into it, and let it rest in her hand in her lap. She was sitting far from him on the wooden wagon bench. After the first mile, she glanced around her like something was missing. It was the incessant Irish brogue of Lefcadio Hearn.

"Where is he? Did you kill him?"

"I didn't, on my honor."

"Honor," she snorted. "Where is he really?"

"He had to wait for money to be wired from his editor."

"That sounded modern. Tired of the I-don't-know-what—?"

"No, I just listen."

"Let's go back and wait with him."

"No time like the present. He'll catch up. I'll be good."

Maggie moved over on the bench even more. "I am carrying the gun in my skirt pocket."

"A very wise decision. You don't know what knaves and rogues we may happen upon."

She turned her head over her shoulder and stretched her vision as far to the horizon that her eyes could see. "Will he be coming at all?"

"Yes, he will. On my honor."

She didn't scream at him or jump down and walk back toward Kelton. He half expected her to pull the gun on him, not just threaten him with it. There was no scene and so he knew that, with little choice, she was giving in again, letting apathy reign.

"Did you read all of my father's book then?"

Mac laughed. "Why shouldn't I?"

"Indeed, why shouldn't you? Seeing how a moral man lives?"

"You are too kind." He bit into a sandwich.

"Are you converting, as Lefcadio said? Wondering what the other side is all about?"

"Froissart, the author of your book, was not a realist. He wrote of what knights should be, not what they were."

"Ah, as if you knew him. Really... what were they then, pray tell me?"

"Many of them professional soldiers. Poor at that and paid to fight. Their expenses were larger than their incomes. If you want to add the work of saving women, which no doubt you do... then work without fee.

"Their armor was heavy and getting heavier, a full suit...four stone. Have you ever worn a helmet, bevor, besage, rondel, couter, vambrace, or gauntlets while swinging a long sword? As the suits became more complete, new weapons needed to be designed to pierce them. Regular swords would not slash them, but long, tapered swords, pollaxes, and halberds found the weak points in the armor. Longbows could pierce the plate, and then crossbows were created... and guns. Guns were coming."

He glanced at her and laughed to himself. Her face couldn't be more sucked in if it was a prune. The straightness of her back could work as a plank. He slapped the reins on the horses' rumps. He feared he wouldn't be able to suppress his laughter and go on. And go on he intended to do.

"In the end, a knight's purpose was to plunder and to get rich and then go home while he still lived, increase the size of his girth, sire children as the head of what once was someone else's estate that the king or queen had given to him as a prize for valor."

Maggie stared at him. "Is it possible for you to be more of an ass than you already are? I believe it is." She huffed away, tears and heat in her eyes. "Leave it to Randolph McMillan to miss the obvious."

"The obvious then...men walking around encased in steel was obviously impractical." His temper felt hot from her flame. He did not know why he needed to disillusion her. He had lived as a knight and died as a knight, but that encasing, that old body with its scars and its disabilities, had been a weight around his neck.

He'd had no peace in that life. He wasn't going to pour glossy lacquer over it and encourage superficiality. He wanted to be real to her. Suddenly tired of women using him, and right now wanting to feel the warmth of her skin against his, he slapped the reins against the mules' rumps. Which, because Maggie then moved over to the very edge of the seat, seemed to signal to her that she had been hijacked. His luck with women—things never changed. Mac thought of the lovely little waitress. Maybe he should be the one turning back.

With the journey once again in a silence that seemed to fit the flatness around him, the mules, never very fast, seemed to be moving more like sloths after a night of heavy drinking. At nightfall, he stopped the animals. He found that in the high desert, spring evenings were cold. He built up a hot, pungent fire with sagebrush that crackled. The restaurant basket was empty. He watched clouds come in with the last bit of light.

"It's going to rain," he said. Any conversation other than the weather seemed too emotional.

"It never rains in the desert. That's why it's the desert."

"So I've been told."

Maggie rubbed her hands together as the night temperatures dropped to very cold.

"How do you think that these daisies survive then?" Mac picked one and handed it to her. He expected her to stay bundled, her knees to her chin and her arms around her legs, ignoring the flower, but she turned her head to it and watched it for a while— a light breeze lifting the petals. She raised her hand to take it and in doing so, touched his fingers. She looked at him and he gazed back, and she didn't glance away.

"Is there anything you don't know?" she asked.

"I know that we have far to go, and we haven't even started."

"Maybe I am like my mother."

"If she is a passionate and brave woman, then I agree."

"She enjoyed the company of bad men." She took back her hand without the flower in it. "We can't waste water on that daisy. It's now doomed to an early death."

He tucked it behind her ear. "Happy flower. Does that mean you enjoy my company?"

"How do we clean these plates with no water, Mr. I-Know-It-All?"

"Sand and a bit of rubbing." He smiled at her. She rebuffed the amusement in his face but kept the daisy in her hair. Mac watched her retire, her shadow a dance of movement in the gaslight against the canvas of the wagon. He wasn't going to sleep much tonight.

The thought was more prophetic than he anticipated when the sky opened with a heavy rain just after midnight. The moisture fell straight onto the sand and was soon running in rivulets underneath the wagon, soaking Mac.

Wet and freezing, he finally ripped the wet blankets from him and stood. While trying to quietly step up onto the back of the wagon, his foot slipped, and his chest hammered onto the wooden side. Climbing less delicately this time and swearing with a medieval tongue, he groped his way inside.

Through the canvas opening, he could see the pure white of the upper half of Maggie's nightgown, upright and facing him. "I have enough sense to come in from the rain," he said to it. He shoved one dirty boot into the wagon, then the other. Rain dripped from his clothes, bringing the weather inside.

"Couldn't you be sensible enough to come in before getting wet?"

"I was trying to be *chivalrous*." His tone was hard and dripped with enough sarcasm to create another puddle. He grunted taking off his shoes, and next went his shirt, pants, and long underwear. "Make room."

"Not on your life. I'll pass you a blanket."

"I want to sleep lying down."

"You planned this."

"So you keep telling me. I seem to be a planner of infinite energy. I told you it was going to rain, and you said it's not, and that I should sleep under the wagon. I followed your plan to the red letter."

He moved as he spoke and when the bed compressed with his weight, Maggie shoved over quickly like a white sand crab. She sat with the covers to her neck in a brittle posture as he settled.

She didn't speak again, and he didn't either. It wasn't long before she knew he was asleep. It annoyed her that he was already comfortable and slumbering. She wanted to kick him onto the floor, except that nocturnal sounds, the occasional stuck inhale, the steady flow of his breathing felt comfortable, less lonely. The open air around the wagon had intimidated her slumber.

With him next to her, the desert felt less empty. With her mind quieting, she slept, and when the strands of sunrise were slowly lighting the interior canvas, she woke to dawn-washed trunks, and sacks, and to passionate dreams that she was getting used to.

During the night, Mac had moved closer to her or her to him. He slept on his back. She listened to his soft breath. His hand lay lightly by her thigh. From her position on her side, she studied the shape of his mouth, his jaw. He looked lighter in sleep, less intense without the power of his blue eyes, less threatening. Rain began coating the canvas again in the drum of the drops. Feeling comforted by his presence, she drowsily sunk deeper down into the feather bed.

She couldn't stop gazing at him; his covered naked nearness drew her sleepy mind. Her gaze tracked to the lip of the blanket at his hips. He smelled of rain still, and with a single finger, she smoothed a lock of hair from his forehead.

His rough cheek and jaw lightly filed the delicate skin of her finger. She traced his throat, pausing at its lively vein, reassuring in its pulse, and then down over the top of a bead-like nipple. Her finger sifted the dark hair that grew thickly there, and then in a quick movement, his hand covered hers. Her gaze jerked to his, and she startled to find his eyes open, assessing her, and deeper blue in longing. The look he gave her made her warm, and when he drew her head toward his, his kiss was easy, tentative, and as soft as the dream that still held her. Sweet skin against skin, he nibbled and licked and deepened, and her lips parted under the tender siege.

She entwined her legs with his and the white linen sheets, and he rolled, coverings and all, on top of her. His hand weaved into the length of her hair, holding her head. The other moved lower on her hips and pulled at all that covered and kept her from him. Just as he took hold of the neck of her nightgown, a bath of cold water drenched the bed.

More rain sluiced onto Maggie through the rip in the seam of the canvas top that had been filling throughout the night and morning. She screamed and sat up, sputtering and trying to disentangle herself. Her nightgown's buttons burst because Mac still held onto the fabric. She clung to the front of the garment and hustled off the bed. Mac lay back. The rain fell on him. His eyes were closed. Good. She wouldn't have been able to turn away from them if they were not.

"Dear God." Her teeth chattered as she swaddled herself in a wet blanket. She couldn't tell him that because he'd been so close, she could smell the earthy scent he had brought in with him. He had been near enough that she could define the length of his lashes, the fullness of his mouth, and the deep tan of his skin.

Mac laughed, the water a pool around him and soaking into Maggie's mattress. "This is all your fault. You planned this," he lightly accused.

"Oh yes. My wet mattress." She sank onto the corner edge of the saturated bed. She glowered at the puddle on the top of a cask. "We'll never get all this dry."

"As you said, we're in the desert." Mac came to a sitting position and began kicking the sodden blankets in a heap. "If I could get that miniature, greasy merchant in my grasp, I'd gut the bugger."

With the sun coming up and warming the earth, Mac detached the canvas roof at the wagon wall. He grabbed the pool that the mattress had become and shoved.

"Oh, my God, what are you doing? Stop...stop...stop!" Maggie's arms flailed to impede his progress. "Would you ever stop? What are you doing?"

Mac caught one of her weapons in his grasp. "It needs," he put that arm behind her, "to dry."

She tried to slug him again with her other hand, with the same result. He had both her arms behind her and his arms around her. He held her more tightly as she struggled.

"I would stop that if I were you," he said between gritted teeth.

She stilled, but she couldn't stop her heavy breathing and her breasts stirring against him. Like a man who had come a long distance to see it, he gazed into her face.

"Don't kiss me."

"Why?"

"Because I didn't mean what happened between us. Because a kiss means nothing from a man like you."

He sighed and let her go. "Are you sure of that?"

Mac climbed down and strode away. If she still watched, he had done his job. He couldn't glance back. Instead he sauntered into the sagebrush to find the animals. He left her standing in the wet of the bedclothes, the mattress, the pillows, and the blankets. Let her decide what to do with them. He hadn't wooed a lass before. He never thought it to be this exasperating. The Morrigan had set him a steep task. It would take forever for her to see past his face to his actions. Damned if she wasn't the most single-minded woman he had ever met.

While foraging, the animals had wandered far, but never out of the sight of the wagon. There were few places Mac had ever been that no human at all inhabited. This flat, mealy land stretched to where the sky and the earth joined at the edge of the world with no hiding places. He turned in a circle.

The danger here was at night. Darkness concealed bad men. Mac realized that even if a man could see his enemy coming for miles, he also had nowhere to run, nothing with which to build protection. It was a challenging place. It had rained, but he figured the sky couldn't be depended upon for water. He'd have to keep an eye on their stores.

He pivoted in the direction of the wagon and laughed. The mattress must have fallen through. She was pushing the soaking mess back in through the rip of canvas, and she was using her breasts as a resting place. He watched the mattress tip and weave, and Maggie with it, until it leaned against one of the pieces of bended wood that framed the ceiling over which the canvas laid.

The wood held. The mattress wouldn't go in. She was going to harm something, either the wagon or herself the way she strained. Her arms were over her head. She had thrown a dress over her corset-less body. The skirt clung to her damp legs. He heard a call of triumph as the mattress slipped into its sheath. Even from his place yards away, he could hear it fall onto things in the wagon, knocking some over, breaking others.

He put a rope around the neck of the mule. He walked toward her, hoping the two bottles of whiskey had been spared.

The woman was all thumbs.

"Don't say anything," were Maggie's first words to him. "In the first place, it's your fault for trying to throw it out."

"What was the point of having it all slosh around in the water in the wagon?"

"How do we dry it out here?" Her arm flung out towards the treeless horizon.

"We hang it from the side of the wagon so it can drip down to the ground."

"Which you didn't do. You just got it all dirty."

"Which I was going to do but was attacked by a mad woman."

"You don't know mad."

The naturalness of the dress over her curves, her hair long and untamed, reminded him of the softness of her countenance at dawn. Her lidded eyes had been tender in sleep. Her lips had been parted.

Now her hands were on her hips. He wanted the day when her face was as the dawn, only in the late of the afternoon. His arm swept before him and he bowed to her. "A thousand pardons, milady. I had a soft woman in my bed, her finger trailing down the skin of my chest, when a tarp full of rain washed over me. I doubt it will ever happen again."

A bird could have flown into Maggie's open mouth.

CHAPTER TWELVE

Guy drank at least once a week in the establishment owned by one George Burnside Cox. Cox had balls and Guy enjoyed his company. He liked that Cox had gotten into politics, like most saloon keepers, to improve the situation of his bar. While Cox hadn't cried about the daily violent deaths within one hundred yards of his front door, they hadn't helped business. One day Frank Kelly, an Irishman, had suggested Cox use politics to solve his problems. Guy had used Cox's flare for it more than once.

Through Cox, Guy had been introduced to some fine men in the community. Doctor "Conqueror of Consumption" Grayton had a patent on the health belt—a cure all. He sold it by mail order. Joseph "Fire Alarm" Foraker, a judge and now a potential gubernatorial candidate. The boys never machinated anything big, and their power grew from their lack of audacity. It flowed from the lower end of the city through the saloon, and through the higher end of Cincinnati by money and favors.

Guy downed the first whiskey Cox brought him. The owner poured another as he kicked a spittoon closer to a customer who had missed it on the first shot.

"It was a great funeral, well attended," Cox said as he sat. He pulled at his big, black mustache.

Guy drank the glass dry again and Cox refilled it. This time Guy sat and let the booze enter his blood stream.

"I have your horses," Cox said as he filled his own glass. "They were parked outside, and I recognized them. The two riding the animals blamed McMillan for stealing them."

"Good to know the word is getting out that she's with him. Mitchell's closed down all accounts. McMillan Senior will probably be on the hunt after I spoke to him. I need someone to follow the man he sends out."

Guy allowed himself to be studied by the large man across from him, while he drank his whiskey by sips, letting the drink dull the compulsions within him. Old McMillan had treated him like he was pig shit under the Hog King's feet. His hands were still shaking slightly from the experience. He wiped his face. He needed to shore up. He hadn't expected the emotion he'd felt at the funeral, and it had all been bad ever since. He knew that's what Cox was looking for—how changed he was. He had to prove he wasn't. He'd press the old man's face in his own pig stink. Life was a son-of-a-bitch. Just when he thought he'd found his own peace... love.... *Oh fucking, fucking, fucking horseshit.*

"At first I was livid with Maggie for leaving," Guy continued. "I thought she'd beaten me for a moment." Silence. "But now I've decided that on the strength of her actions, I can have her committed. When I get her back."

"Will you get her back?"

Guy tipped up the last of his third whiskey and backhanded moisture from his mouth. "In a heartbeat. I already know that she has taken a train to Utah."

Cox signaled to the bartender. "Bring a beer." And then he said to Guy, "If it's all so easy, how did you so thoroughly lose her? You've been hitting the booze a lot lately. It's getting around. Fortunately, they're mostly thinking you're in mourning, and not that the money's slipping through your fingers."

"Money! It's the money with all of them," Guy said with a growl. "Why should I be any different? Pig King is no saint."

"But Grace was. Hitch your horses to a saint and a saint you must be. They will refuse to have Grace corrupted. She brought out the best in them, and they appreciated that. They will also be limited in what they will allow to happen to Maggie."

Guy's eyes closed. He felt the thumping vein in his temple.

He could taste the smoke in the room. He needed a cigar.

"I heard William is gone," Cox continued.

Guy slipped a smoke from Cox's shirt pocket. He clipped and lit it, drawing the burn in rapid puffs until the end glowed steadily.

"I'm worried about you," Cox said. "It seems that all the rats at your home have jumped ship. Doesn't look good."

Guy smoked with his eyes closed. The beer tasted like water to his tongue, which was calling for stronger stuff, but Cox was slowing down his drinking. Cox didn't think much of drinking when a clear head was needed.

God. He hadn't anticipated any of it. Cut off at the knees. Stupidity in easy steps, and he hated Cox for pointing it out. No one could have seen it. Maggie abandoning her precious mother, no one could have foreseen that. Hooking up with Randolph McMillan. Guy just shook his head, and then he laughed—low and deep and then louder and longer. The humor in it all rocked the ribs in his chest. Garth hadn't been left to him. The will, when it was read, would appoint him Maggie's guardian until marriage. Linden had been right. Guardian of what? Guard her? He'd already lost her, for Christ's sake. Without her, and with his luck, the place will go to some distant cousin instead of to the sister. He definitely would be replaced by a person of Garth blood.

Him, missing Grace. Maggie with McMillan. Will gone for days without asking for money—disappeared by all counts. The kid must have stopped eating, not that it would hurt him much. No one was working within character. Guy rolled the cigar round his teeth.

He met Cox's gaze and said, "Spread the word that my son can't accept the death and has abandoned the place Grace lived. For all I know that's what really happened." Guy brushed some ash from his shirt. "Same for the servants. I've been left to deal with everything alone in my own grief. I'm going to be the worried father. Remember, we've all had a profound shock. We've lost the dearest person in the whole world."

"You're a cold bastard, Guy, you know that?"

"Go to hell. Both of us, you and me, we were born at the bottom, and we've had to beat our way up. Why shouldn't we want more? We know how hard it is to turn over a dime."

"You need some sleep."

"I need some help."

"Ask Frank."

Glasses clinked and Guy's edgy nerves lengthened. A discussion at the next table got louder, and Cox went over to calm the three sets of clenched fists. When he came back Guy said, "I need someone to follow McMillan."

"How about the two that had your horses? They owe you. They know McMillan. They know what Maggie looks like."

"Where are they?"

"Down by the docks."

Guy staggered out onto the pavement in the yellow night. He paused and adjusted the collar to his jacket. A fair woman, well rounded in her exposed breasts, breathed an offer of sex into his ear. He hadn't been thinking of that, but... Her gaze made promises to him when he glanced at her face.

She smelled of soap, distant soap, but soap just the same. Guy put his hand on the swell of her chest, and she smiled. Good teeth. Not a bad whore all the same. How long had it been? His thoughts swelled him. Such a long time. All through the illness. Celibacy had never been his greatest feature, but the opposite would never have been forgiven.

Strong perfume lingered under his nose. He was dazzled and aching and drunk. Semen seemed to drip from him as he walked with her, his hand at her buttock. He needed this. He needed to shake off the death, clear his head. Revive his juices.

In a bright room with a long mirror, he lunged for her, tearing her bodice and exposing a red nipple. She laughed and poured him two fingers of brandy, and then she stripped, layer by layer, down to her paper-white skin. Churned butter before the added yellow dye.

This must be Cox's doing. She held out the drink at the end of her tapering arm. While he drank, she undressed him, touching every part of liberated skin. Pushing his pants to the floor, she kneeled naked to take him into her mouth.

Lust expanded Guy. He was Priapus, god of male sexuality. He was deep in her mouth when the flash of a camera discharged into his face. Blue smoke rose languidly to the ceiling behind a dressing screen. Lust and rage released from him in a single loud roar. In his white blindness, he blundered toward the screen, and then Mitchell, the lawyer, stepped from behind it, a gun in his hand.

"Get dressed."

Guy was limp, but he stood straight up, and his vision was clearing. He unsteadily picked up his pants.

"I was a good husband to her."

"She hasn't been dead three weeks."

"I haven't had sex in over a year," he roared at the man, and then tried to pull himself together. His head pounded. He rubbed his temples. Her perfume still filled him. He'd been set up with the perfect whore.

"Grace deserved better. I don't know what she saw in you."

"My redeeming qualities, but this isn't about Grace, is it?"

The whore, now dressed, slipped past him and out the door. Drained, Guy fell back onto the bed. He waited. Mitchell dropped a document next to him. No doubt to release the money.

"Sign this."

Damn the headache and the booze. Thoughts slipped through Guy's shaken brain. He thought he had done it, finally backed Maggie into a corner. She'd been like a caged tiger, always snarling, but he'd thought she was contained. And now—the little bitch—his signature was barely legible, and then he rolled over and shut his eyes. He hoped Maggie would never know that in the end she had her money.

Maybe it was all over. He'd lost Grace. When he was alone, it was still hard to move. Not being an introspective man, much of his thoughts of himself sickened him. He hated the self-pity that sapped his will. Sleep. Let the alcohol clear out. Things were just getting interesting. Let the alcohol clear.

———

The next day, his head hurt. In the gray morning, sheltered under the brim of his hat from the slight rain, Guy rode one stolen horse and had the reins of the other, and he headed toward the Ohio River. Large women with broad asses swept the human muck out of bar after bar and shook out useless mats. He passed over a dark and quiet Third Street where the banks were closed, and where in a few hours Mitchell would be arriving to wire Maggie part of her fortune.

Guy felt no sting at the thought. Let them all sleep well and rise confident. They would not be watching. He worked well from the grave, from the place where others thought he was dead and buried. Laughing, he moved on until he got to the wharf, to Rat Town, where snoring painted ladies and still-sloshed sailors lay on top of each other in alleys or dark corners.

The horses tossed their heads at the smell of the place, of a sloppy river, open sewers, and human chaos. Guy reined in his ride and gazed at the area. He would not go back to a life like that, if he had to kill her himself.

Guy dismounted and pushed hard at the midsections of the two men he had been looking for. Doofus and Dullhead, the two who had taken his horses, friends of his son Will, and of McMillan. They hadn't realized whose horses these were, or they would never have taken them. When the thieves opened their bleary eyes to see Guy over them, they both started.

"Shit," said Doofus.

"We didn't know, for feck sake. We took 'em from McMillan."

"Stupid. And you let Maggie Bathurst slip through your fingers. Now you need to remedy that, especially as you know what she looks like."

"We wasn't looking at her. She was behind a horse. It was dark. Besides we couldn't take our eyes off McMillan—every fecking second they were on him. You got your damn horses back."

Doofus rolled over, turning his back on Guy, who then grazed the man's shoulder with a bullet. Doofus scrambled to his feet, hands out in front of him, palms up. "None a that then."

"You have your choice. Bring her back for a good amount of cash, or go to jail."

"You got the horses." Doofus whined.

"Not from you two. I'd shoot you through the foot right now, but you'll need that foot."

"Ah feck so."

"Right then. Last I heard she was in Kelton, Utah, just off the train. You've got four weeks. That's what you've got. After that, I'll send bounty men after you both. Bring her home in a pine box if you have to. Won't matter, just blame McMillan."

Guy threw some money at them, remounted, and wheeled his horse around. He didn't slump in his saddle until on the suspension bridge to Kentucky. He felt the heaviness of his body as he lifted his leg over the saddle, and then he leaned against a steel girder and watched the Ohio River—brown, high, and full of debris; the same flotsam that seemed to be broken loose in his head.

Opportunity could be so random. The thought hurt behind his

eyes. He'd been born unlucky. He'd tried to compensate by cunning and craft, using what he had to its best advantage. Luck bruised him, or at the least it shunned him at every opportunity—in favor of others—happy others who had no notion of the battle.

Some days the hate in him ate black holes in his brain, painful dark moments that blinded him. They all had come to the funeral thinking they knew how he felt. They had no idea, and he must return to the drawing rooms of their houses. He must eat and drink with all Grace's friends again, be the shattered husband. Quickly, too. Cox was right. They'd become uncaring soon, and then the death would be useless to him.

Just before Guy put his foot to the stirrup, he saw it, a well- laden chaise with the McMillan crest—trunks upon trunks, like a heavy lump of dried clay moving forward on over-pressed wheels, in the direction of the train station.

Men never traveled with that much stuff.

She is going west after her son. McMillan is sending his wife. She's probably the only one with any control over her son. She will be able act as a chaperone.

Guy heaved his bulk into the saddle, and his spine rolled as it curved into the back lip of leather. He watched the wagon and stroked downward on his mouth as he thought. He didn't know if the lady was traveling because only she had some semblance of control over her boy, or whether she was being sent to chaperone Maggie back.

Guy turned his horse to follow. God, she had packed quickly. His mood was lightening. That meant the McMillans saw this as a very large problem. The lunch had not been a bust after all. This was an unexpected development to be used to his advantage. His luck had been so bad lately, though, he didn't want to misinterpret this. He wanted to think and to watch her get on the train—He wanted to make sure she was going west and not on a visit to her aunt or some other rich relative.

Her travel trunks were being unloaded. Then she arrived and

alighted, a slight woman who was padded heavier with corsets, layers of thick fabric and large hats. Her mouth looked small and tightly wadded. When a man approached her, Guy sat up and cursed himself that he hadn't tried to get closer. He was losing his edge. His sweat dripped as vital fluid, weakening him.

At a scuffle next to him and some shouting, Guy slid down the right side of his horse. He hid behind its neck should she glance over, and then he heard someone behind him laughing. Hate slithered up Guy's body like a slinking, smothering snake ready to choke him. Linden! Guy made the laugh feed him, give him strength.

He realized Grace had been draining his potency, and then he knew that he'd let her. More secure in his place and in the needed goodness of it, of her, he'd allowed himself to relax. No such rest-time now.

Linden had his uses. Guy could smell the old man's cologne in his nostrils. He inhaled deeply, into his flesh. He had become too soft.

"Well, well, well, you're up and off of your fainting couch," Linden said.

"Is that a Pinkerton's man with her?"

Linden glanced above Guy and the horse.

"You know that I haven't the slightest idea. There are so many, and they're always hiring. He does have the right mustache and firm thighs. Her hat, God. You're not looking much better, by the way. Are you living in your clothes now instead of in your house?"

"Is that Pinkerton's?"

"Such wonderful naïveté, like a boy in breeches. Dull as a Catholic virgin. You know McMillan has his own men."

"For once in your bloody life, tell me what you know. Why would the mother be going?"

Mistake, Guy knew it. The asshole Linden would press harder on Guy's vulnerable bruise until the blood pressed farther out under the skin—wider and more discolored. That or he'd clamp his jaw shut tighter than a horse's sphincter and nothing would ever come out. The mother and Maggie would arrange to destroy him.

Cold—the wind on his perspiration-soaked shirt chilled him. No clouds, except in Guy's mind as he watched Mrs. McMillan end her conversation. His feet felt numb as he walked forward. She had all the power in the world, all the money, all the connections. Hatred froze his joints and iced his thoughts except one. He must follow her —never let her out of his sight.

"Give me whatever money you have, Linden. I'll triple the payback."

"And if you don't live?"

"Here, sell this." Guy handed a set of reins to the man's creamy hands.

With a first-class ticket in the same coach as Mrs. McMillan and some cash dearly paid for, Guy leaned his head against the window. Maggie had bested him. More faithful connections, stupid luck, his own blunders, but she had done it. Damn the little bitch. He'd just sold his beautiful dappled grey horse, a present from Grace on their first anniversary. Maggie hadn't planned but a trace of any of this, and that's what fractured the little sanity left to Guy's mind.

The luck he had felt at seeing Mrs. McMillan flushed from his veins. He gagged bile into his mouth and had to sit up to choke it back down. He wiped at this mouth. Thoughts piled upon themselves now like the acid that had laid his throat raw. He'd been sucked in. He'd told Mitchell he'd get her back. No one sucked him in. Dead or alive, Magnolia Bathurst. *That's what happens when a man gets to the point when he has nothing left to lose.*

CHAPTER THIRTEEN

At the end of two days in the desert, in the shimmer of intensifying sun, in the empty, dusty, far reaching landscape, space had become a swear word. Maggie's brain and bum felt the same, sore and flaccid. Both nights she spent under the stars while Randolph had at least the base of the wagon over his head. The blankets had dried in a good easterly wind. In fact, a gale always blew across the flat topography, getting sandy soil on the blankets, on the food, in her ears. She aired the mattress each day, and each day it became a little less of a wet dog. The bed had ceased to be her comfortable haven in the wilderness of the desert that it had been the first night. How could the boxes in the wagon be so dusty and the feather bed continue to be so wet?

In the mornings, she rearranged the interior of the wagon to lift the bed. She'd shift the big things on her own with a passionate energy turned inward. *He's a rake and an opportunist*, she had thought as she pushed a crate of potatoes. A confirmed libertine who had almost undone her. She'd cry and then smear a wet dust over her face. No excuse. She had known with whom she was dealing. She had known what he was like, and she had fallen for it all.

Straining under a small barrel of flour, her fingers had given way and gravity had done the rest, right onto the top of her bare foot. With a main vein broken, blood had swelled under the thin layer of skin, by the pint. It looked like she was bleeding to death internally as the skin stretched and ballooned.

"Randolph! Dear Jesus, Randolph!"

He sprinted to her. The earnest intention in his face as he climbed the lip of the wagon soothed her. When he saw her wound, he pushed her onto the bed of feathers and lifted her foot.

"It's nothing. Let the blood drain in the other direction for a space," he said and then as fast as he had come, he left. Comfort left with him and the mattress seemed even more cold and damp.

She shook her head that he had become the person she called in panic with every expectation that he would come and that he would rescue her. She was in over her head, and she had to think what to do about it. She had noticed that Randolph hadn't as much as hummed, much less spoken to her, throughout the whole of the two days.

Another day ended, with them both as mute as ghosts while sitting next to each other on the wagon seat. From time to time, she couldn't help but glance at him out of the corner of her eyes, from under low lashes. He had bought a hat with a broad brim. He casually looked out at the endless plain of sand and scrub. She admired the whole of him. With his sleeves rolled back, his well-shaped forearms tanned in the sun. Even under a light cover of dust, he appeared fresh. His dark hair tossed. His eyes stared, steady. His hands appeared an extension of the strong leather reins they loosely held.

Her glance left him and favored the landscape again. Long cotton sleeves covered her own arms, and her gloved hands held a summer parasol. They looked respectable enough, she mused. She frowned into the void of unwound dullness that was the desert and tried to ignore an excitement that thrilled though her— the impetuosity of rubbing against such a man as this. She had been feeling it all morning as she'd moved furniture.

This, this feeling, this was how the Randolphs and Guys of the world got on in life. They took advantage of the desires they created in women. They used their guiles without guilt and without looking back.

"What about chivalry? What about courage? What about romance...love?" she mumbled to herself. She jumped when Randolph answered.

"Do you think that men incased in tin and walking around like ducks were courageous or romantic?"

"I know this: women would be much safer if you had been born a eunuch."

As if struck, to her surprise, Randolph's spine straightened. He leaned in, pinning her back against the canvas behind her. He pressed in. The fabric of her shirt rubbed against his as the wagon swayed forward. With his left hand, Randolph held her just at the small of her back. He yanked her forward, closer. She strained away.

"Never say that again."

"Are you saying it isn't true?"

"I'm saying you don't know anything. I've saved your complaining hide," he said, his look piercing.

"I saved yours." Her lips practically moved against his.

"You were caught."

"You lost our horses."

He kissed her like her lips had been earned.

Mac let go of her abruptly and said, "Women will always idealize men." He clicked the reins too hard and the mules jumped.

Stunned, Maggie hadn't meant to start something. Her thoughts lived too close to the surface. She noticed that cool air rushed into the void Mac's presence had left. Even with the pressure of his body gone, her nerves quivered. She closed her eyes. She didn't bother with slapping him. They seemed beyond that. She adjusted her hat. He flipped the reins.

Thanks God, she thought when she heard from behind, "Hooray, whoop...thanks be to Mary and the babe in his cradle that I've finally found ye in this Godforsaken place." Lefcadio Hearn. She was not undone.

Later in the day, Lefcadio, unpacked and leaning against his saddle in front of a sage-fragrant fire, said, "In spite of the story, I've been cursing myself for coming. All the way here. The turning of the divil himself isn't worth all this dust." He had been making loud honking noises to clear his nose and throat of dirt.

Maggie walked to him with a bottle of whiskey, no glasses. In her path, a bull snake was coming to life in the cooling evening and hissed at her. She dropped the bottle and smothered a scream. She picked up the whiskey and furiously beat the thing with the heavy container. She wasn't going to give Mac another reason to save her. She surely wasn't going to idolize him. She wouldn't be beholden to him.

"It's dead," Randolph said as he passed her and took the bottle. "You are not to be in charge of this any longer. In fact, never touch it again."

She found a stick and flung the snake into the night. Her heart was thumping hard, but she'd done it. Silly to feel so triumphant about a snake, but she did.

"That could have been dinner."

Maggie glanced back at it. "Oh, Lord, no."

"I brought some Irish chocolate, so I did. Just for the lady. Miss?"

"Lefcadio, you are a shameless hustler." She sat next to him and, after brushing off her hands, took the sweet.

"I am so."

Maggie sat on the bit of blanket Lefcadio had been patting for her. She arranged her skirts as he said, "You killed the serpent."

"I'm afraid that there are many more where that one came from."

"No truer word has been spoken. You're far from home, and with that reprobate, McMillan. That's got to be a fine story in itself."

"And not one I feel like telling now. Are you bleeding? It's just that I see some wetness on your arm in the firelight."

"A disagreement on the price of the horse."

"It must be deep. You'd better let me see it. Turn...no...yes...that way...toward the fire. It's appalling. How have you come all this way? It must be stitched. *No*, it must be. Thankfully, I brought a needle and thread as suggested in *A Traveler's Companion*, which someone I know thought was an overreaching book."

She walked into the dark with trepidation and picked her way across the ten yards to the wagon, her skirts lifted as she placed her feet to climb. At home, right now, Cook would be bringing her hot milk. Cook in her fluffy soft shoes and her night robe would smell of the residue of laundry soap and sugar.

There, Maggie certainly wouldn't be killing snakes or sewing up strange Irishmen's arms. Lifting her arm to reach into the wagon, she noted her sweat and odor. The smell of raw work and heat, not the smell of a lady. She couldn't find the sewing kit initially and had to lift the lids of box after box, throwing the contents of each on the bed. Finally, her hand dived for it, jabbing her finger on a nail in the process. "Damn the cursed, bloody box to hell and back in a handbasket.

What?" she said as she walked back from the wagon into the fire light and into the stares of both men. "It took me awhile to find the damn thing."

Dropping next to Hearn, she jerked his arm practically into the flames. "I can't see," she grumbled. The fire had gotten hot. It, and the work, made her sweat even more. She'd never worked with slippery, bloody skin. His skin was soft and white, like a woman's. She couldn't keep hold of it. It helped that the needle passed easily through it, though.

"I'm sorry," she kept saying. When she tied off the thread and had poured a good lot of whiskey on it, Hearn complained about the waste. He remarked that he'd improve faster with the whiskey poured into his mouth.

"That was a fine job for such soft hands," he said, his Irish lilt slurring.

She poured what seemed like drops of water over her hands, and then, holding them up in the air, she considered a towel. She glanced at her skirt and then just left her hands up in the breeze. The Irishman next to her bumped her shoulder from time to time as he swayed and sang to himself.

She had devoted her life and her soul to becoming the perfect wife and mother. Now here she was, sitting on the ground with no water and no towel with two men who were not her husband. One a drunken reporter leaning against her neck and the other, by his own words, a man hell wouldn't take.

She smelled of smoke and sweat, and her hands seemed to permanently smell of the sagebrush she had had to tear out of the ground for the fires. Yet without Lefcadio's quiet song buzzing into her ear, she'd feel the vastness of the sky and desert, and she realized that even if things had gone perfectly, she'd hate being at her planned destination all alone.

Maggie glanced at Lefcadio's wound. If she was asked a time in her life that she was proud of, this might be the one time. Useful.

How interesting to feel the taunt thread as his skin pulled together. She hadn't even gotten lightheaded. She studied her hands. They seemed changed, more capable. She wanted Randolph to notice. She said to the Irishman, "How is your arm? Better?"

The Irishman touched it with the pads of his fingers and winced.

Alarmed and feeling guilty that she had somehow hurt him unnecessarily, she added, "Don't touch it."

Hearing the man across the fire chuckle, she turned back to Hearn and asked, "Have you known Randolph long?"

"Ah, we've just a literary acquaintance."

"You read the same books?"

"People write about him, and I read it."

"What is he up to then? As you see it?"

"That's the very thing I've come to find out."

She was hoping for a reaction from Randolph. A slight stiffening...a glance. A rebuttal. All he did was pick up the coffee pot and pour himself another cup. "What say you?" she called at him into the darkness.

"The Morrigan," his voice said with his back to her.

Lefcadio laughed until he wheezed, upsetting her repose, and nearly upsetting the bottle in his lap.

There she was, between Hearn laughing his head off and Mac, who was still acting indifferent, and she not knowing over what with either of them. The situation was not what she expected.

They were becoming closer, and she was on the outside.

"What about the Morrigan, then? Spit it out if you brought it up. Let us all in on the joke. What is the Morrigan?" She was warm now, her cheeks flaming.

Randolph was always one step ahead of her. He couldn't be flattered, not that she'd tried much, or at all, or cajoled. Her thoughts mixed and ran into each other like dizzy children. She was surprised that he seemed serious now, a little wistful, even, and sad.

Lefcadio must had seen it too as he handed Randolph the bottle. "It's a good night to consider the Morrigan. The goddess of death," Hearn said.

"And rebirth," Mac quietly added.

"And rebirth," Hearn repeated, nodding as if the phrase was the wisest thing ever said by a human being in all his time in the world.

"What do you mean, the goddess of death? Whose death?"

"Any death," said Hearn. "But especially in battle. She moves the living through their death to the next place or plane. Another name for her is the Banshee. Her cry is the cry of death. She comes as a crow, you know. If a warrior finds favor, then he is given rebirth."

"You've been reborn? Is that what you're saying?" She stared at Mac, whose face was in a flickering light as the night deepened. "Why not?"

Her gaze locked with his. He seemed immaterial; to her, it seemed his face jumped from one likeness to another in the flame light. She wrapped her shawl tighter around her and broke the stare first.

"I'm tired. What nonsense." She didn't move, though, because it was warm in the circle of the fire. The air behind her felt cool to her back. She'd rather be in the light, in the flame, in the heat.

Hearn watched her. He gave over the bottle of whiskey to her.

She sighed and took it. After drinking a slug of whiskey and then coughing, she gently wiped away the moisture left burning on her lips. "My name is Magnolia Bathurst."

"Magnolia, Magnolia Ba—" She heard him suck in air.

He stared at her. "Jaesus." He took the bottle from her. Lifting it, he said, "To the Morrigan." He drank and then passed the bottle around. "I sniff a change in the air. First, by God, let us Wake the Dead." He drank again when the bottle reached him. "To Grace Bathurst, the loveliest of lovelies, the kindest, gentlest woman who ever lived or died, so she was, so she lays." After drinking a good amount and handing the bottle to Maggie to do the same, he added, "May she rest in the arms of the God who knew more of her good days than the very few of her bad." He began to sing again.

CHAPTER FOURTEEN

Maggie had never woken up with a hangover in her life. She lay in her bed with her forearm over her eyes to block out light. Mac rounded up the mules from their nightlong pasture with a full-throated bawdy song. The man liked his voice. A fog bell would be quieter. She could hear Hearn clanging pots.

She rolled over. She wasn't here, surrounded by God-awful sand. She was at home. Her mother was about to come in the door and say, *"Lazy Suzie"* to her for sleeping so late. Maggie listened for the sounds of home. The woodpecker that loved the maple just outside her window, the hooves of her precious horses on cobblestone. All she heard was a damn ass braying as Mac harnessed him to the wagon. Another day of a landscape that was as steady and monotonous as a man picking a field of cotton.

An arm struck through the hole in the canvas. Hearn or Randolph's, she didn't know which, until the man behind it said, "Here's some coffee, nice and hot, with a little whiskey in it. Hair of the dog. Drink it down or you'll suffer the day through." He sat it on top of the barrel, and then peeking in, said, "I'd drink it before the whip hits that long-suffering donkey's ass."

Maggie lifted her head two inches and thought better of it. "That's the spirit," Hearn said as he smacked the side of the wagon.

If those two thought she was getting up, they were idiots.

"Drink it, lass," Hearn said again from somewhere outside the canvas. It seemed he knew the power of a sore head. Every inch of her body groaned as she moved just enough to poke out a hand from the blanket to snag the cup. Of course, then she had to sit up to drink it. She heard someone climb into the seat of the wagon.

A glance from Randolph through the round front opening, a look she would have sworn was no more than the interruption of a sweeping movement of his eyes to see if all was well, had Maggie thinking that if he wasn't careful, he was going to have to be reborn a second time. With the whiskey and coffee at war in her system, she fell back to sleep.

She slept on and off through the day. She ate and then went back to bed. Hearn had the coffee on the fire when she woke for good the next morning. The coffee at the fire tasted sweet with plenty of canned milk and sugar in it. She shaded her eyes to search down the road that stretched to the edge of the sky and then vanished into the blue. Every day she looked hard down the bald ribbon of dirt, and each time saw only the trick of more road at the end of the earth. This time, though, a fair bit away still, but before the horizon, a dwelling. From the distance, it resembled a large cockroach hunched low in the sagebrush.

Two hours later, the abode became a place of planed lumber that had sun-dried and been desert-sanded to a fragile brown-gray. The place was as alone as God before creation, and her hopes for a bath, a bed with a clean bolster, a sand-free cup of coffee, and something baked, dissolved.

Maggie stepped inside like she was walking into the dark entrance to a cave. "Napkins on the tables." Her thoughts, the words, her joy, jumped through her lips. The almost-white linen was the most civilization she'd seen for a long while. She would have wept into those white squares of cloth, if the proprietor of the City of Rocks Home Station hadn't walked in behind her.

She introduced herself as Mrs. Trotter, a square, impacted sort of woman that wind nor rain, or even rattlers could shift. With a positive smile and a wave of her brown-spotted hand, she sent Maggie back out the door to drag out their sheets and ticking to wash and hang to dry.

"In this wind, this here will be dry in no time." The squat Trotter woman chattered to Maggie as a woman who didn't get to chat often enough. "Dear, you have no color. Maybe you'd better sit, let me finish, and then I'll get you a coffee. No, reverse that. Back inside. I'll get you a coffee first."

She did feel pale. Her great adventure had become the colorless desert of flat, white dirt and the dusty blue of sagebrush and one increasingly endearing friend. She could hear Lefcadio. Who couldn't hear him? His voice lifted her as she glanced through the lines of coarse shelves of leather books on one wall.

She thought of her father's books on mahogany shelves. Somehow the dusty and ripped jackets of these in front of her seemed more precious. She heard someone whistling across the front of the way station. She knew who it was. She knew before he got there. He was always singing or whistling. Lefcadio talked and sang. Randolph sang and whistled. They'd have a chorus if they knew the same songs.

McMillan sauntered into the room. Even if her back were turned if he was near, she couldn't ignore his presence. Some part of her seemed to reach out to be nearer to him. He didn't walk up to her, didn't acknowledge her; a ghost would have gotten more attention. Damn. If he were manipulating her, at least he could do it properly. Oh God, what *was* wrong with her?

Mrs. Trotter trotted over to her. Maggie almost laughed. The Trotting Trotter. "I heard your mother just died," she said as she sat Maggie down and brought her coffee. "How are you holding up?" She looked into Maggie's face with her brown head tipped on its axis and her tough face open and concerned. "Your husband told me." Maggie gulped her coffee, and then grunted as she burned the palette of her mouth.

If Mrs. Trotter had then glanced at Maggie's ring finger, she wasn't saying anything. She understood in that moment how profound Mr. Mitchell's warnings had been. How different things had turned out from her looking down the kaleidoscope from Garth as she'd planned the adventure of going west. She was more vulnerable here than she had ever felt at home—even with Guy living there. She should never have left, and yet, her thoughts paused. She shook her head.

"We held an informal wake."

Mrs. Trotter patted her hand. "That explains your color. I'll get some beans. And we've got corn bread."

"And napkins."

Mrs. Trotter laughed. "They are appreciated. Small price to pay for the work they add." Returning with a full tin plate, Mrs. Trotter said, "Magnolia, an unusual name." She put the plate on the table and disappeared again, returning with her own cup of coffee.

"My mother's favorite tree. It grew outside her bedroom window," Maggie said as she put a napkin on her lap.

She thought of how Mrs. Trotter must see her, a pale girl in black silk, probably circles under her eyes that topped her cheekbones, and no ring.

"I've seen it all," Mrs. Trotter said as if understanding Maggie's thoughts. "Out here one can find some strange bedfellows. Everyone's got secrets, and most times, they should keep them, but if you need it, the talking is free. See the sign?"

"The food costs, the conversation is God given," Maggie read.

Mrs. Trotter brought two more plates as the men arrived. She was a big bosomed woman who felt like a warm blanket, like Cook.

Hearn ate noisily and voraciously as only skinny men did. With her stomach full for the first time in weeks, her mother cried over, and a steaming coffee in her hand, Maggie felt tucked in and soothed. She closed her eyes to savor the moment.

When Mrs. Trotter asked the men their names. Hearn answered sprightly, and then it was Randolph's turn. This interested Maggie. Though she figured that Randy-Mac would not be known here, she didn't think he'd use the name.

"James MacArthur."

No! She coughed up corn bread and had the nimble Mrs. Trotter pounding on her back.

———

Mac let her cough. He had lost things, too. He had lost his face, his name, his friends, and his life. He understood the lash of battle—its unpredictability. He wasn't complaining that he had died, or that he was here. Being here was a gift. Mac sure didn't expect that in saying his own name he would once again feel a sword in his hand, or inhale the smell of England, but the only thing he had left to him was just that.

To Maggie, he was a storybook character. She had him in flesh and blood but couldn't see it. As Padric had always said, "Ye're always in the field when luck is on the road." He had decided to see how it sounded in this time and place with this nice woman, Mrs. Trotter. A woman he'd never see again.

Be damned and come what may, they needed to know. Over his food, Mac began with his childhood, the fire, with his adopted family and Elizabeth, the castle, the rescue and his death and rebirth. If Hearn kept up with all that, he could just say that Randolph McMillan had really gone insane, Mac's plan all along.

During the entire recitation, Maggie made scoffing sounds through which Mac pressed on with his tale. As the story length-ened and deepened with details as real as the sun in the morning and as fast as the tick of a clock, she quit, and listened.

"I became a knight by running away from that hateful place and giving myself in service to William of Tancarville. He knighted me in the field and girt with sword and then delivered the coulee, a slap to my face that nearly broke my jaw.

"Only a man of means could afford a horse. I had to win mine that day. The last thing I did as a knight was try save the woman who was my only friend from a marriage to a man who would beat her, and to end the FitzAlan line, if I could, by killing its heir."

"Did you?" asked Mrs. Trotter.

"I heard him cry out from my knife."

"And Elizabeth?" Hearn coaxed the end out.

"I gave them every amount of time that I could."

"So you don't know?" asked Mrs. Trotter. When Mac shook his head, she added, "You must go back to England someday and find out."

"I killed a good number of men, and probably Malcome too, or maimed him. That should have given Padric plenty of time. He is, or was, very good, although he was in the boat with women. They may have thrown him overboard."

The door opened and Mr. Trotter came in loudly. "They hitched up Abigale again," he snarled about the stage that had just arrived. "She's too old for that run now. Where's the liniment? Didn't you use it last night?" He took up a jar, took in the party inside, shrugged his shoulders and swirled back out.

"Oh my Lord, the stagecoach. I didn't even hear it," said Mrs. Trotter as she bounced up.

On Mr. Trotter's heels, eleven weary souls walked in, and Mrs. Trotter had only enough time to say one thing. "There's a sort of nobility to it, don't you think?" Mother-like, she put her hand over Maggie's and patted it and began serving endless coffee and beans and cornbread.

Maggie still watched him. He was aware that his story, for all his lectures to her, had been full of chivalry. He had lived as a character from Froissart, and damn the man's hide for writing it. Padric had always thought him a fool for it. Still, there were bad knights in it as well.

If she never saw past his face, he couldn't blame her. He let himself gaze at her now—thin-lips that he had only kissed twice, and now suspicious green eyes that once had turned darker in passion. He stood, turned, and strode outside. Might as well see if Mr. Trotter needed any help.

He picked up a pitchfork and scooped up dung. *Malcome always said he'd rearrange my face. Guess he succeeded.*

Hearn found another tool and worked beside Mac. "It's a sight more believable than the redemption of Randolph McMillan, so it is. My problem is how to make this believable enough for the non-Catholics. Ye might as well be whistling jigs to a milestone for that one back at the house. She's deep enough, but stubborn. I have a great respect for her ability to stay that way."

"A statue is more pliable," Mac said. "My Irish friend, Padric, would have said that the sea was full of fish, especially now that my fishing pole works."

"As well said as a man could ever say it. She wants her father, who is dead, and a man in a picture book. One day, God help ye, she'll want a man who's living."

"Amen."

"If ye don't mind, I think I'll stay for the ending."

"I'd have begged you to stay if you weren't," Mac said as he planted the tips of his pitchfork into a bale of hay. He wiped a hand on his pant, and extended it to Hearn.

While shaking hands, Mac knew he agreed with Hearn. Telling the story might have been the stupidest thing he'd ever done. He should have just extolled the virtues of knighthood and repainted Randolph as a saint, but then she would have been right to call him false. She would have always been waiting for him to give himself away.

Enough. He wasn't going to run from it. Mac wandered to the door of the barn for some air. Maggie was beating her beloved mattress with a hard hand. He understood her dilemma, even sympathized with it. He watched the touch of the girl she had been, still was, as she stopped to push back her hair. She had the air about her of a woman who was trying to adjust to what the world really was, to what she'd never, ever, figured it could be.

She hadn't had enough experience in life to determine her own destiny like this. Mac sighed. He and she were alike. They were orphans. He squared his shoulders. One thing he figured, in all her pampered years, she had learned how to stitch. She needed to use that skill, maybe her only one, to piecework herself together.

"Did that book of yours tell you to bring a tarp needle and some good sound thread for the canvas?" he called to her.

She didn't stop working. "It told me to be sure of my travel companions, that my life might depend on them." Winters were warmer than her reply. "That name came from a man, a real man, a good man. It wasn't a fabricated fairytale of miraculous courage and unending love for a woman that you say you died for. It's not myths about gods who cradled your lifeless, broken parts." The words were spat at him as if he had killed her father himself.

"I didn't come here to argue. If you want that mattress to stay dry on the next downpour, you'll tell me where the needle and thread are."

———

She didn't answer that time. She quit swinging the duster. A quiet, yet heavy breathing had come over her. He'd come a very long way just to lose her because he didn't look like anything she wanted. He knew he didn't want to leave her behind, but there was nothing to be done about it.

A new man rode in as Mac and the Irishman struggled with the canvas. The stare from the arrival as he passed the wagon told Mac the man knew him. Mac studied the back of the lad until he lost sight of him. He jumped down when he heard Maggie scream.

As he ran around the wagon, she was chasing the stranger with the beater. She grabbed the first gun she saw, a gun that was leaning against a wall. She struggled to cock it. Her hands shook, and she swore. Once cocked, she aimed it at the man. Mac dived for her waist and tackled her where she stood, the gun shot wild, and then the weapon flew from her grasp.

He wasn't dead. She wasn't either. Maggie scrambled in the dust to reach the butt of the rifle. Mac held her waist. She shook him off and kicked at his legs, trying to knee his groin. She turned over and slapped at his face and reached again, only he now had a good hold on her forearm, rolled on top of her and pressed.

"No, no, no," she yelled as she struggled. "Get off me."

"I will when you are still and come to your senses." Her mouth puckered, maybe to spit.

"Don't do it."

"I've been found," she cried instead. "Him! Let me up, you big oaf."

"For Christ's sake, woman, what are you talking about?" Mac stood and lifted her to her feet. He was about to restrain her again, but she was too quick. She dove for the rifle. As she managed to get a shot off, the newcomer, already on the ground, moved crablike behind the wagon. The shot sprayed dust where he had been. Mac jerked away the gun, wrenching Maggie's index finger. She put it in her mouth and sucked on it.

"Damn it," she said, her tongue knocking ungainly against her digit and making the words sound irregular. "Shoot him."

Mac picked up the stranger's hat and hit it on his thigh. "I will not." He walked over, still watching Maggie, and handed the hat to the man.

"She's insane. You could have killed me," he yelled at her over Mac's shoulder. "Look what you did to my hat."

Mac warmed to the stiff, insecure line of the boy's body, the soft young eyes on the hard face. Not a stripling, but colt-like, with an air of juvenile lack of respect. The young man was fighting the personal indignity of being shot at by a mad woman with all the invincibility that he could muster.

A wild bullet streaked by Mac's shoulder. Christ's blood! Another gun. He'd get that gun from her and break it in half. For all he knew, she was also shooting at him. She looked madder than a stuck boar and just as dangerous. Even with Mac in front of him, the young man once again danced behind the wagon.

Mac eased toward Maggie. "Give it to me. You don't want to kill anybody. You couldn't kill Guy. You won't kill this guy either." Only the expression on her face said she did.

"I couldn't kill Guy because the damn gun was empty."

Hearn threw a rock at the side of the building, which made her turn. Mac fell on her again. Wrenching the gun from her wrist, he fell with her to the ground. On top of her again, with his whole weight against her spine, he talked into her ear.

"Cease and desist."

She spat dirt. "He's white trash."

"Trotter has come around the corner. He is trying to decide whether to shoot you or not. As the man you are shooting at is behind a wagon, my bet is on you. Behave yourself."

"Was it that little idiot who told you about me? Who helped you plan?

Mac wanted to spank her. Instead he glanced back at the face of the young man, the only part of him visible behind the wagon.

"He's the son then."

"Oh for the love of...of course he is, and don't pretend you don't know him. He's your pet Rottweiler. Let me up!"

"Promise me."

She fought him then, trying to turn, butting her head into his chin. He held her until she slowed. His nose hurt, and he had a split lip. The new blood in him didn't taste any different. He began laughing then...at women over time, of their problems and tempers, which made her mad all over again. She bit his nose.

He roared, deep and loud, and her face changed. *Good*, he thought, as he moved off her to roll her over, her face in the dust.

He put his knee in her back.

"Okay, okay," she said.

He pulled her to her feet, and she swung at him.

"For Christ's sake, woman."

Her arms were at full stroke. He took one in the chin before pinning her arms behind her, her length against his, and there he held her. She had never looked so alive. He almost had to shut his eyes to her flushed, bright face. The desire to take her had never been so strong in him.

"All right!" She looked away from him. "Let me go. Let me go," she said again, quieter. She must have judged the look on his face. She was panting when he let go, and then she purposefully walked past the gun and into the dark interior of the home station. The baffled looking Mr. Trotter stood with his gun, taking in the scene.

Mac could feel the imprint of her body on his. He licked his damaged lip and called out wearily to the boy, "Come out." The son of the man Mac had hit square in the face within Mac's first moments newly alive inched out. Father and son did resemble each other in dark looks. This boy's brown eyes asked for no man's help, but his uneasy body did.

William Didsbury stepped from behind the wagon with an enforced swagger and a sneer to his face.

"I saw you both leaving. From my window."

Maggie burst out from the door. "How did you find me?"

"Me! You!" William's smooth face looked younger in anger. "You wonder how I, me, how I could follow you? Anyone, a five-year-old, could have followed you...you and this particular man."

Will's face shifted to uneasy as he glanced at Randolph.

William had obviously remembered who was listening.

"So you've become a bounty hunter?" Maggie asked.

"No! No."

"Where is Guy?"

"He's not here. I came on my own."

"What are you up to then?"

"I could ask you the same thing. Why with him? You are Grace's daughter."

Maggie stilled in her steps forward from the door. Only her hair and dress moved in a warm wind. Mac picked up his own hat and hit it against his knee. He knew William hadn't been sent. Never a lad was ever sent to do the work only a man could stomach.

He eyed the young man and appreciated the skill it took to take them by surprise. Maybe he wasn't as unskilled as he appeared. Damn it, though, here was another direct acquaintance of Randolph's to deal with. Whatever. Mac had to chuckle at this raw youth who seemed to be "chaperoning," a bit from afar.

Another person in the ranks who wouldn't believe his story. Oh well, he'd told the story and now he could leave it to the natural taleteller, Hearn. Mac felt gratified that in the space of a moment, with his real name and life aired, he didn't care about the details of who his face represented. The rest of his party, they were now the only ones who would be losing sleep.

He would be himself.

And so, when once more on the road, Mac talked of hunting wild boars with kings and peasants and dogs and how the peasants were bait.

William, probably thinking Randolph was talking about a trip to England, said that he had been born in England in Clifton and then he moved to Nottingham. "There's a pub there named The Trip to Jerusalem at the Foot of Castle Rock. Someone carved a 'j' in the gray stone fireplace there. The proprietor said it had been there since the thirteen hundreds."

"Don't tell me it was you who put it there, Randolph?" asked Maggie in the dry voice she'd adopted since the home station, moisture-free as a dead well.

"I used to serve customers there for a bob or two when I was eight," said William.

"The thatch used to rain bugs into my ale."

"It wasn't thatched."

"Things do change in five hundred years," said Maggie.

"I used to play in the yard of the Ferry Inn and watch the boat move back and forth. My mother used to take me down Barker Gate for leathers, or Pilcher Gate to haggle with the pilchers."

"What's a pilcher?" asked Lefcadio.

"A man who makes clothes from furs."

"I used to play Robin Hood," said William.

Mac sat straighter and winked and began,

"Lythe and listin gentilmen that be of frebore bolde I sahll you tel of
a gode yeman
He name was Robyn Hode
Robyn was a prude outlaw
Whyles he walked on grounde
So curteyse and outlawe as he was one
Was nevere non founde
Robyn stode in Bernesdale
And lenyd hym to a tre
And bi hym stode litell John
Agode yeman was he
And alsoo dyd gode Scarlok
And Much, the miller's son
And Much the miller's son...

That's all I know. I wasn't a bard. It goes on for hours. As the tale goes, Robin did steal from rich priests and nobles, but he kept it," Mac said.

"Now, William, if that doesn't sound exactly like you and Randolph."

"Grow up, Maggie, my love. You've had some hard times, but mostly you're a spoiled brat with a shrew's tongue." Mac snapped the reins.

"Why Miss Magnolia, I do believe that's the first tongue lashing I've ever heard given to you," said William.

She stuck out her tongue.

Hours later, the wheels of the wagon turned, but seemed to go nowhere, the pace so slow that his hair grew faster. William had talked incessantly, as if his mind, his voice, his thoughts had been set free. Maggie sat next to Mac, now and then a hand would graze, and knee, or two shoulders would brush.

Mac pulled back on the reins so hard the mules tossed their heads. "I need to walk for a while." He handed the reins to Maggie.

Just as Maggie picked up the reins and was about to slap them against the flesh of the mules, the animals startled at something and ran. Maggie pitched back through the hole in the canvas.

"That screaming will make her hoarse," William said as Mac pulled him out of his saddle.

Mac, riding fast, overshot the wagon as one of the mules tripped. It didn't go down and the stumble interrupted the run. The wagon, with grace, slowed and the stopped

Mac stuck his face over the top of her knees and through the hole in the canvas.

"Don't you laugh!"

"I'm not, although I have wanted you on your back on this bed the whole of this afternoon, but without so much drama."

"I could have been killed." She pulled in her knee and struck him in the chest.

"Oomph." He grabbed the wagon to keep from falling off.

"Damn all men. Every blasted one of them."

CHAPTER FIFTEEN

Maggie held a cast-iron frying pan, her wrists bent from its weight. She walked to the fire, where she placed it over the heat. In her pocket, Mrs. Trotter's recipe for biscuits was stained with pools of melted butter and sprinkled with flour. She took it out to reread it. Somewhere she was going wrong. She let her hand drop. Her hand. It had become rough and appeared as red and dry as the feet of a laying hen.

A day without wind in the high desert was a dear one. She wiped a grain from her eye. She knew the sand would be in her dough, such as it was. When Will passed by and told her he was sick of her burned food, she flicked a little more sand into the flour bowl. She wasn't hungry anyway. She hadn't been hungry since leaving the way station with her stepbrother in tow.

He'd said that he'd seen her ride away with McMillan. He had owed it to Grace to follow. What a pack of liars she was with. She brushed hair back from her cheek with her forearm. Her hand dropped onto the rim of the tin bowl.

"The pan's getting too hot," Will said.

"The pan's getting too hot," she mimicked. For three days now, she had put up with William saying nothing good about anything.

He had sworn up and down that he hadn't been sent. He behaved differently here. He got up in the mornings. An enigma. And apparently, he could cook.

"It is."

"You do it then."

"Thank you." He took the bowl and dumped its contents on the ground. He ignored a strangled cry from his stepsister. He mixed the cream of tartar into the flour and then rubbed in the lard. Maggie hadn't added the lard when she did it. "You add milk instead of lard or water," she said.

"What does it matter?" he had retorted. "Either way, you burn the ass out of the bottoms."

That first time she had tried the recipe, after squealing at the charcoal smell, she had whipped the pan from the fire, and then stepped into the batter bowl. The iron frying pan fell on her knee as she hit the ground on her bottom. She couldn't walk the rest of that day.

Maggie glared at Will. Her fists were clenched, as was his jaw. Mac had taken her gun for good. He must have noticed she was about to sock her "brother" in the jaw because suddenly she was over his shoulder and leaving camp.

"You're not anything like your mother," Will called.

"You are everything like your father," she called back.

"Quiet," Mac thundered. He stopped at a sandy edge of the Snake River, dragged her with him and threw her into its icy waters, and jumped in after her.

Maggie surfaced sputtering and cursing. She came up seething and jumped for Mac's head, trying to take him down. He let her.

"Damn it!" She came up for breath and dragged herself to shore. Her saturated skirts bound her legs and weighted her down. "Damn you. You didn't need to throw me in. This dress will take ages to dry."

"Oh, I disagree. We gave you the choice of returning to Kelton."

"And miss all of this?"

She lay on her back and gazed up through the cottonwoods to the sun. "What would that have done for me? A woman alone. You all could just get on your horses and follow me back. All I want is to be allowed to live my life in peace. Is that too much to ask? I don't want to be begged, borrowed, or stolen. I am not anybody's solution, not yours, and not Guy's. If William is such a good cook, let him do it."

She heard Randolph sigh. He had rolled to his side facing her, bent his elbow, and rested his head in his hand. He was beautiful wet, his hair just slightly curling, the rich hue of his dark hair enhanced, making his eyes a clearer deep blue. She almost felt the graceful slide of a drop of water down his cheek. She reached up, her hand froze midway, and let it drop.

"You all have me. I'm surrounded. What is the plan? Do you know why I left with you?"

"Why?"

"Because we are still heading away from Garth. We're still going north. The opportunities to bring me back have been numerous. To kill me, too. And also, Idaho? You all collectively thought back in Kentucky to take me to Idaho? Guy wouldn't wipe his feet on Idaho. He's just like that. So I guess that maybe all our plans are a wreck. Maybe it's interesting watching the great Randolph struggle. That story you told, I mean...after all."

"The story is true, and my only plan is waking to your eyes, your face every morning."

God, she wanted to believe him. It broke her heart that it wasn't real. The words were too precious for a guy like Randolph to say. She could cry, but she snorted instead. "You've got creativity. I suppose you would, being who you are. Hearn came, too." She focused on the clouds. "Besides," she said quietly, "There's nothing to go home to... but Guy."

"He'll be here soon too, no doubt."

———

He watched her expression change. Instead of remaining in a semi-relaxed pose, with her hair spread upon the sand like an overlay of silk, the delicate curve of her neck less tense, her soft pink lips parted, she frowned. He was sorry he said it. He didn't get to see her un-frowned very often. He had wanted to lick the drops of water that wet her lips. She had moved her hand over her eyes, her palm up. Grains of sand were imbedded there against her smooth skin. Coveting their place, his body swelled. He now had to suppress the urge to run his fingertips along the inside of her forearm, dislodging more of the offending grains.

Instead, her wide gaze left the sky and looked fully into his steady one. Fear made her need him. She looked as if she'd never glance away, as if she hoped to find something there in the blue of his irises. He followed the connection to her lips at first, just licking the wet there, and then kissing them fully and endlessly. No woman had felt more natural to any man. He shifted to kiss down her neck. Mac lay back with his side touching hers, and one of her legs still bent, and the sand indented where they lay together.

"Why is it I feel safe with you? I shouldn't." She was crying.

"I mean, William couldn't seduce me, so you were commissioned?" Her words brought him such pain that he didn't answer.

"Maybe I am an easy mark. I am my mother's daughter." She sat up and brushed sand from her arms. "If I become a fallen woman, I have to marry someone. I assumed it would be William by default, and now he is conveniently here. You share Garth with Sir Guy. Be a knight, Guy says to you. She's crazy about them. It must be killing Guy that he can't marry me himself."

She sobbed on an inhale. The words were costing her, too. As if silence was unbearable, she stood and shook her skirt. She began again. "You're right. He is coming for me. Just remember, I won't marry anyone."

Mac knew he'd regret his next words, but she wasn't the only one the words, like daggers, cut. Anger boiled hard in him and somewhere the heated steam held these words: "Christ's blood.

You're a hard woman."

Maggie was startled to quiet.

He knew he was glaring at her as she gathered together her sloppy fabric to ring it out.

"You will never plant your bad seed in me." She left.

It was then, still lying on the ground with Maggie's footfalls raining sand in his face that Mac realized it was now possible to do just as she had suggested, and yet he still wasn't spreading his seed. Then it occurred to him, whose seed would he be spreading? Randolph's? He thought of it with shafts of sunlight all around him, as if in epiphany. The thought froze his bones more than the water had. He had the thing between his legs, but it seemed he was destined to never use it, and maybe the life it held wasn't his.

The Morrigan had been wrong to send him here.

She had been walking slowly, and he caught up to her when William met them coming the other way. Mac heard her say to William as she passed him, "If you're so good at cooking, you may have it." She was still crying.

Mac decided he needed some time away from being "Randolph." Let them kill each other. He kept walking until the flat desert rose into rust-colored, bald, sedimentary rocks. He climbed layer after layer, slipping now and then on loose pebbles, but rising up the craggy splendor toward the sky. He settled on the rounded top. A slight breeze blew without any tension. Ants moved around him. He could hear the sounds of animals and see the curve of the river. He closed his eyes and let the wind cool him.

Mac remembered the swordplay between Padric and himself. After, they'd throw themselves into the sweet, cold Lee and stuff themselves with his sister's hot stew. He missed the rain and the green in Ireland, the mist and the mystery.

No mystery here. From the trace smoke of their fires, he'd been able to see that someone else had been following them since yesterday. Varying the pace of his wagon, Mac had been testing them, and they'd been consistent. He'd been watching Will, too, to see if there was any communication.

He rubbed his hand along his face. His clothes were dry. He had been here too long. Jumping from his rock, he decided he needed action and wished for his broadsword. The Morrigan had appointed him her protector. From his vantage point, he could pinpoint the camp of the new arrivals. He'd like to see who and why.

During the two-mile walk, Mac strategized his approach to the camp with no natural camouflage, and he decided that the only way was as a snake on its belly. Closer to the thread of smoke from what was certainly a sparse soldiers' fire, he settled in the sagebrush for an uncomfortable wait.

Checking his firearm, a gleaming thing in the afternoon sun, he marveled at its shape and convenience. Still it felt strange in his hand, foreign. It was not good to go into battle with something that wasn't second nature. He lay in the dust, feeling the metal in his palm, picturing his responses with it. He wanted his brain to react, not think. He hoped that their pursuers' brains were lethargic from an afternoon meal.

In spite of the marvelous instrument in his hand, he wished for his broadsword, the hilt in his fist, arm and sword one being. He liked the gun but didn't have an instinct for it yet. So he loosened the leather flap of the knife at his belt as he lay in the sparse shade of the coarse sagebrush. He'd have to decide on sight how to take whoever was dogging their steps.

Mac sweated as he inched, belly in the sand, closer to his mark. Grains had penetrated his shirt and grated on his elbows. Dust blew in his face. He chewed on grit. In Mac's mind, Padric was laughing at him—all this for a woman who treated him like horse excrement. Hundreds of years later, a whole new body, and look at him, still on his belly in the dirt with a weapon in his hand—for a woman. It was hard to smile with grit against teeth. Things had and hadn't changed much, and then Mac felt Padric's absence. There was no one at his back.

One of the men yelled out. Mac lowered his head until his chin touched the ground. The man spit out his drink. The coffee was either disgusting or too hot.

Witless crouched about ten yards from the weak fire with *Lackless,* the two who had stolen their horses at the beginning of this journey. They were still grimy and unshaven, with the same dull cunning about their red eyes. They snorted ugly words at each other as one took the coffee pot from the fire. The other had the bottle and was drinking freely. They weren't planning the attack for this day, anyway.

Mac watched them fight each other, and watched Lackless cook with surprising grace, half sloshed. The man obviously loved to fill his belly. They answered each other's half-sentences like an old married couple, and they never lost sight of their weapons, which were lashed to their hips. The gun handles were the cleanest things on their bodies. They wouldn't want to tangle with McMillan again. They were here because they had been sent.

One against two, and they probably wielded their guns like Mac used to swing his sword. They'd all be firing. Mac wondered how to keep them alive. How to keep himself alive. He needed answers. He wanted to know more about his real adversary, Sir Guy Didsbury, and his plans. He needed to know how important Maggie's life rather than her death was to Didsbury, and then he remembered that the two would recognize him as McMillan.

Brilliant, it was like Mac had put on a costume. He had a role to play. Mac crouched onto his legs and stood, his gun and his knife in his hands. He had been practicing with the gun, but if he shot from here and missed, they wouldn't.

He wondered how long Randolph had ridden with these two, and whether he had been straight with them. Was there a bounty on Maggie, or himself? It amused him that they were in no hurry. The bounty must be high enough that they were following, but not so high that they were rushing in. Or Didsbury wasn't paying them at all, and they would put off the final scene for as long as possible.

They knew that in stealing those horses, they'd gotten lucky. They also knew that Randolph would remember the slight. They could see him now, if they were watching, but they weren't. The two idiots with the smoking fire felt safe. Mac measured the distance. He shortened it by degrees, always watching. He pointed the gun at them and yelled.

"Are you bringing my horses back?"

The two hesitated but did not capitulate. Mac realized late that was probably why McMillan had been riding with them; they were good shots, and they knew it. Kill or be killed, that's how they saw it with their old partner Randolph. In their surprise, Mac had time to shoot twice. As they scrambled and shot back, he ran toward the horses for shelter or a way out.

One of them had the same idea and beat him to it. Mac took a slug while aiming, a second as his took his shots. It had been a short run in this new life, he thought as he fell. Consciousness slipped from him, again. Once more, he hoped the other two were good and dead. His last conscious thought this time though was not of Elizabeth, but of Maggie.

CHAPTER SIXTEEN

"T'is past noon, and Mac's not shown a bit of himself," Lefcadio said. "Where did you see him go off to?"

"That way," William said. "He just walked away."

"Surely Randolph wouldn't leave without a horse." Maggie, redressed, stared in the same direction as the men.

She rounded on William. "What do you know about any of this?"

"Nothing," he yelled back. "Jesus, get off your high horse, will you? It's you who fights with him."

"Oh, I can't remember ever asking you if you knew something. If we leave without him, he's on his own. Are you sure that you don't know something, because if I find out later that you did, I will have you gathered up by the sheriff in the next town for stealing my earrings. Do you understand? For God's sake, be a man for once in your life. Call honesty your friend. You might like it. It'll make your soul lighter and you might sleep at night."

"What do you care so much about Randolph anyway?"

Maggie's mouth snapped shut. "I don't," she muttered.

She kept busy, collecting sage for the fire, and then later washing up after dinner. She didn't inspect the dishwater red of her hands this time. Instead, she gazed at the road Mac had taken. She began throwing pots into the wagon. She sent William to the river with the bucket.

"Where would he have gone?" she asked Lefcadio. "Do you think he's dead or something?" She'd never envisioned Randolph dead. He gave off a capable aura. Invincible, almost mythological in his exploits. Someone death didn't touch. She was startled to think of him in more human terms, that he might be alone and bleeding somewhere. She could see the road stretched out in front and behind.

"Could be the Blackfeet. We'd better stay armed, all of us." But no Blackfoot, single or otherwise, did she see.

"Serves him right, going off alone like that," she said. "Now we've lost a whole day waiting." Still she watched for him, expecting him to materialize in the distance in the glare of the sun over the brown-white sand. Damn him. She didn't care, she wouldn't care. She wiped her hands on her apron as she surveyed the landscape.

She looked long in each direction. The air tumbled and rolled over itself in waves. It was hard to understand what she saw in the surreal of sun-glinted brown sand. She had never seen so much human-free land. Lone wolves died here and then their bones sun bleached to the color of the earth. In this aloneness, if they left him, he would die. Later, one last time, with her hand over her eyes, Maggie peered again down the path, this time the yellow light of the low sun blinding her.

"Come on, William, and don't complain or I'll shoot you as you stand. Hearn, stay here in case he returns. I'll take your horse."

They'd ridden in the direction that Mac had left for about half a mile when William said, "How much farther should we go?

It's getting dark. I mean, how far would he walk?"

"I don't know. I don't know." She'd been riding with her hand on her pistol in her lap.

"Maybe we should go back and wait the night," William said.

"He'd be back if he wasn't—" Maggie felt her throat close.

"Dead? If he's dead, then there's no point looking."

"And if he's wounded? No honor among thieves, William?"
William gazed at the landscape.

"Where are those tracking skills that got you here? We actually need them now."

"I'm not a footprint in the sand kind of tracker."

"Pity."

"What help are you? Anyway it's going to get dark soon. We should head back."

As she turned her horse, Maggie replayed the weeks she been with Randolph in her mind. That Randolph might be gone choked her more than all the dust she had inhaled traveling through this wretched desert. Something deep in her, a place she didn't under-stand regretted that he'd never again kiss her lightly, swing her up over his shoulder, pick leaves from her hair, and hold her on a horse as she slept. She'd never catch his blue-eyed gaze taking her in, surrounding her with sky.

"Shhh, wait, listen," William said. "Did you hear that?"

"What?"

"*Listen.*"

"I don't hear anything."

"God, would you just listen? That way, I think."

She stretched her neck to hear. "I still don't hear anything."

"It's stopped."

"Of course, and next you'll—"

"I think it was gunfire."

"Gunfire! Are you sure?"

"No, but now that column of darkish cloud?"

"What, damn it?"

"Now I think it's dissipating smoke from a campfire."

She kicked her animal into a run. William called to her to wait. He would have to catch up. She saw the camp, the men on the ground. She jumped off her skittish mount. "Oh, dear God, no." She recognized the men from the road. "Move the horses away from the blood and then check those men."

They had seemed invincible to her, her father, Randolph McMillan. She hovered over him, unbelieving. Her own heart failed to beat. "Oh Jesus, oh Jesus." She shook her hands in front of her. "William! William! Over here!" If she touched him, she would confirm he was dead.

William dropped to his knees and pressed his fingers to Randolph's neck.

"You can't die," she said. "Neither Lefcadio nor William like to dig."

"He's got a beat." William sat back on his heels. She glared into his regard of her, daring him to say a word. After a heartbeat more of looking at her like he had never seen her before, he said, "Those two are dead." He straightened and stripped them of their shirts, tearing the garments from the men's backs. He squatted next to her. "Press these into the bleeding."

She watched the blood seep through the dirt on the shirts. "You should go back for the wagon."

"And leave you here?"

"Yes, yes, you'll have to. You and Lefcadio will hitch the mules faster. Don't spare them."

"What?"

"Just go," Maggie yelled.

She heard every pound of the hooves of the horse as William rode away. Glancing back at the two other vermin that the buzzards would soon have, she remembered their faces, and she remembered this was what she had told Randolph to do to them. Her words felt so brutal now.

Maggie peeked under the cloth. The bleeding hadn't slowed. She had no idea what these particular men were doing here. They couldn't tell her, and maybe Randolph wouldn't be able to, either. At first, in that initial recognition, she thought he'd come to meet them as planned, but they were dead, and he almost was, too.

How had he known? The campfire. He'd seen it.

God, his face was the color of the sand his head rested on. Wind whistled past her ears. In the middle of nowhere, and under her palms, Randolph's life dripped from his body. "How could you be so stupid to come alone? You in a gunfight? Damn it. I'm going to save you and then kill you. Do you hear me?" She felt like she had been entrusted with a gift and had dropped and broken it. She couldn't tell if he was breathing, so she leaned in to kiss his white lips.

The wagon roared in, the mules snorting from the dust in their nostrils. Lefcadio dropped to her side. He rolled Mac. "The bullets have gone through."

"Get the whiskey—"

"Didn't that wee book ye brought have ye bring iodine?"

"Get the damn whiskey and my needle and thread."

She poured most of what was left of the bottle through the holes in his shoulder and stomach.

"Easy there, lass." Lefcadio took the bottle and swigged what was left.

Mac gasped at the liquid burning his open flesh. His eyes opened, that clear blue that warmed Maggie.

"Wha...where am...the Morrigan?" He spoke like the whiskey had been poured down his throat instead of into his wound.

"Ye're still here in our forty days and nights in the desert. The Morrigan hasn't moved ye to a better place. She's a capricious woman who likes a good laugh. We're going to have to move ye to the wagon. William, take the head. Up now."

"Put him on the bed." Maggie said as she searched for the needle and thread.

"I'll get water and soap and wash his shoulder," said Lefcadio.

Her fingers trembled as she carved the first stitch. His shoulder reflexed back, and the needle caught the skin on one side of the wound. She bent into her task, now and again wiping the damp from her forehead onto the sleeve of her dress. After she finished, she shuffled around some boxes, opened one and took out a bottle of scotch. There comes a time in every woman's life to start drinking.

She uncorked it and poured a generous amount into a tin cup. She managed to swallow two fingers' worth in one gulp. She didn't know if she would breathe again. After blinking away tears, she took another, smaller drink. Maggie sat back against the tarp and on a barrel.

"I brought me own cup."

She filled it and another for herself. She liked how hard it was to swallow, and how warmth fanned through her stomach. She cradled the cup on her lap between her hands and let the bottle lean against her hip. "The last of my father's rare collection. I've been hiding it from Guy for years, and now, well…"

"It's a drinker you're becoming, then."

William climbed in next, and then rooted in the crates for a mug and sat next to her on a box.

"Get off," she said to Will.

"Are you joking? Just a little, for God's sake. Don't be so mean."

She knew she had to. She knew that refusing him just now was her usual reaction in another world. "That was a good job you did. How you got the skill we can all guess."

"You couldn't end that nicely, could you? Actually, you don't know anything about me," he said as Hearn poured into his cup. "And you shouldn't get into the habit of drinking alone anyway. It's not good."

"So you say."

"It's not."

William leaned against a canvas post and sniffed then drank. She glanced away from his look of genuine joy. "You're still pushy and mean—"

"Give it back." She reached for his cup.

He held it out of her reach. "You are an absolute, ranting slave to your convictions—"

"What do you know about me?"

"But," William continued, "I've never seen you so brave."

The air went out of her. "What do you know about those men, William?"

"They ran with him—" William glanced toward Randolph. "—from time to time. That's all. I never ran with him. I just, you know, was there with him in bars. I tried to copy him."

She snorted. "Copy him? Fine, let's let that stand. Why?"

"To learn how to be sophisticated."

Maggie bowed her head and swept her drinking arm out. "He taught you well."

"To see how I could best my father."

"And be the bad king of all the land."

"You are nothing if not consistent," William said with a growl.

Maggie put the cork into the bottle and then hit it with her open hand. "Neither of us has bested him. Maybe the real Randolph, not the copy—" She glanced at William. "—will have better results. Like a western shoot out. Randy Mac and Guy, guns on their hips. My money is on Randolph. I hope there is a good hotel in Boise, and that we get there soon. The real Randolph has my bed."

———

Mac woke to the smell of water, or the lack of dust. From the sound of lapping, he guessed the wagon was near a ferry to cross a river. He had come in and out of delirium, during which there was her hand giving him teaspoons full of broth. He moved his shoulder. He had lived after all. He was still lying in the same place with his heart thumping in his wound and it occurred to him they had all come after him. The sheet that had been tucked tightly around him was a little damp; his fever had broken. God, he was hungry.

He heard the mute sound of wood hitting wood and then William's voice urging the mules on, the slapping of the reins on the animals' rumps. The wagon rocked as it passed the threshold from ferry to land. Mac quit breathing with the pain and almost wished the Morrigan had taken him again.

"How much farther to Boise?"

Maggie's voice. She said it as if she'd ask for a Christmas gift that seemed impossible. She sounded like she wished she had never known the word "west" as a hopeful idea.

Mac pushed with his good arm to sit up. He stood carefully, waiting for his brain to reset to the altitude. He eased his way up and out and pawed his way through the debris that was the wagon bed. He opened the wooden box that had in it eggs cushioned in straw. He broke two into his mouth, one after another, then two more. With the raw taste on his tongue washed down in part by a slug of whiskey, Mac eased himself back to his pillow. The wagon rocked him, and he slept until it stopped.

The canvas flipped open. "So ye didn't fly off again to another era." Hearn turned his head and yelled, "He's among the living. Not before time," he said aside to Mac. "She's making you eat and drink in your sleep. She's been touchy as a bitch in labor, and here she is." Hearn waved her in.

Maggie studied his face. He enjoyed the worry there. He thought he'd never see it again, and he was right in thinking it wouldn't last. It rearranged itself into something bland by the second tick of a clock. Hearn glanced at Mac and shrugged.

Mac noted the bruised tinge under her eyes. "Where's the black silk?"

She glanced briefly at her change of clothing. "I'll never get the blood out of it."

She wore an apron and her hair was mounded at the base of her neck. She disappeared and then returned with rabbit and onions and potatoes swimming in a bowl of broth. The smell made his stomach growl, and she looked up when she heard it.

She smiled just a little.

"One good thing," Maggie said to him as she settled him sitting up against the boards of the wagon, "you're too lame to be a nuisance to me."

She was sitting close to feed him. He leaned in to kiss her cheek.

She pulled back. "Oh, stop. Eat this. Keep your mouth busy." As she was sitting farther from him now, she moved the spoon slowly over her precious bed.

"Just put the bowl on my lap. I've got one good arm and can feed myself."

"All right then," she said as if the soup had scalded her. "We are about four days from Boise. I've been thinking that it's a good place for me to settle down for a while."

"I'm better and how are you today?" She sniffed and turned her head.

"William's here. He's not so bad. He's come all this way to make sure of your safety. Maybe you should marry him and trot back to Garth. All will be forgiven. Or, as you plan, in Boise, you can find a more moral and upstanding man who will fall prey to those lovely eyes and the artful use of the lashes around them. I'd find one that shoots well. Guy is coming."

Maggie sprang up. The bowl on Mac's legs unsettled and brown juice spilled.

"Oh no." Maggie grabbed between his legs for the bowl and then for potatoes and carrots. She stripped off her apron and jammed it down between his legs, dabbing at the mattress over and over.

"Jesus, woman." With his good hand, Mac grabbed her wrist.

"My bed." She met his eyes. He met hers. A conversation they never had in words held them. Truth wrapped around them like the tight binding of a satin ribbon, until Mac, so hungry for more than stew, reached around to her shoulder and laid her back, down to the sheets. He took her lips like they were his, like he'd come for them, like he'd die for them. When he lifted his head just enough to still feel her breath on his face, he fixed his gaze on hers, daring her to move away or even glance aside.

Maggie didn't. Mac took her lips to his one more thorough time. If he died again tomorrow, she'd remember him.

CHAPTER SEVENTEEN

As Randolph lifted his head from the kiss, as Maggie lay on her back with his face inches from the sound of her voice, she realized that she loved at last, the wrong man. It broke her heart and freed her tongue. "This is an impossible situation."

He rose onto an elbow. He picked up some of her hair and rubbed it against his cheek. "If you can be open-minded about what I say, if you can let even one chink of light into your dark thoughts...one possibility of truth. Because if you can't then there is no reason for me to say anything at all, is there?"

"There is no reason to say anything at all if it is not honest."

"I have been as honest as the day is long. You don't want honesty; you just want to hear me agree with what you think is the truth," Mac said.

"And you just want to twist my thoughts."

"You don't want to listen."

"*You* just want to get away with this little scheme of yours."

"You two better be quiet in there before little Willie and I decide you're both as cracked as me grandmother's tea pot and we pitch the lot of you into a ditch. If ye're feeling that feisty, the both of ye can come out here and help track down the mules so we can get to the fair city of Boise and find some comfort in a fresh bottle of Jameson's."

"Mind your own business," she and Randolph said at the same time.

"Boise is near." Maggie moved from him. "We can part ways there. I'd say it's for the best."

———

"There, that one, the Overland Hotel." Maggie climbed down and then in a few minutes, came back up saying, "It's good-sized and clean, although the noise from the stagecoach office adjoining it will be annoying, and the dining room doesn't have linen on the tables. Let's try that other one we saw."

"Hart's Exchange," Will offered in a barely interested voice. They'd been up and down the roads of the town as Maggie checked all the hotels' entries.

She went inside and came back out with a man to lift her trunk of clothes.

First, she planned to order a bath. It would most likely be a bath-house, but any bathtub with hot water would be a luxury. Randolph could pay for it. She'd saved his sorry life twice at her count. She didn't want to see a man for at least twenty-four hours.

Later, as she undressed for the first time in what seemed like ages, she knew dust was ingrained in her pores. She'd been chewing on it for miles. She coughed and then sneezed as she pulled the dress over her head.

She dipped her foot into the clear, hot water. As she slid in the rest of her body, the water lapped against arms and legs, and in between and under like wet silk. Water was so much better with one's clothes off.

Her head back, her mind relaxed. With the water on her bare skin, she thought of his hands on her hips and then on her thighs.

Not as soft, more pressing. Taking up the soap, she soaped the skin of her arms and then her legs to her thighs. She thought of his lips again. If his mouth could do that... the rest of him! Maggie lifted her hand from the bath to her forehead. Drops ran down her arm.

With her eyes closed, his face appeared in the darkness, a face of a man of all seasons, with his barbarous chin hair sweeping forward. Eyes that matched the sky. In that moment, naked, her legs relaxed and open, had Randolph been near, she would have taken his knight's sword that he claimed to use so well and thrust it between her legs herself. Her body felt too light without him.

Maggie's eyes jumped open. She sat up, sending waves of water against the tub and over the side. She lathered her hands and then scrubbed at her scalp with a vengeance. Sitting back to rinse, she closed her mind. The water had gone cold. She rose out of the tub, mourning the loss of a peaceful bath. She covered herself with the shield of her clothing and walked to her room.

As she brushed her hair out, she wondered where he was, if he'd seen the doctor, what the doctor had said, and then she called herself pathetic into the mirror. Damn it! She weighed out her alternatives.

She'd had it all pictured in her head for so long, since the days that she and her father had sat together on the porch swing. A knight, he'd said, would come for her, a man of honor and integrity. That knight would take her hand, and, as light as a whisper, he would kiss the inside of her arm just at the crux of her elbow. He would woo her with stories of bravery. He would build her a castle. The wedding would be white, with gardenias and orange blossoms. Her father at the altar with her, giving her hand to a man who would keep her safe and well loved. She very much wanted to be cherished again. She began crying, her head on the top of the vanity, the hairbrush and her hand in her lap.

Her mother's voice came to her: "You're spoiling her, Edmund."

"No," her father would say back. "Nothing is too good for Magnolia Bathurst. The world is hers."

"And then you died," she yelled and pounded the vanity. "You shouldn't have died." When she sobered and pronounced herself done in the mirror, Maggie realized that while she was going to eat chef-prepared food at a linen-wrapped table, food without grit in it, she was going down to eat it alone. She suddenly wasn't hungry.

This was no way to go on. Maybe she'd like Boise. Maybe she should stay here. She strolled down Main Street. Her heels sounded on the raised wooden platform sidewalk. The thoroughfare was scarred and creased with rut lines now full of leftover water from a spring shower. Here and there a planted tree leaned away from store porch roofs, seeking better sun. She wished she hadn't put on her finery. Her hem was already darkening from damp soil. Boise was a man's town, but in the midst of it the Falk Brothers' window, showing genuine lace collars, also furs, stopped her progress. The hats and glassware were dusty. Next to that was W.H. Nye's Drugstore, and two doors down, Peyton and Taylor's Saloon, a creaky wooden place that seemed shabby next to the better brick buildings. She felt better the whole town wasn't made of clapboard and that it was bigger than Kelton, three streets instead of just one.

The women who passed seemed less shapeless, more attractive than those in Kelton. The men sat in the corral talking. She saw mules munching on hay. Then there was a blacksmith, shoeing shop, another saloon, Peter Cohen's Variety Store with Candies, and then John Lemp's Boise Brewery, where she stopped to scan the inside. No one she knew.

She crossed the street in front of a wagon with tired-looking nags. On it sat a middle-aged man with a grizzly beard and an old woman on a rawhide seat with a pipe between her teeth. On the other side in the window of Jimmy Hart's Grocery and Bakery, Sample Room, she read, "The indigent, sick, idiotic, and insane will be fed with clam chowder at Jimmy Hart's tonight as the hospital is undergoing a frescoing." Boise wasn't a temperance town like Kelton. Lefcadio would be on a stool in the back. The Irish.

She peeked into the dark interior. Long and narrow, she could just make out gaming tables in the far back. She enjoyed the fiddle and banjo before a patron nudged her with the door. Feeling her cheeks redden, she walked on. They were in there and she was outside.

She moved on to another type of bakery, one with only buns that advertised tea, but just had coffee. Maggie sat at the window and drank. She picked at the doily. She fiddled with the cream pitcher. Coffee in a teacup at a window with her white gloves seemed tame, even boring and silly in this town.

She heard an Irish brogue in the street. In turning toward the window, she knocked over her cup. As the owner helped dry the table, Maggie glanced again out the window. She saw no one she knew, and now her handkerchief dripped with brown liquid.

"New here?"

"I'm so sorry about the mess."

"It'll clean. Staying or passing?"

"What, sorry, ah, pardon?"

"Staying put or passing on through?"

Maggie continued to move her saturated handkerchief through the puddle on the table. Her thoughts felt a little like electric bolts, brilliant, chaotic, and short lived.

"Ah, yes, or no. I'm not sure."

"Where you coming from?"

That question seemed to make more sense and she answered quickly. "Kentucky, just the other side of Cincinnati."

"Lemp's from there."

"Of Boise Brewery?"

"Beer King of Boise, and our esteemed mayor."

"He's German, of course. I don't know any Lemps myself, but there is a Lemp in Cincinnati that I know of. He's in hogs. It's rumored that he has an illegitimate son who's not right in the head that they keep locked in the eaves of their mansion. The Monkey Boy, some called him. Oh, dear lord, I'm sorry, that was ill-mannered," she said as she stopped mopping and looked at the woman. *Stupid*, she said to herself. She heard her mother rebuking her, "Only a few people in life get away with saying anything they want, and it generally requires great age or great wealth."

"Don't bother about it. Mrs. Lemp comes here every Thursday. Come back tomorrow at two-thirty, and I'll introduce you. She'd love to hear the news."

As the woman poured a fresh cup, Maggie thought, *Why not stay?* All her careful planning gone with the money. This town seemed decent, friendly.

She was getting in deeper and deeper with Randolph. Another woman would make life easier. Maggie knew she had to meet Mrs. Lemp tomorrow. Maybe they'd like each other. They had Cincinnati in common. It was a start, as long as she didn't talk about monkey boys. She needed someone of her own sex to talk to.

———

The next morning, she hadn't heard from any of her male friends, even Lefcadio. At least he could have checked on her. Probably too drunk. She knew she was straying when she missed drinking with them. It was a beautiful sunny day. She wouldn't think about them. She was clean, and her hair was up, her hat on. She was a picture of respectability. When she met with Mrs. Lemp, hopefully the older lady would insist on having her to dinner.

On her stroll to the coffee shop in the early afternoon, she noted the loud laughter coming from Jimmy Hart's. The men had been "sampling" already.

Down the street, a man in rolled-up sleeves loaded a Peasley transfer wagon, the workmen calling positions to each other as they pushed a piano, their arm muscles bulging. Military men from the local garrison joked with each other and tipped their hats to Maggie. Her skirt brushed the dust that usurped every surface, vertical or horizontal, in the whole of the desert town.

She ordered coffee and glanced at the watch pinned to her blouse while she waited for it. She had grown restless in the hotel and had arrived too early, by three hours. Maybe if she sipped very slowly. She wished she had a book. The luxury of a book. Her father's library.

Stop it, Maggie. You can't sit here and cry into your coffee.

"A Southern woman if I've ever seen one, and a sad looking one at that." a man said to her as he doffed his hat. "I was born in Syracuse, New York, but don't let that bother you. I attended St. John's College in Cincinnati and taught there for a number of years. May I sit and help you become less homesick?"

The man was long-legged, with white trousers to his brown boots. He was a goatee under full lips sort of man. His own accent was an accented drawl, as if he worked hard to keep his musical tones from fading. As he sat, he sighed. Maggie smiled. She knew the type, men who liked to lounge with their feet out and with a long, cold drink in their hands.

His face was tanned and unlined, still the skin didn't appear to be the tender covering of youth. He put his broad-brimmed white hat with its black, thin band on the bend of his knee. "I think you're new to this fair city. What do you think of us?"

"It's more civilized than I expected after all the desert."

"Not nearly as beautiful as the green fields of the South, but we do have something to say for ourselves. I plant orchards. I bring the trees in from all over. Great climate for them. Lots of sunshine. They just need watering. You should let me show you."

"Mr..."

"General Edward Cartee, and you?"

"Miss Magnolia Bathurst."

"I like the miss. Magnolia." He said it with his head tipped back, rolling the vowels off his tongue. "Beautiful. Lovely name, lovely tree. How I miss that graceful, white flower. Are you alone, Magnolia Bathurst? If you're whiling away the afternoon, why don't you have a stroll with me to my orchards? They're not far. I have a house full of a few nieces and two sisters, so if you are comfortable, we can all have cold tea and cucumber sandwiches together. That's a fair introduction to Boise. What do you say? It's only six blocks. Sons and daughters of the South must stick together. You must not think we're all about sand."

Tea, and why not?

It's not like anyone one of her so-called companions had knocked on her door for dinner last night or for breakfast this morning. They might have decided as a group that the plan hadn't worked, and they were returning to Cincinnati. She had won. They were all gone, so she could walk out on this gentleman's arm to his orchard. She would flirt and bat her eyelashes and meet Mrs. Lemp later.

She put on her best smile walked with her hand just at the inside of Cartee's forearm from Seventh Street to Third and then turned onto Grove.

"That's my barn," he said with a sweep of his hand.

Maggie staggered to a halt, and then glanced at Cartee, who smiled at her reaction.

"It's thirty-two feet by forty-two feet. It has sixteen feet posts and two floors, one for the carriages and one for the hay, and inside stairs."

She noticed on top of the roof and on top of a cupola was a steeple with a spire running up from it. Mounted on the spire were the four points of the compass and a trotting horse.

"Fifty-two feet to the top."

"Are those windows in the cupola?"

"I can see the entire town and the mountains."

As she passed the building, she saw behind it another cupola, steeple, and spire, thirty feet high and with a rooster on top.

"Yes, isn't it beautiful? You see, in another life, I was an architect and builder in Pennsylvania. And now—" He waved with his arm to encompass a selection of buildings. "Over there, Boise's first greenhouse. Are you hungry? Let's skip the cucumbers and have lunch and cakes on the veranda and then I'll show you inside.

"I intend to import trees, flowers, shrubs from all over... China,

India, Japan. Impossible, you're thinking, but I've already started planting. Twenty-four acres between here and the river. What do you think? Look, what would you like to drink? I bet you've had coffee to the gills. How 'bout lemonade?"

The general's long legs took him inside and Maggie walked to the edge of his porch and gazed out onto the orchard that was nothing more than loam-less desert soil with twigs of trees sticking out of the ground like toothpick-soldiers and dug-out ditches in between for watering it all. She wouldn't let him see her disappointment. He saw things in a big way, the way it would be, like her father had, and maybe she could see its promised beauty in the new blossoms there.

When she heard the slightest sound of glasses clinking against each other, she turned and put on the biggest Southern smile she could find within herself. "This will be the most beautiful place in Boise in the springtime."

"I would have a Chinaman to do all this," he said as he laid out the drinks, "but the little buggers are so angry all the time. The one I just fired was breaking things now and again on purpose."

He offered her a glass and took one himself, raising it in her direction. "Here's to your lovely countenance gracing my home."

She gave him another warm smile. "And to the lovely sight of apple blossoms."

He even had fan-like white wicker chairs and bamboo in pots. She'd passed a room with rows of books. He had tasseled velvet at the windows and stained glass overlooking the stairs. She sat back to relax, almost closing her eyes, worry unknotted. She could stay here.

"You didn't come all this way alone, did you?"

Maggie wanted to say yes, intended to, but she hadn't seen even one of her traveling companions' concerned faces for twenty-four hours. Anyway, it was a tactical mistake to think about Randolph now, where he was now and what he was doing, whether his shoulder was healing and whether he was caring for it.

"I have a footpath along the river," he was saying. "Let's stretch our legs a bit and then lunch will be ready."

Maggie put her hand on his elbow. She felt the delicateness of her touch there. She smelled his aftershave. It was light. She noted that the Edward Cartee didn't assault her senses, like someone else she knew. He soothed them. She felt the sunlight of the day as she walked easily beside him. He expected nothing but her presence. He wanted nothing but her conversation.

This is refreshing, she thought and then said it out loud. He tightened his elbow with her hand linked through it against his side. Under his guidance, Maggie let her mind wander... eventually to Randolph. She shook thoughts of him away several times. She looked up at her partner, as Southern women will, with a slight tilt to the head and with an intentional smile.

He told her of the difficulties of getting nursery stock from Kelton to Boise on the wagons through the desert. Ditches ran along the walk that lent the air the cool smell of water.

"I have the boys of Hailey's stagecoach line trained to soak down the packages at streams they're crossing, to keep the roots damp. Once they soaked through a package of paper meant for the surveyor general's office."

She laughed into the pleasant afternoon as he spoke.

"Hard to keep the cherries up through the spring freezes."

"It freezes here?"

"High desert. Snows and all in the winter."

She stayed for high tea as well and met his sisters and nieces, and then he walked her to the hotel. He kissed her cheek, just at the corner of her mouth before letting her go. "May we have coffee again tomorrow?"

"That would be nice." Maggie let her hips sway just a little as she knew he watched her retreat inside. Maybe she could stay here. Maybe she should thank Randolph for getting her this far. He'd said Guy was coming, but Guy would never leave Garth; he'd worked so hard to possess it.

———

Mac surveyed his surrounds. Jimmy Hart's Sample Room was a long, barely put together wooden room. End to end it took some time to walk from the light-blinding door, along the rotund kegs, to the back, to the bar. While the walls hadn't seen paint and the floors were misaligned, the bar was loved-kept. The carved and polished mahogany top glistened like the mirror behind it. As Jimmy Hart was Irish, Mac sat beside Hearn at the bar and spoke Gaelic with them. Hearn knew how to get a free drink.

"Now I know your story is true," Hearn said in English for William's benefit when Jimmy moved on, "and that the Morrigan is on your shoulder."

"She must be. When I touch my shoulder, it burns." The air was foul with the scent of spit, tobacco, ale, and men. He had been listening to Ireland's mother tongue. The alcohol had him humming along with Hearn's Irish fighting songs. Mac sang his own in full, off-key baritone.

"Would ye ever tell us about the other woman? The one ye died for. She must have been something, that one, to have a man die for her."

"She was no beauty." Mac waved his finger in front of his listeners. "Men die in scores for beauty. It's a waste. Beauty is not to die for. No, she wasn't beautiful, but she had goodness, even in the likes of that castle, with the likes of her father. He had no soul, had sold it to the highest bidder. I would have given three lives for her."

"Ah then, it sounds as if ye loved her purely."

"I carried her favor with me. What she felt for me was too much entwined with pity, though, and I couldn't get her with child. She was meant to be a mother."

William knocked back the rest of his ale and slammed the glass to the bar top. "Listen to you two. What a pile of rubbish."

"Tisn't Randolph McMillan beside ye, Boyo."

"Really? Who is it?"

Mac pushed back from the bar. "To hell with it, Lefcadio. Don't bother. It's why I left Cincinnati." Mac threw coins on the bar and walked away. Hearn would write the story. Randolph would be considered insane. Maggie should stay here. William, too. It was plain that William felt he had a debt to settle with Maggie's mother. If anyone could keep Maggie safe from Guy, it would be Guy's son. Homesteading in Grangeville, that's what he was going to do. Mac wanted land, his own land. He had saved the lady, brought her safely west. His debt was finished.

Outside, on the dirt street, with riders on horses coming in and going out, Mac remembered how he used to ride along the outside edges of the land his father had forfeited, feeling the pull of it. It would have been his, should have been his, all of it. He remembered a small, clear creek he used to play by with his mother in the summer months. He bathed there. The maid always got soap in his eyes. He'd fought furiously for the next king, hoping to be awarded land, but FitzAlan had been too strong an influence at court.

Mac considered Jimmy's words again. "The land is given to you, just like that—well, that and a hundred thousand miles of split-railing later. After two years, you'll have an ax growing out of the end of your arm, natural like. The soil's good and black, I've heard. You sell to the Indians and the miners.

"The closest flourmill is in Walla Walla. Got to pack it there. It's a one-hundred-and-thirty-mile trip to Lewiston and back for supplies. It snowed last winter starting on an afternoon on the twenty-eighth of February until the thirtieth. The storm dropped twenty-six inches and the temperature dropped to zero.

"There's no doctor. They lost a good few this year from scarlet fever. The government is pushing so hard on the Nez Perce, so as you wouldn't know they are a peace-loving tribe. A man named Johnson stopped in on his way back East. Just yesterday, he said that anybody who wanted his place could have it. Far as I know, it is still up there for grabs."

Lefcadio joined Mac outside the bar. Mac could see they were both up to their snouts in drink. "I think I will take Mr. Johnson up on that and God bless him. Now I need some sleep." Leaning on Lefcadio, and Lefcadio leaning back, Mac's eyelids closed while walking, and weaving on the road. He jerked them open and the bright rays of the setting sun burned orange red into his mind. Wasn't that the hotel they'd dropped Maggie off at? Mac veered Lefcadio right. There she was.

By all that was holy, she cleaned up well. He followed her to the door. There, he watched as Maggie turned toward a goat-like man dressed in white. She smiled the blessed smile that Mac had only seen once. The goat kissed the back of her hand and then he kissed her on the side of her smiling mouth. There wasn't one cross word out of her lips. The smile that remained seemed to mock Mac. *This*, it said, *is only for goat-men*.

"If I'm not among the favored, then..." Mac flopped the hat in his hand onto his head. He redirected Lefcadio in a difficult about-face to the stables. William found them as they walked.

"Stay with her, William."

"Plenty of fish in the river, Padric, yes, there are." Mac was not going to be Randolph McMillan one moment longer.

CHAPTER EIGHTEEN

R andolph?" She saw him from the corner of her eye just before passing over the threshold of the hotel. "Randolph! What's wrong with you? Would you stop?"

She ran after him and didn't catch him until he was in front of one of their mules. Maggie breathed hard. He didn't even turn to look at her. "Randolph, what in the world—"

"Don't call me that."

His voice was so hateful, she stepped back from him. Too astonished to say anything more, she watched him sit Lefcadio on a bale of hay. His back to her felt so solid and airless, like a wall without a window.

While she continued to stand behind him, he bartered for a horse and saddle, and after giving the horse his full attention, he walked with the reins in his hand and the horse following past her. He didn't speak, although he paused to gaze full on her face. His rich blue irises sparkled with, God, pain, anger. He took her shoulders in his hands, his fingers gouging. He kissed her in a way she never expected existed, both hard and soft, loving and hateful.

The extremes had her touching her lips when he released her.

"I thought it wouldn't matter, but it does. It matters who I am, and it matters that you hate who I appear to be. You can't see past your upturned nose. Stay with the goat-man. Have his babies. He's the gentleman you want."

She heard the leather of the saddle creak as he lifted himself into the seat. The brass of the bridle chimed as he turned the head of the horse, and then he was gone, into the last bit of orange as the sun slipped below the horizon.

Maggie once thought that life was simple. She'd plant persimmons and pecans and help when it was time to render soap. Like her father, the man she married would sit with their children on the porch swing, and they would all play croquet, and she would never, ever have to cook!

The men at the door of the stable stared at her. Cartee had followed her. She gathered her skirts and lifted her head and tried to move as if her heart wasn't broken.

Cartee followed her back. At the hotel, he doffed his hat and said, "I am at your service."

"Thank you. You are the kindest man. He...." she gazed at the direction Mac had taken.

"Is a sore loser," said Cartee.

"Yes, I suppose." Maggie smiled a quick smile. "Well, goodnight."

"Coffee tomorrow? Four o'clock?"

"Of course."

She traversed the lobby, and then paused just before she stepped up, her hand on the rail. Just like that, the extraordinary events were over. She couldn't feel anymore the threat Guy used to hold for her. God, it seemed so long ago. One heavy step after another, she ascended the staircase. She pirouetted on the landing and went back down and ordered a brandy. To sleep, she told herself. When William walked in the door, she told the desk clerk to make it extra-large.

"Drinking again?"

"Find somewhere else to be."

He laughed. "Thought I needed to see if you were still here."

Maggie swept her arm across her body and then curtsied. "Still here. Randolph is gone."

"Gone?"

"He is on the road out of town. He got tired of the game." She took a long drink.

———

In the morning, Lefcadio and William joined her for buttered toast with real butter and apricot jam, grown locally, bacon and eggs, and coffee.

"Gold mining has petered out," William was saying. "We're too late. Everyone is selling to the Chinese."

"Are they now?" Lefcadio said while paying attention to Maggie. "How do the Chinese get along then with the gold gone, and themselves still squeezing the orange?"

"They use a rocker better and have a hell of a lot of patience, I guess. They mine the dust. Lots of Chinese in town, from what I hear. Some guy that sold herbs and opium was run off last night. They followed him to the Snake River. After he crossed, he yelled back at 'em, 'You go to hell'ee.' Do you know what the Chinese are taxed here? Three bucks a head. I was told they hide people to save money."

"I would," said Maggie. She noted that she'd never heard the boy talk so much or so freely. The West was good for him. His table manners were still pathetic, though. Sighing, she put down her knife and fork. Food wouldn't pass by the constriction in her throat anyway.

"Where is he going?" she asked Lefcadio.

"Where the loam of the field is darkest."

She gritted her teeth. "And where would that be?"

"A place called Grangeville comes to mind."

"Where is that?"

"North."

William watched her. "You're not thinking of following him? He knows the game. He plays it with exceptional timing. "And you would know," she snapped at him.

"You are not serious? You ran away from my father. This guy is one hundred times worse. That's Randolph McMillan."

"I'm not after a gentleman. It's a knight I was promised." Maggie lifted her napkin from her lap and tossed it onto the table.

William turned to Lefcadio and said, "What is she talking about? Would you talk some sense into her?"

———

Maggie emerged from the hotel in a much shorter dress, thick shoes, and a sunbonnet. Packed away were any hint of a trailing skirt, kid shoes, and hats of fashion.

At the wagon, she found that Randolph had already taken her white sheets and comforter to the Chinese laundry. William had somehow added a sheet-iron stove. While she had been walking orchards, they had been cleaning. William arrived with a cow and a butter-churn. Maggie stared at the animal and the heavy teats underneath her. "Milk. William, I could kiss you."

"Hold that thought for at least a few hours. If I had my way, I'd tie you to a bed until your madness subsided. I promised your mother—"

"What did you promise?"

"Milk and butter. You strain the milk into the churn, cover it closely and then tie it to the wagon. It's much more sensible to let the wagon do all the work."

"William, what did you promise?"

"You know what, Maggie, it's just none of your goddamn business what I promised." William moved from her line of sight. She heard the rope threading through a piece of the wagon.

"Much more sensible," she said to the mooing cow. There was so much about the humans that peopled Garth she had not known. She sat down on the bed and watched William pack fruit in with the flour and lard and bacon. He had buried eggs in the beans for safe-keeping. She had no idea who this person was.

She felt lousy; maybe a cold was coming on. She was sitting list-lessly on the fresh sheets when someone rapped on the end of the wagon. If it was the general, she had no idea what to tell him. She pushed her hair back hurriedly, and then let her hand fall back. It didn't matter and anyway, it wasn't Cartee, just a woman delivering another picnic basket. Crying, she crawled out of the wagon to stop by the coffee house to leave Cartee a note. She needed to be a nicer person.

When she came back, William was leaning through the opening and over the lip of the wagon, his rear-end faced her as he seemed to fish for something.

"What are you looking for?"

"Not looking for, storing the lager. You've become such a fine drinker that Hearn decided you'd want some for the trip."

"Good man."

———

The town of Horseshoe Bend was a single track of wooden side-walk, which one descended or ascended by a set of double planks. Every other pine building was a saloon. No bush, no garden, just heaps of deer and horse dung. An Irishman lived in every town and hollow.

Lefcadio left to have a beer or more and gather information. William replenished stores. Maggie sat with the resting mules in the shade of a building and fanned herself. The first of June had turned hot at the bottom of the desert that was Horseshoe Bend.

The track now followed the Payette River. The water ran so clear she could see fish swimming. They began climbing from the desert floor. The canyon walls created by the river became spotted with white pine. She filled her lungs with the fresh scents of water and pine. Snow pockets remained under trees and in the shade. Where there was water, snow, and runoff creeks, there was mud and puddles. At times, she had had to drive the wagon while the men pushed. When her clothes were mud-hardened, a spring rain washed them, and then at nightfall, the temperature dropped to near freezing.

Maggie had her hands out to the fire. It smoked, the wood was wet, but it was wood. Compared to a sage fire, it smelled like lavender.

"There's bear here," Hearn said. "I've been warned to keep watch."

"Is that all?"

"Ah sure, there's a few mountain lions, some bobcats, and the elk aren't too nice either. The bears have cubs this time of year, which is all the more reason not to encounter one. You wouldn't want to come between a mother and her young."

"Don't tell me." She gazed at the water. "Have you ever seen a river move along like that?" It pounded down from the mountain as white water. "It's as if the law was after its hide." "Trout in it," William said.

Maggie was getting used to William knowing everything. She hardly blinked an eyelash. He didn't leave his arrogance behind with his father, but it had taken a different, more useful form.

The canyon widened into a long, narrow valley that was closely surrounded by yellow pine, fir, and tamarack-fringed mountains. The flat land was carpeted in bunch grass and wild red top that was knee-high to the horses. She stared at the uncultivated spread of white grass flowers, and red and pink birdbills, blue camas, and yellow buttercups, and in the distance, a thread of smoke.

Homesteads dotted the flat, ranching land. Mostly log houses that looked like the building in which soap was rendered at Garth. The sides of the houses had the mottled color of weathered, planed wood that had been through a winter or two.

One had a flat mud roof. Nearby were a corral, a shed, hay piles, horses, and chickens. A hen flew passed Maggie as she walked a path to the door. A vegetable garden grew along one side of the path. The man came toward Maggie, wiping his hands on pants so faded as to have no color at all. He smelled like carbolic and animals. Hearn had told Maggie that on the nights they ended close to any homes, the settlers took in paying guests, sort of like small hotels on the road.

"I've got coffee on the stove. Let those mules run. They had a task getting you up from the desert." The man introduced himself as Jim, and he took Maggie's elbow to lead her inside to a good-sized log room with glass windows that faced north and south.

An entire log lay on a robust fire in a stone fireplace. At a knife-scarred table, Maggie sat on seat made of black pine poles with flat wooden slats across the backs. She sat lightly on the woven rawhide seats that still had red and white cow hair on them. One small window in the back had a flour sack tacked in the frame. Afternoon light illuminated the weave of the fabric around the black letters, "Jasper's Best for Bread."

She tried to control any shock on her face as she glanced across the hard-packed dirt floor at a bed with a blob of a mattress near a cook stove that radiated heat. On another table, a headless chicken twitched in its last death throes. As he handed her a cup of coffee, Jim said, "If you start pluckin' that chicken, I kin help them with the livestock."

"I've never plucked—"

"Ain't too hard. Just grab on the feathers and pull."

He left her alone with the corpse. She considered calling William. With one cup down and another poured, Maggie paced around the chicken. She petted the bird's feathers, and then grabbed one and plucked.

"Not so bad. Not so bad. I'd better speed up or we'll be eating it tomorrow." She put her cup down. With half a handful, she tugged, and the entire bird fell to the floor. She squealed, and then looked around to see if anyone had seen her. In her research, reading about the West, women were always plucking chickens. "Just thank your lucky stars you didn't have to kill it," she muttered.

Soon, Jim and William and Lefcadio came stamping in the door, Jim talking. "You're lucky to get here in springtime. The Pottengers arrived in end of October and took one of the abandoned cabins. They intended to go back to Boise to stock up for winter, but from that time 'til the first week of November the snow came. Piled up to eight feet.

"Come to think of it, J.W. did go down later by cooning the ferry cable across the river and then skiing down. They were lucky, too. It wasn't till the last of March that all the seasoning, shortening, and what have you they bought ran out. After that, they was grinding wheat on a coffee mill and eating it as bread and mush with nothing added. They lived on one biscuit a day and mush. She said she never left the place until the snow was gone." Jim paused to dump two more headless fowls on top of the partially nude one Maggie was working on. "You ever scrapped a potato?" he asked.

"Yes, of course," she lied. "I think we are going to Grangeville."

"Grangeville? Yep, been there. Call in on John and Sarah Aram. They been there ten years. Came in the sixties. Their cabin is about a mile from town. Funny, I just had another feller come by asking about Grangeville. There's a new flourmill. Only the Nez Perce are unsettled up there. You could stay here in Long Valley. The Perkins just left. We're close to the Emmett fruit orchards and to Boise. Some real nice hot springs, and a real nice lake just twenty miles from here. It's more ranching than planting here, though."

"How long ago did the other man... I mean, several days ago?" Maggie asked with what she hoped was a casual tone as she tried to wipe feathers from her sticky fingers on a flour-sack towel.

"On a week now, at least."

Her heart skipped a painful beat. At least they knew he'd been here. *Fine thing. Here he was leading them all on a merry chase, through bears and lions and dead chickens.*

He is still alive and going to Grangeville, it seems. She closed her eyes tight, trying not to let the tears of relief fall. *Damn him.*

Jim talked through the cooking of the meal and the meal itself. It seemed that wherever they stopped people had a lot of conversation stored up in them. He stood to clear the table.

"I'll do it," said Maggie.

Both Will and Lefcadio looked up, startled...like she'd offered to clean the stables or something. To hell with them. She washed every pot, fork, glass, spoon, and plate. Her hands felt as dry as the damn desert when she was done. Lefcadio, of course Lefcadio had brought in the scotch. Maggie noticed they had put down a glass for her.

She took it to the fire and sat in a rocking chair, trying to ignore a moose head staring down at her.

"There'll be snow in the mountains tonight," Jim said.

That night Maggie pulled the rug on the floor over the top of the blankets to add warmth. She put socks on her feet and hands. "You'll have all the best," her father had always said to her. She closed her eyes. Her father had been wrong. She wasn't sure she wanted to live with that.

CHAPTER NINETEEN

I*f you show you can do something, it is yours forever.*
Who had told her that? Cook, probably. Maggie had plucked a chicken and peeled potatoes. Her life was never to be the same. As they traveled farther north toward Grangeville, Will was teaching her to cook breakfast so he could help find the livestock that had wandered and grazed through the night. He had also taught her to milk the cow.

The feeling of raw dough between her fingers next to a campfire each morning seemed appropriate to their surroundings. She could get Will's little oven to a temperature hot enough to cook the insipid balls to a golden brown. It helped that there was tree wood to burn.

As if on cue, Will pointed and said, "That steam. Do you see it?"

Maggie glanced along the point of his arm. She put her hand to her mouth and then moved it slightly to say, "It looks like smoke. Is it a fire?"

"I believe that it is nice hot water to bathe in."

"What are you talking about?" She turned to press the heels of her palms into the dough.

"It is, I believe, a hot spring."

"What is that?"

"Only a pool of hot water issuing from the ground."

She ignored the dough and shaded her eyes as she stared at the plume.

"I'm going—" "You can't—"

"No, you don't understand. I am going."

She had never walked so fast, so far. Maybe the men trailed, maybe they didn't. She didn't care. Nearing it, Maggie lifted her skirts as her stride increased in pace. William had promised her a warm bath. She thought of the rose-scented soap in her hand. Oh God, the soap. By now she was running. Steam rose in the chilling late afternoon air, so thick that she could just peek at the clear, clean water. Staring at it, she unbuttoned her blouse and left her skirt to drop. The heat warmed her bare feet and then her knees and thighs.

"Wa hoo, join right in." A man's head came out of the steam. She fell back and tried to crab-walk up the lip of the pool when she noticed the skeletal body of a man in full whiskers. He held a bottle of rye above the water and when he smiled, he had no teeth. No, she would not give over this pool, this haven of warm clear water. Maybe he thought she was close to insane when she told him to get his naked rear-end out of this public place. His face lost its leer, and the man did reach for his clothes, and then Maggie heard a bullet whiz past her ear. She dived for the dirt, her face planted in a cottonwood bush.

As Will reached her, she grabbed his revolver. She cocked it and shot back, full six shots. The miner made tracks, his back end in full view.

William wrenched the gun from his stepsister.

Maggie stood, saying, "He shot at me!"

"He missed. On purpose," Will said. "Pity."

"He shot at me."

"Don't shoot back unless you want to die. What did you do?" Will countered.

"Nothing!"

"What did you say?"

"Nothing! I just asked him to get out as he was naked in a public place."

"Jesus, you are the most crazy-assed female I've ever met. No wonder your mother said you were high strung and over-raised."

"What? You are lying. She would never say that."

"I am not lying. Believe me. I mean, God, just look at yourself."

A white body ran past her just then, like a streak, and jumped into the water. A wave splashed over Maggie and William. Will stripped and joined Lefcadio. With her hair and the dress on the ground water-plastered, Maggie felt sour, standing at the edge of the pool.

"Damn it," she muttered. All she could do was jump in with them.

She paddled in the very hot water, letting it relax her thin nerves. She thought of William's words. Her mother had been like a goddess to her. Grace had all the graciousness that a human woman possessed; to Maggie she had been perfect. Her mother had loved her father, but... Maggie realized, as she floated, there had been a physical bond between Grace and Sir Guy; her hand always on the shirt that covered his chest, or on his forearm.

Grace had preferred Guy. Her father had been too whimsical to her mother's practical. Grace depended on Guy, and Guy had treated her well. He had been grateful to her for giving him what he wanted, but Grace had died. Guy's dreams had died with her. With that guardianship clause in the will, Grace had left her daughter as a pawn for Guy's ruined ambitions.

She didn't think I could do it. She didn't trust me to run Garth. Sometimes truth could not be suppressed. Damn them all. Maggie slapped her hand on the surface of the pool of hot water.

———

It was a long, quiet nine more days for Maggie. She had been a cherished being. She had been her parents' world. At the hot springs, William had drowned her spirit, her image of herself.

Even Lefcadio had gone quiet after the week of helping the mules trudge up the mountains and back down them to the Camas Prairie and the Town of Grangeville, and he was parched. They had run out of liquor. After helping to settle the animals, Maggie trailed behind the men as they headed for the six wooden buildings that comprised the town. She lifted her skirt, which had no starch left in it, and stepped onto the boards that were the sidewalk. She heard the song before she recognized the voice:

Bryng vs in no browne bred, fore that is mad of brane, Nore bryng us in no whyt bdred, fore ther in is no game But bryng vs in good ale.

Her heart skipped a beat. She pushed back her hair and smoothed her skirts and had her hand on the swinging door of the drinking establishment when William's comment about her being crazy pushed through her brain, and her foot hesitated. She couldn't, bold as brass, walk into a saloon.

"He is there, by God, the prodigal son," announced Lefcadio as he sauntered past her into the bar.

Maggie stepped closer to the opening, trying to listen. She peeked into the dim lighting.

"Come on in," a slurred baritone called out. Men glanced at her. Randolph saw her. He tipped his hat and then turned away.

"He did not just *thank you mam* me."

William followed Lefcadio and smiled as he passed her.

She grabbed his shirt. "Would you tell Randolph to come out? I would like to speak to him...please." His head knocked into the swinging doors.

She leaned against the wagon her arms folded over her chest.

She would wait and see how long they left her here in the street. She set her mind for the game. She watched the White Bird stage as it approached town with mud on it as thick as a poultice. The driver whipped backwards as the harness broke. Maggie observed him with single-minded interest as took off his suspenders, patched the harness, and then came the rest of the way into town.

She followed the progress of not a few drunks as they avoided getting run over in the street. She gazed upon a man too sloshed to ride. Every time he fell off his horse, the animal would stand and wait. That horse, she could use that horse as a friend instead of the ones she had.

William arrived smelling of whiskey, and Maggie pushed off the side of the wagon.

"He said that's not his name and—"

"I have come hundreds of miles to talk to that man. If you and Lefcadio value your peace of mind and my peace of mind, you will get him out here."

William disappeared into the bar. Soon after Randolph walked out or sauntered out like a man with all the time in the world. "I told William to stay with you. I thought Boise would be good for you. It looked like a good idea."

Maggie cupped his ears. She kissed him as soundly as she knew how. The action, the desire surprised her. Her fears for him lengthened the contact. He tasted like whiskey and she drank him in. His tongue burned her mouth. It was a kiss born of anger, though, and when she pulled back, she said, "Never, ever again make decisions on your own about my life." Her spitfire gaze held his.

"Then make up your mind about what you want."

"I came all this way."

"Only because you paid me to come, and you wouldn't be left." He kissed her again like it was owed to him and then let her go. "Thanks, that part was nice. Let me know when you've got it all sorted out." He walked back into the dark recesses of the bar.

She could hear a piano. It sounded much more fun inside.

William had been returned to her.

"Arg. Send me Lefcadio."

taste of dirt was in her nose and mouth. Clean windows reflected the rose and orange of the setting sun. She put her hand at her back and stretched. Work, it had an element of satisfaction to it. The house certainly looked better. She needed to pick some wildflowers. No vase. She needed to get a vase.

When William asked her if she wanted to bathe off the sweat and exhaustion, she didn't feel she could walk the hundred feet to Graves Creek.

"Ah, come on. I have soap and a towel."

The path to the creek was well beaten by heavy use. The Sumners' had trod it often. She had walked back and forth on it at least five times already today for water. The clear river was inviting until it was up to her chest. "It's freezing," she called to no one.

William replied, "Refreshing," as he gathered kindling.

She let her hair float in a wide, calm part of the water. He was right. The cold made her skin come alive. The scent of pine refreshed her senses. When her body began to feel numb, she scrubbed it clean and got out. Her ears ached from the temperature of the water. Her skin was pink. Her thin blouse on damp skin did little to warm her. She headed back to the house and hoped William had started a fire in the fireplace she had cleaned.

Maggie had her hands out to the flames as he cooked the pheasant he had shot out of a tree, and then he pulled out a bottle that Maggie recognized. "That's your father's—"

"Fifteen-year-old scotch."

"You can't open that without Lefcadio. Where is the Irishman? Ahhh, he's with Randolph. Avoiding cleaning, no doubt. Closer to the saloon. Open it."

"Why did you do it, leave with McMillan?"

"I didn't intend to. I sort of ran into him, and then I thought I could control him. He's a person who could be smarter than your father."

"Stupid."

"Yes, I suppose it was."

Because the inside of the house became hot from the oven, Maggie and William sat outside. She poured the rest of her cup of coffee onto the dry ground and presented it empty to William for filling. She smelled the scotch and couldn't remember when she had disliked that earthy scent. She had come to like the first taste when it burned and was hard to swallow and when the warmth spread in her throat and tongue and stomach. She had come to love that feeling. She cradled the cup on her lap between her hands.

"Garth has been in my family for three generations. I did what I did to try and keep it."

"You mean keep the pedigree."

She scoffed. "Yes, yes, I guess. There are still parts of my plan in play. I'm here, starting my own place."

"You should have stayed."

"You say that, but you never won a fight with your father. Oh, let's not fight. We've worked hard together. I've never seen you do so much cleaning, and don't say me, either. New things for us both. I'm going to bed."

The first night in Sumner House, in the same bed that she had bought in Utah, the one in which she had slept with Randolph that first night after they'd left Kelton, she tossed and turned. When she closed her eyes, she would see his face and have to open them again. The dark felt lonely. The calls of the animals looking for each other were lonely.

Magnolia Bathurst had just crossed the vastness of sand and scrub of Utah and Idaho in a wagon. She had brushed her own dresses and made biscuits, and on the way, she'd fallen in love with a criminal.

An ear-splitting sound reverberated in her overtired brain. It seemed to come from under her bed. Someone dying slowly. She thought she had becoming numb to the constant drama of the last month and a half, but this sound had her to her feet and out the door in search of William. She couldn't imagine such a tortured sound existed from any living throat.

"What is it?"

"Some big cat. A cougar maybe. Under the house."

Maggie clung to his arm. "It's dying."

"No, it's just calling, but we can't go out while it's here." William peeked out the window.

Maggie hung back.

"I think there is a person out there."

"Oh, my God. What is he doing?"

"Watching the house."

"Are you sure you see someone? Maybe it's a tree trunk. It's so dark."

"No, he's there. He's not hiding."

Maggie sat on a stool and hugged her knees to her chest to let her nightgown cover her freezing feet. There was no warmth in her blood.

"Why would he be watching the house?"

"I don't know. He's slipped into the trees." William gave her his revolver. He retrieved the rifle. She hummed to herself and rocked slightly. Later, in the quiet, with William still at the window, she went back to bed and slept the morning away.

She ate the cold breakfast that William had left her. She saw him come out of and then go back into the barn. With a few dishes to wash, she hummed as she scooped water from the river. Across the rapids, an Indian stepped from the cottonwood. William had told her to carry a gun. The pistol weighted down her apron pocket. She slid her hand into the pocket and held the metal there. *If he moves,* she thought, *I will shoot.*

But he stood there, firm as the tree next to him and looked at her as if he wanted to see something that wasn't there. She must have blinked because she didn't see him anymore. Two hands grabbed her shoulders. She screamed, tried to squirm away. Next thing she knew she was over a shoulder and moving back toward the house.

"What the hell are you doing?" She recognized the clothes on his back. "Put me down."

"You're a bloody fool. You know that, don't you?"

"So I have been told more times than I can count on this trip. So many that I'm sick to death of hearing it. I went for water. There is no indoor plumbing in this castle you chose. I took a gun. What are you doing here? I thought you were not speaking to me."

"Where is William?"

"He can't be nursery maid every minute of every day," she yelled. "Last night, a Nez Perce killed a settler and burned down his house. I came to see if you were all right, and I find you staring at one."

"I was getting water. It's not plumbed in. I had a gun."

"That was still in your pocket."

Randolph set her on her feet close to him. She had missed his proximity. Oh God, she was glad he was here. Everything within her reached out to cross the inches between them. She pressed her lips to his, couldn't help it. She missed him. He'd shortened her life by all the months that she thought she'd never see him again. There was no anger now. She couldn't sustain it any longer. He kissed her back with a kiss that said he'd worried about their progress from Boise. It was a kiss that said he'd missed her and her him; and when he stepped back her lips felt fuller from the love there, the absolute yearning that had begun at the first moment when she had saved his life, and then he had saved hers.

"Hey." It was William.

Randolph let her go and stepped back so abruptly, she had to reach out again to steady herself.

"Jesus and all his saints," Randolph sputtered. "Is there never a sane moment? There's been an Indian here." Mac wrenched Maggie's arm, pulling her behind him.

"There wasn't anyone here this morning. I checked," countered William, his own lips pressed together in disapproval. "But he may have been here last night. We had a big cat under the house. That may have scared him off."

"Look," Maggie said as the same Indian walked into the open.

"Easy." Mac put his hand over William's rifle. "If he wanted us dead, we would be dead already."

The Indian's features appeared like clay under a sculptor's hand, the same reddish-brown color, the same chiseled lines for mouth and cheekbones. His low forehead made his face round. His eyes were small but attentive and forward-looking. The man dressed simply in worn buckskin, some feathers in his long hair. His right hand was out and away from the knife at his waist. His smell was of animal skin and sweat.

The Indian stood at Mac's height. He had come toward them with purpose, but also with a rifle in a semi-relaxed grip in his right hand, pointing to the ground.

William moved and Randolph held him back. "He's well-armed but not threatening us."

The Indian kept coming until he stood face to face with Randolph, the two close together. In front of Maggie were the three bodies, Randolph, William, the Nez Perce, all blocking the sun in a way that glowed like a halo around them. When the Indian talked, his voice had an edge of resentment that he should have to reveal himself here and now to the man in front of him, and also with a respect that Maggie couldn't understand.

"You have traveled through many lives," the Indian said to Randolph. With a straight back, the red man offered his hand, palm open to Randolph. He reached out with his right hand after shifting the gun to his left, expecting Randolph to do the same. The weapon for both of them was on their less coordinated side.

The Indian spoke again. "I was told that you were coming. The Tamuluit are the strength of each person of the Nez Perce. This creative power comes as dreams, but not to dreamers, to the aware. It is unusual that a vision be so insistent or have the face of a person. I saw your heart being cut by a hundred knives, as one who laughed looked on. My dream told me of your coming."

"I killed the one as he laughed."

The Indian nodded his head. "He is dead. The world rid itself of him. Your shape is different now. This thing has cost a part of you." The Indian studied Mac's head to his feet. "I suppose it's to be expected with such a rearrangement." The Indian regarded him. He seemed to measure the worth of a man who had been so chosen. "You were honored."

"I am just here to serve a purpose."

The Indian's dark eyes softened to the color of deep suede. "It is not that you were honored, but the question of why she was as well." The Nez Perce fell quiet. Cottonwood snowed fluffy seeds onto the ground.

"My dream puzzles me. How could it speak to me about the future? Kol-kols-ne-nee gave his permission to the first settler to plow a furrow in this Nez Perce prairie. He said he would not have said it, except that he didn't think the settler could do it. We didn't understand them. Our first mistake.

"My father was the first to see through the white man. Governor Stevens came to my father and said the only way for us to live in peace was to separate white from Nez Perce. We would have a place set apart, and that we must stay there. My father wanted to be a free man. He said, 'Do not take any presents. They will say that they have bought the land with those gifts.' My father planted poles around Wallowa, and he told the whites that behind the poles was ours."

The Indian stopped. He regarded the house, the corrals, and the horses in it. "I thought we could drive the white man away, and then all of the Nez Perce, living and dead, would live together in great happiness. So why did this dream come to me of you and the many knives?"

"Because the Nez Perce are not yet meant to die?" Randolph answered.

The Nez Perce could have been a hawk, so piercing was his gaze. One heartbeat... two... three. Maggie saw the boiling resentment in the man. She considered her options should the Nez Perce strike, if he decided that Randolph held no value for him any longer. Three more heartbeats as Maggie thought about the heaviness of the gun still in her apron.

"Maybe that there is life here after life, but it doesn't look the same," Randolph said.

The Indian's features saddened. "We have always lived as we do. We have not changed, but there is resilience in change."

"There is value that can't be altered in each of us," Mac responded.

"The Crow was right to bring you forward. Spirits such as yours are needed in all times."

"The Nez Perce may die to what they know but will come back with a new face."

"Yes, you speak well. I see the dream now. It is both of our nightmares."

"You will accept change?" Randolph asked.

"Some of us. With our traditions, each man is his own chief, each man follows his own heart. Even you, Of-a-Hundred-Knives, did not come here without a fight." He filled his lungs with the water-scented air. He closed his eyes and turned his face to the breeze, and then he looked to Randolph. "I'm sorry," he finally said. "From time to time it occurs to me to enjoy what we were before it is gone. We will see."

The Indian walked into the trees, then like a spirit through them until he had truly disappeared. Maggie stared after him. She watched his straight back and the ripple of his leather clothes as he walked. He had insulted her. Why her, he had said, and then Randolph; Randolph had said he was here only to serve a purpose. Well, she had her own dreams and nightmares. Dreams of being loved. Nightmares of being used.

Her chin quivered and she put her hand over it. They had as much as said Randolph was her gift and she was not worthy. She inspected the blisters on her dry, rough hands, her muslin dress, and her braided hair. She remembered Randolph... Mac's hands, mouth, tongue.

Everyone in her circle seemed to get it, some depth of knowledge that she couldn't see. She'd never thought of herself as stupid, but she struggled to... to find clarity. Lefcadio called Randolph Mac now. William had had confidences with her mother. The Indian... none of it, none of it made any sense, except to everyone else, including strange Nez Perce braves.

Lefcadio arrived. Oh, he'd be upset when he was told what he had missed.

CHAPTER TWENTY

M aggie walked straight to Lefcadio to tell him about the Indian, and she needed to talk to someone who would understand.

Another person rode into the yard, his horse lathered. The horse reared as he pulled back hard on its mouth.

"All hell's broken loose. Dick Devine is dead. This morning. The Indians stayed at his place and ate his food. So is Elfers, Bland, Bacon, Baker, Chodoze, and Horton. Manuel's place is burning. His wife and daughter are captured or dead. I'm gathering any able man to strike back. They're building a stockade at Grangeville, that's your closest point."

"How far is that?" She thought of the Indian. He had been so close to them, his cold presence, she had felt his determination. "Which way?"

"Six miles. See those two dead trees? Head that direction. You'll see people."

"Now's the time to shoot this," Mac said as he handed Maggie the rifle he'd twice taken from her.

"You're not going to leave me here. You said I shouldn't go a hundred yards to the water, and now you are leaving me? You are not. We are all going together."

"Lefcadio and William will stay with you. It's only six miles, and it's better if we keep them busy as a united army than have them pick us off individually, one by one."

"No, no, no, no, no. I don't know how you have the gall to tell me you're leaving. Randolph McMillan, Indian fighter, is just plain ridiculous. You don't put yourself in harm's way. We should all get to Grangeville together. You won't leave me. You just won't."

"McMillan, my dear, has turned over a new leaf. Whether you want to see that or not is your own problem. We will find the Indians and deal with them. You only have six miles. Lefcadio, William, guns and horses."

"I have the mule."

"Get it saddled," Randolph said as he kicked his horse down the road.

Stay with me, her mind cried out. "Some of us only have the one life," she yelled instead. "Damn it. Where are you going, William? No, William," she called louder.

"We won't be alone," Lefcadio said. "There will be other people on the road heading the same direction. When we find a group, we will stay with them. If the men fight, we will be protected."

"Damn them to hell where the sun never shines." She threw a rock down the road. The gun in her apron hit her knee. She patted the pocket. She'd forgotten about it. After fishing it out, she cocked it to check the chamber. "I'll get whatever bullets are left in the house. You saddle the mule for me." She threw Lefcadio the rifle. "Can you shoot?"

"I'm better with me fists."

"We don't want them to get that close."

When Lefcadio lead the mule out of the barn, she walked out of the house. "Do I lock the house? Oh God, let's go." She kicked the mule so hard it jumped. She turned its head down the road, toward the two dead trees. "Just six miles," she muttered. "What can happen in six long miles? Everything."

"Of open prairie." It occurred to her that Indians were invisible unless they wanted to be seen. Her body felt solidified, the paralysis of standing on a spotlit stage with the sound of the audience all around, their coughs and whispered words, their boos and hisses, only the boos and hisses were arrows, the road the stage, the bright midday sun the lights.

"Take the road, or thread through the grasses? Maggie? What do you think, the road or through the prairie? Are ye with me, lass? Jeasus, the road then. At the least it will be faster."

"The road, yes, the road will be faster."

"That's it, stay with me. Just keep looking around."

She didn't see anything in front or behind, other than a sparkling sun warming a spring day. Lefcadio kept talking. He stayed close. They could have been riding into town to buy a hat and a pint.

"The posse is keeping the Nez Perce busy," he said.

She began to believe him. Still, she had a gun across the front of her saddle, and her grip on it was embossing of the logo of the handle into her palm.

As Lefcadio predicted, within the half-hour they overran a woman in a wagon. She was cracking the whip over a mare that had no spirit left to her. The nag could barely pull the family forward. Closer in, Maggie saw a boy hardly in pants holding a rifle across his lap and a girl sucking her thumb and crying.

The pressure in Maggie's brain to keep going, to get out of open land made her head ache. Sick with fear herself, as she pulled up next to the wagon, she could see the woman's face and the under-eye bags down to her chin. The woman talked to herself as a long, breathless mutter. "The Injuns have been jerking beef. I told everybody the Injuns have been jerking beef."

Maggie inhaled deeply and closed her eyes. She had made all these choices. She was here because of her own decisions. She had another choice here. She blew out her breath and said, "Your mare is spent. Let's change horses and then we can all get to where we are going together faster. All right, Lefcadio?"

The woman kept whipping the animal. "I can't stop."

Maggie understood the anxiety that pushed those words from the woman's quivering lips. Maggie had been swallowing her heart back down into her chest as a repetitive action.

God, she was a girl from the deep South...chocolate in bed in the morning...lingering on the front porch swing in the afternoon. She was also fighting the urge not to stop. She wanted to run the heart out of her mule.

She knew she would forever dream about the crunch of every stone, of waving grasses and two dead trees and a mountain that must be getting closer but didn't seem to leave its oh-so-distant place, damn it. Each movement of each blade of grass meant more than wind.

The woman muttered. Her sanity was leaking from her mouth with each word, and still the trees grew no larger with proximity. When Maggie finally smelled the pine cut stockade logs, maybe her fingers would quit tingling.

Riding beside the slow wagon up a blind rise in the road, up one side like a turtle, Maggie was about to address the horse change again, when at the crest of the hill, the woman screamed. Her children wailed. Maggie's mule must have smelled the blood.

It shimmied and danced, and then tripped. With her knees, she gripped the flanks of the animal as it stumbled. She tried to jump free as it fell. Her knee scraped the washboard of the road. The body of the mule pressed her thigh into a rock. The mule was not sticking around. It stood and ran.

"Go after her, we need her," Maggie called to Lefcadio. She stood and rubbed her thigh. A damaged muscle burned, her knee refused to bend. She tried to walk it off by heading toward the still scene just fifty feet from her.

"It's the Chamberlins," the woman said in a voice so shrill it scared birds. Mr. Chamberlin lay in a pool of blood. Close to him was a boy with a bleeding head. A baby had the beginnings of a cut across her throat. The woman, shot through both legs, had once held the baby girl, but blood loss had left her arms useless.

The horses were dead in their harness.

"We've got to keep going," the woman screamed.

Maggie turned her head and threw up her breakfast, that sweet meal in the calm of the morning that seemed too long ago already. Maggie could see that Mrs. Chamberlin was breathing. "We have to get Mrs. Chamberlin into the wagon."

When the woman raised the horsewhip, Maggie said in a voice reserved for idiots, the deaf, and William, "If you strike that horse again, I will take your wagon to ground and cut your harness."

"They're not good neighbors themselves," the woman spat back.

Maggie lifted the baby and said, "This one is also alive. Hold this baby," she told the woman's boy, and then to the woman, "Help me. What is your name?"

"Amanda."

"Amanda. Take her legs." Amanda threw down her reins.

Maggie and Amanda dragged Mrs. Chamberlin a few steps, when the woman's eyes fluttered.

Lefcadio returned with the mule, tied him off, and then helped raise the woman into the wagon. "It's like lifting me drunk brother off the streets of Dublin. It's like me mother after a dram of whiskey."

"Don't make me laugh. I won't be able to carry the weight."

"Ah, I wouldn't so."

The boy was light, but the man... Maggie thought from the burning pain in her thigh that her leg would give out.

"Is he alive?" asked Lefcadio.

"Heartbeat." They, more than not, threw the father into the wagon. Maggie leaned against the wood and rubbed her leg. "There's another man behind those dead horses." Maggie shut her eyes just like a blink.

"Praying I hope." Lefcadio said as she pushed herself forward.

"I don't know."

Maggie felt the man's chest. "He's breathing." For a moment she knew that she'd hoped he would be dead. "I'll take the legs again."

The man moaned when moved.

"Let's switch their horse for the mule. What do you think, Lefcadio?" She said over the nearly dead body.

"Yes, it's best. He's used to the harness."

———

Amanda swore like an unpaid prostitute at the time slipping away. Maggie puffed out as she walked with the weight. "Stop a minute." She let the man's hind end drop the two inches she'd managed to lift it. She inhaled twice as she rubbed her leg.

"Hurry up," Amanda snapped.

"Get down and unhitch your horse and tie him to the wagon," Maggie huffed as she and Lefcadio rolled the man into his wagon.

When Indian riders appeared from the direction of Lake Tolo, Amanda started screaming. With the horses and the mule attached to the wagon, Maggie yelled over her, "Lefcadio, take the reins and get that animals into a dead run."

"The mule won't like it."

"Damn the mule. Make it run. Children, lie down in the wagon, your mom, too. I'll shoot from the back." She gathered all the guns they had as the ruts in the road tossed the contents of the wagon.

"Don't tip over," she prayed.

Their ponies fleet and unencumbered, the enemy was catching up. Maybe Amanda had been right; maybe they should have kept going. Either way, she would now be in trouble.

Maggie shot out the back of the moving wagon until the gun in her hand clicked. She threw it into the wagon and grabbed another, then another, until she had only the rifle left, and it had to be reloaded.

She felt as if she were sending bullets into the air. No Indians reacted as if hit. None fell from their horse. They all kept coming, getting closer. They didn't shoot. Why didn't they shoot? *Because they can't hit us from there. Because they don't want to waste ammunition...or arrows.*

She didn't want them close enough to start firing on her. She aimed. The recoil knocked her on top of Mr. Chamberlin. Scrambling back to her post, she loaded again. She had twelve shells left. How much farther? Maggie glanced forward. There was nothing there but road. Six shots out, two more. She had hit someone. She had killed a person. Oh God, she had killed someone. Well, she'd had to. Damn, that also meant they were within range.

The Nez Perce would give them no mercy now. Down to her last bullet, Maggie prayed for a miracle. She placed the rifle against her shoulder and stared down the barrel. Another Indian joined the pack from the left. As she was about to pull the trigger on her last shot, the Indians pulled back.

"They've turned," she said, then again, "They've turned. Oh my God, they've turned." Maybe they were regrouping. But no, the band picked up the shot man and rode away, except one. She saw one lone Nez Perce left there, the horse quiet as the man. She knew he looked at her. She knew who he was. He had saved her. Her hands shook. She tipped her head down for a second as if bowing. He only turned the head of his horse to ride away.

They didn't slow down until Mount Idaho. They didn't stop until they were within a fort constructed on a hill of two parallel rail fences filled with rocks and downed trees. The wall was approaching four feet. She wanted twenty. Anyway, she had gotten there.

The Grangeville folk carried away the family. She hadn't wanted to save them any more than Amanda had, but she did, she did. Maggie closed her eyes as she sat in the wagon. She had no energy, no legs to move.

Sitting on the wagon bed, she could see over the stockade wall. She wondered, if this was war, whether they'd last the night, and where were Randolph and William? Lefcadio, always good for a drink, handed a flask to her. He lowered himself to sitting. More people took over the horse and mule. The wagon moved under her toward the stockade wall to be used as protection.

"Time to move, I think," Lefcadio said.

"Do you think tonight's our last night?" she asked him.

"If it is, I hope me old mother is there to greet me. I haven't seen her face in a while."

"She's dead?"

"So she is."

"No rebirth for her?"

"Not so as I've heard."

"Do you believe Randolph?"

"Yes."

"On your saintly mother's grave?"

"On me mother's grave, is it?"

"Do you believe in the Morrigan?"

"There are a few things. Sure as the first point I would say is that the Randolph McMillan I reported on seemed to work off his perfect understanding of human nature and his charm, rather than an extensive knowledge of medieval history. I have heard the only words he ever read were ones about him."

"He didn't arrange, so much as seduce and charm his victims?"

"That's the McMillan I know. He wouldn't have nearly died that day he went after the two men following us. Randolph would not have been with a rescue group. He would not be in Indian Territory during a war."

He turned to look at her. "Point two. I've never known him to stray this far from home. His family protects him. I would say now that there isn't enough money in your family coffers to interest him in being here, and that he'd a killed ye long before now."

"The very man...James MacArthur though? Maybe Randolph has gone insane?"

"According to Mac's own account, he seemed to be ready to

move on, whether that is insanity, or the lack of it... well, you'll have to make your own mind up."

"Is he James MacArthur in the flesh?"

"Not in the flesh."

Her head dropped.

"Sure as why don't you see how that baby is, and the other people you saved? Ye've transformed a wee bit, too." Lefcadio said as she stood.

"How so?"

"Ye don't sound so much the same as Amanda as you used to."

Behind the stockade logs, men and women moved in and out of weak firelight and a few remembered lanterns. She heard sharp voices call to children. Men sat with their guns across their laps and drank coffee. Everyone already looked haggard, and they still faced a sleepless night.

Maggie too. She felt like the West had been aging her more rapidly than one day at a time. The group Randolph and William had left to join hadn't returned. Some part of her had come to think of Randolph, or Mac, as invincible, more like a myth. His story was defusing throughout her ideas of him. Randolph McMillan was already larger than life; he couldn't die. He said as much.

The Morrigan on his side or not, when he and William did ride in, her knees weakened. They'd all seen danger. She had to touch him, to hear his beating heart. She ran to him and he swept her up into his arms. Maggie met his kiss and then took in the beat of his heart, his scent, as a part of her every breath. He was warmer than the air around them. Her own heart beat joy through her. She pulled him closer, wanting to crawl into the joy forever.

"You made it," he said, his lips near hers.

"It was horrible," she said, and then she sobbed. "How could you leave me? I needed you. I almost died." She felt the emotions break. The balloon-encased fear popped. She beat his chest. He held her until she quieted. "I want to go home. I am going home. I don't care if that Indian saved me. I do care… b-but….” She sniffed loudly. “Did you see those people, the ones Lefcadio and I saved?”

“We were shot at, too,” William called. “It’s like that everywhere. Geez, Maggie. You were ten when Kentucky stopped fighting the war with the North. Don’t you remember any of that? How could you live your life in such a fishbowl? This is life. Get used to it. Go home. My father will be glad to see you. For pity’s sake, you’re crying on the shirt of Randolph McMillan. You are so stupid.” William stalked off.

“I wasn’t there in the war,” she yelled back. Would people ever stop saying things like that to her? She pushed away from Randolph. “Yes,” she yelled after William. “I was raised in a fishbowl. I can’t help that.” She wiped tears that wouldn’t stop.

“Do something about it,” he yelled back over his shoulder.

She sank to the ground and held her head in her hands. It was all too much. She realized that, once again, she wasn’t coping.

CHAPTER TWENTY-ONE

M ac leaned against the newly cut pine stockade. God, she made him crazy. After picking herself off the ground and wiping her tears, she'd run to Lefcadio, and Mac left her to the Irishman. He should go back, hold her. She'd gone to Lefcadio. She always did that, run to other men. As he was about to turn, his ears picked up the sound of horses, lots of horses. Mac studied the road and spied the glint of metal catching the sun. Alert, he waited and considered his choice of action, being without his rifle.

His heartbeat slowed when the shapes clarified. Ad Chapman and eighteen other settlers rode alongside the horse cavalry into Grangeville. Venturing outside the walls of the rough-built stockade that encircled Grange Hall, the settlers cheered them on. The force was small. Mac estimated about a hundred. They traveled light, without any additional arms. No need for siege weapons. As the soldiers stiff-legged their dismounts and eased their legs into walking, Mac studied their dust-covered faces. A First Sergeant McCarthy, Mac heard him named, called to the boys to get some beans cooking before the night guard.

"Will we be here for the night?" a pimpled lad with an Irish accent asked.

"I damn well hope so, goddamn saddle sores," said another, sounding German. "Twenty-four f-ing hours in that goddamn saddle."

Mac took in a long breath. These men in their sky-colored coats were the elite, the new knights. They were what fighting had become since the advent of the gun. *Of course, the Irish are here*, Mac thought as he shoulder-pushed himself against a stockade log to full standing. The boys in the blue jackets appeared more haggard than a man's parts over the age of seventy. Picketed, even the horses were lying down to rest.

Mac saw barely bearded young men in brand spanking new blue coats with silver buttons that had picked up the sun. He saw pride in their wilted faces, though, even arrogance, as if the uniform coats they wore were a kind of soft armor, the silver buttons a safeguard from evil. The casing of warfare had changed, but not much else in five hundred years. He still saw boys, dust coated, easy to kill and stiff from the saddle.

Mac walked through the acid smoke of multiple campfires toward the line of horses. The lack of substantive light, the fuzzy shadows, and the common scenes moving slowly before Mac's mind's eye caused a schism of reality to a Scottish moor and the heavy smell of damp, peaty earth. Iron lids clanked against iron pots. Swords sounded sharp against honing rocks. He heard the sound of Padric's laugh. That Irishman always laughed before battle. Mac had never before fought without Padric at his side.

God-of-all-the-saints, that captain must know not to take this sorry lot into battle until they get some rest,

But Captain Perry was surrounded by voices that had endured too much, and they argued that the Nez Perce would be gone by sunrise.

"Where are your volunteers?" Perry snapped to Ad Chapman. "I was told there would be volunteers."

"I've got volunteers. There's many a man here who'd like to catch those Injuns up the ass. I'm telling you another thing. Those bastards are real yellow. Cowards. They get real brave when they got numbers on their side but take a good force like this against them; they'll turn tail. They is just thieves and murderers; they ain't soldiers."

Perry strode off and signaled for his captains to follow.

Mac wasn't surprised when he heard a horn calling the men to action.

There was going to be war. Mac had to try to bring a few of these young men back. As he walked to his horse, he felt the absence of Padric at his back. Another difference between this battle and the many others Mac had participated in: he'd never had a woman to come back to. Or maybe he didn't. Her body, her lips, her breasts, all of that, she had all but given to him. It stirred him to think on it. Still, her mind, her heart, he wanted those, too.

"Prepare to march...prepare to march...prepare to march," The words echoed. Officers kicked dirt onto fires. Someone next to Mac yelled, "Men, you heard our orders, be goddamn in your saddle when the trumpet sounds."

Mac threw a blanket on his horse and then a saddle. He mounted and kicked the horse forward to the group forming near the mouth of the fort. William was there.

"Damn it, I wish you'd stay with Maggie. Isn't that why you came all this way? There's enough young men over there in uniform."

William shrugged.

Maggie hated that shrug. Mac could see why.

"Somebody has to stay. This place is not secure."

"Get plenty of extra cartridges," a man in blue said to Mac and William in passing.

"Why are you going, then?" William asked.

"I'm trained to it. I'm fresh. That could mean the difference to a handful of these men's lives."

"What do YOU care about other men's lives?"

Mac sighed. He said what Randolph would never say but should have said before the passing of the rich man's miserable life, "Maybe now's the time of atonement. You've got nothing to atone for, William." But William was determined to become one of the good guys.

The bugle called again, long and insistent. The holdback soldiers threw the dregs of their coffee on low fires, hitting flames that sizzled and bucked. Mac watched those already mounted form a professional column.

The silver buttons on the blue coats will act like mirrors when the sun comes, Mac thought. He wondered if these pimpled boys with quivering chins could hold a line. He'd seen younger cut down the enemy with fierce purpose, but they'd had the spark of personal grudges, and they hadn't lasted to the end.

He'd try one more time with the boy. "For the Nez Perce, this is the end of a way of life," he said to William. "A hard fight becomes more intense from bitterness. And these cavalry men, the ones who think their enemy is scared, all of them will fight badly if they underestimate their opponent. But whatever the odds, these guys are paid to do this. It's not a moral fight for them. If the Indians take the day, this rude piling of wood could become a slaughter pen."

William didn't dismount. He didn't realize that he would be another distraction for Mac.

James MacArthur sighed and felt the absence of his scabbard and sword. The carbine rifle had a different balance that annoyed him. His weapon should be an extension of his hand. Nothing he would have to think about. With the firearm, he felt clumsy, a boy himself. Still, he rode forward on the orders of Captain Perry.

For the hours left of daylight, while riding to the lip of White Bird Canyon, Mac had noted the faint smoke of signal fires moving with them. At dawn, the word "halt" came back to, Mac as a whispered wave from soldier to soldier. He dismounted and stared down the neck of a canyon.

"Goddamm it," Perry said. "Get me Chapman. Where the hell is that idiot?" the captain whispered. "What the hell? We are at the top of a cliff."

As he walked back from the precipice, Perry kicked the hand of a private who had struck a sulphur-headed stick into a bright flame. "Goddamn it, put it out," Perry growled as best he could at a low-throated volume.

In a pale shadowy light, with the mist rising from the canyon bottom, and with orders set, Mac was the first of the civilians to kick his horse down the butte. Mac glanced back up at the silhouettes of the mounted troop that extended across the entire smooth-topped ridge bow. The shadows of men created regular peaks along the length. He watched as the shapes began to spill over the side.

"You okay?"

"Yeah," William answered. "You?"

"Keep a good eye."

Approaching the bottom, the scouts were easy to pick out. The two rogue Nez Perce were easy to see, with their stiff backs. Mac checked his horse, the weapons attached to the saddle and to his body.

A lone shot that hit the bugler began the war.

Mac and the eleven civilians around him hunched behind their designated knoll of prairie. He watched the bugler slide from his horse. "Shit." Without the bugle blowing orders, the troops would be directionless.

Perry charged the last length of the canyon. "Get ready. We have to hold Perry's flank," Mac called.

"Don't worry, we have two to one odds. They won't touch us over here," said a farmer.

Mac swore. "Get your guns on the enemy, now," he yelled.

A Nez Perce horde spilled across the valley leaving in their wake a red stain on green fabric. All the civilians ducked when nearby brush peppered them with bullets. Their horses reared and bucked. The volunteers shouted at each other.

With the Nez Perce rushing forward, their war cries in Mac's ears, their painted faces in front of his eyes, his blood surged from his heart to his head, his hands, and his feet. This was what he'd left. This was what he knew. Bullets rang past and into the dirt with sprays of dust. Rifles puffed a dark, acrid smoke. The enemy charging them was stripped down. Mac hadn't seen see any Nez Perce fall. He sensed the strength of their enchantment. The Morrigan was on their side.

Close to him, Mac heard one civilian cry out and then another. Who was down? Mac glanced around, and saw a horse try to buck off its rider and then tear up the hill with the civilian hanging on. As he reloaded, Mac noted that all the farmers were diving for their horses.

He fired more shots and shouted at his band to hold, but they retreated to the next knoll. His rifle at his cheek, Mac covered their retreat and then joined them.

"God-damn-me, we're about to be surrounded. We're gonna be in the soup if we don't get outta here," said Chapman.

The shrieks of the Nez Perce so close sounded like death. William mounted his horse. "Come on," he shouted at Mac.

"Leave me your rifle and shot," Mac shouted back. "And then go, damn it!"

"Get away," William yelled.

"Leave me. No one is covering anyone's retreat. If the soldiers can't regroup, Maggie and Lefcadio are at risk."

William fell in next to Mac. God, he was a great kid.

Mac, with William at his back, shot using his carbine to pin the warriors as long as he could. Just as he thought, the warriors were moving away from him toward the middle. A Nez Perce horseman split off and circled around to Mac's back. He had one shot left. He used it. The carbine in his hand was now useless except as a club.

He assessed the situation. They were alone and watching all the men in blue on the run. The warriors were now between William and him and the retreating troops. Mac and William had given the civilians a head start, but now they were alone, and amazingly whole. He considered their retreat, when he heard the grunt that came from a human being when a bullet pierced their skin.

God, not William.

"It's just my leg," the boy said when Mac turned to him.

Mac shoved William into a thicket of brush in a seam of the canyon.

The boy's feet still stuck out. Mac kicked at William's boots and watched as they disappeared. "Stay there. Stay there! Don't make a sound." Mac dived into the brush next to William. He waited and prayed for the Morrigan to spare William. A squaw on horseback stared at the brush around him like she might have seen a snake slither into hiding but wasn't sure. Mac inched his feet into the branches.

When she left, Mac had William slide further into the seam. At dusk, after he neither saw nor heard movement, Mac helped William dash from brush to brush. Nearing the top of the canyon wall, his heart beat faster. He thought they might get away, but the squaw had been watching. Her head tipped back, and she screamed a war cry. Realizing all he and William could do was run, Mac lifted William and then pumped his legs up the rest of the hill. Too soon, bullets hissed past him. His body tensed, waiting for that ultimate invasion or for the dead grunt from William on his back. There was nothing to be done.

As before, he was outnumbered and had nowhere to hide. Running up the steep slope, he tripped once, his heart and leg muscles burning. Soon Nez Perce, on horseback, would be slapping his backside with the butt of their rifles, playing with him. He wondered if the Morrigan would once again cradle him to another time or think that he had failed this one. He fell again. His head smashed against a rock. Crippled now, his brain swam.

William lifted Mac's arm.

"Come on. It's a horse. Jesus, man, come on." William lifted on his arm again. Mac stood and staggered.

"Jesus, don't spook it."

"Leave it. We have to find a place to hide until dark."

"But—"

"No. We won't make it ten feet until it's dark."

CHAPTER TWENTY-TWO

M ac dug into the earth, releasing the smell of rotting plants and peat. He shook dirt from the root of the Camas Lily, a delicacy of the Nez Perce and why they fought so hard for this land. He shoved it into his mouth and pulled up more for William, who continued to lose blood. William needed strength. The entire battle had only taken three hours. They had a long time to wait for the cloak of night.

"God, that's foul," William complained.

"Eat it and lick the leaves for water. We have a long wait."

The Nez Perce roamed the prairie like crows in a harvested cornfield. Mac watched the sky for smoke, an indication that Grangeville was burning. The good thing was that a substantial bunch of the bluecoats had made it over the lip of the canyon. That they were leading the Indians right back to the fort, Mac had no doubt. Had they stopped to regroup, God only knew. No smoke though.

"No smoke," Mac said to himself. "But their blood is all fired up—"

"What?" William asked.

"Their blood is hot from the win."

"Leave me here," William said.

"There's nowhere to go right now." Mac chewed on more camas root. He had brought them up here to die, it seemed. The Morrigan sent him forward for this. Mac laughed.

The night cooled quickly as the sun left for the other side of the world.

Mac stood straight up and pulled William onto his leg.

"We're in the fucking open, aren't we?"

"They'll be all together now, either celebrating or getting the hell out of here before any more bluecoats arrive."

"I can't hop all the way home. If they're gone, leave me here and come back for me." William relaxed his walking leg so Mac had to ease the dead weight to the ground.

"It's just three miles. For the love of God, you can crawl that. You're soft, man. Get up on that leg of yours. They didn't get them both."

With nearly every slow step, Mac's insides screamed for more speed, but he knew that if Maggie were dead, there would be nothing he could do, and arriving earlier had no advantage. He'd saved one of them, or maybe not. Mac felt William leaning on him more and more heavily.

Mac kept his eyes wide open and let anxiety feed his body, keep him moving, and keep his mind awake. He talked to the Morrigan, cursed her for her part in his friends' destruction. The anger kept him vital. Soon he was all but carrying William.

Half a mile out, he saw the bluecoats returning to the fort with a wagon. He yelled until a man answered him back. A pack of men stopped. They loaded William onto a horse and handed Mac the reins of another. He mounted the horse in a single fluid motion. He didn't wait for anyone anymore.

He would take her into his arms and kiss her until her passion ran hot and her protest ran cold. He should have done that from the beginning. He'd allowed her head, enough that she'd run straight off a cliff. No words this time. He could smell the roses of her skin and taste the flowers on her lips. He would take her where she stood. Mac kicked the horse again. He would let her know that he would never let her risk her life again. It was more precious to him than his own.

The horse flew through the partition of the log boundary. He reined in within a cloud of choking dust. People scattered.

"Where is Maggie Bathurst?" He asked the first person he saw, and then another.

Lefcadio ran up to him.

"Where is she?"

"Gone."

"Gone?"

"I saw her leave. There was some confusion when the soldiers came back. I looked for her then, ye know to make sure of her, and I saw her with a man. He had his arm around her, and she left with him."

Mac expected a crack of lightning, a boom of thunder, so rent were his thoughts, his heart.

"Why am I here?" The words issued forth from his soul. "Why am I here?" Mac said the words more quietly, his heavy face imploring Lefcadio.

The wound to his heart struck by Malcome's knights had hurt him less. Mac turned back to his horse.

Lefcadio grabbed him by the shirt. Mac elbowed his forearm. The Irishman took hold with his other hand. Mac swung. Lefcadio ducked and threw a left jab and then a right and then another left. Like a mosquito, the Irishman buzzed around his friend's head and arms.

"Cease!" Mac roared.

"Ye need food. Ye need drink. Ye need rest. She's not alone."

Mac looked back at the Irishman as if from the end of a long tunnel, a long distance over time. His brain buzzed from the transition of distance. He shouldn't have left her to get to the fort by herself. He shouldn't have left her afterwards with Lefcadio. She was gone. *God, why did the Morrigan bring me back as a scoundrel? Why did she send me back at all?*

"And anyway, are ye of sane mind?" Lefcadio asked, peering at Mac.

"Yes, yes, I'm fine."

"Ye don't look fine. Ye are unhurt then? Where's William?"

"I'm fine. William. William!" Mac passed a hand over his brow and glanced back where he had come from. "Holy Mother of God, William."

"He's not dead, is he?" Lefcadio watched a wagon parade through the encampment. He joined Mac walking toward it.

"He'd better not be," Mac replied. "I left him with a group of soldiers who were bringing in wounded in a wagon."

"He's hurt?"

"Yes, but he lasted the night."

Lefcadio pointed out a wagon surrounded by blue coats coming into the fort. It stopped in front of Brown's Hotel. Mac strode to the bed that two settlers had eased William onto.

"He looks grim, so he does. All the blood that he was wearing in his face, he's now wearing on his trousers." Women dressed the leg as Lefcadio said, "Are ye alive, William, boyo?" William nodded.

"He never was a man for words," Mac said. "That's all yours."

"So it is. Will he lose that leg?"

"I don't think so. There's blood, but not enough." Mac watched the boy's eyes bounce open, like he'd seen death and preferred life. Maybe Lefcadio had concerned the boy over his leg. William's head rose up as many inches and said, "Where's Maggie? She's all right? The soldiers kept them all safe?"

"The halfhearted wench? She left in the company of a new man with a mustache that was trimmer than is possible in this retched West, who had brand new, quite clean boots that were paining him into a slight limp on the left," Lefcadio said. Mac glanced at him. Lefcadio shrugged. "I wanted to spare you, so I did."

"And you tell me now?"

"She's gone?" William interjected. "Are you sure?"

"That she is, lad. I'm sorry. I would ha' said some words to her, but I only saw her leave in the distance. She had no last sentiments for me ear to hear. More's the pity. Ye came all this way and fought the Indians and all."

"It's my fault."

"No lad, it wasn't. She is her own mistress. She told me so enough times."

William was trying not to cry. Mac put his hand on the young man's shoulder. No one could have done more, been more, suffered more than he had. William had not failed Grace.

"It's over for you, lad. You've done well. I'm going after her. If she's going back, I have to make sure she is safe." But he would never go to such an effort for another woman again. Mac felt his age, all of it. Lefcadio must be like Jesus, turning the water into alcohol, because the whiskey in his flask was endless, and merciful. Lefcadio gave William the next sip.

William closed his eyes. "Do you know the man? Was he a local?"

"Sure as I don't know many locals. Does she?"

"She's a woman men take care of." Then Mac remembered her tearing at his shirt in fear. "Why would she leave now, with anyone? The soldiers lost. The Nez Perce are loose around us."

"Be Jaesus, ye're correct. I wouldn't have thought giants could drag her from this fort."

"What did the man look like?" asked William. "Did he have dark hair? Was he kind of well dressed?"

Mac looked in horror at William. "Did he have some resemblance to the boy here, like the man was his father?"

"He did, so, now that you mention it. I thought I had seen him somewhere."

As Mac strode away, he turned only to ask which way they had gone. He had failed. The Morrigan had sent him all this way, and he had failed. He, the knight-who-saves-women.

He burst through the front door of the hotel and turned toward the pine-studded mountains. Anger had kept him alive through his years at Arundel Castle. It had driven him to become a knight of the Realm. Anger had purified the vows he had taken to fight for women as befit that knighthood.

He would find Guy Didsbury and hand him no favors this time. Mac thought of the worst that Guy could do to her and that wasn't to kill her. He could impregnate her himself and put it at the feet of her unchaperoned travel with the notorious Randolph McMillan. He could act like he had saved her.

God's blood, Mac had used all his bullets. They were in short supply after the Indian War. There'd be no loan of any, with the Nez Perce roaming about, drunk from winning the crown.

It was getting light. The man would have had to stop once darkness fell, or risk getting lost. He would know about the lack of safety. He would have had to measure his steps. That would slow him.

Mac set out from the place Lefcadio had seen them, in the direction the Irishman had said they were going. Would she have enough presence of mind to help in her rescue? Mac thought of the fight in Maggie; she had the fight in her, but she was weakened by the distance from the house that had strengthened her.

It had been in Elizabeth. The girl could stare down her father, but in the end, he'd almost had to throw her off the castle wall. Maggie could have reached her breaking point, that point when the struggle felt without point. She'd seemed near it when he last saw her.

At the edge of the stockade Mac glanced at the horizon. Sun was an hour off of true daylight. He thought of Maggie and of what clues she might leave. She hadn't had much time. Seconds, really. He would have her at gunpoint. She would go with him if he threatened to—what? To kill someone else in the middle of the settlers? No, they'd have him in the beat of a heart. She was alone with Guy.

Mac walked forward, scanning the ground, the leaves. He looked for disturbances. Maybe farther out. He shook his head at how impossible this was going to be. He ran his hand though his hair. If he scrounged for a horse, he would be faster, but faster to where, really? He had no idea which direction.

He about-turned back to camp to find a horse to bring anyway, if only for the road back. There, he started to approach a soldier who was asking if anyone had seen his jacket. Mac kept walking. The man didn't have his coat, never mind a horse. They wouldn't give him an army horse anyway. Mac remembered that stray horses had been drifting in from the battle. He set out again with the hope of finding one of those. At a creek several horses with an army brand drank water. Well, they'd get this one back, eventually.

Mac patted his hip for his knife. He carried his empty rifle. He might need to fake it. Guy had walked out of the fort, probably thinking that he wouldn't be noticed. Mac hoped that wherever Guy had hidden his horses, it was far away.

Mac searched for a piece of torn dress. Even if he hunted for a thing that was not there, he had to hope that something meaningful would catch his eye. He could no longer see the safety of the log stockade. If she were going to leave a marker, she would have left it by now. He couldn't remember if her dress had buttons. It must. Damn woman. Either she hadn't thought of it, or he had missed it. The buttons on women's dresses were so small. He glanced out across the acres that likely separated them, trying to think like Guy.

He was done with this slow pace. He'd mount. They were probably mounted by this point. There were horse tracks everywhere. The sun was up now. Mac talked to his horse out of sheer panic.

From the top of the horse, Mac took in the landscape once more. He had to make a final decision which way to ride, and hope the direction was not fatal. He also scanned for Nez Perce. On the horse, time slowed. Mac felt like the saddle was supporting him, as his heavy limbs and torso sank onto it.

His legs had begun to burn again from the short walk he had taken from Grangeville. When he found Guy, if he found Guy, he might not have the strength to do battle. He had no bullets and fading strength. Where was the woman?

His stomach was trying to push its needs into his mind. Mac wished Lefcadio had brought food instead of whiskey, and then he felt the saddlebags hitting against his thigh. He dug into one pocket. Nothing. Figures. In the other he found jerky. Smoky delicious. His mind-stomach connection wouldn't give him time to chew it through. A second piece went down slower.

The third gave him some strength.

Guy must know about the Nez Perce. As Whitebird might still have Nez Perce, the man should be heading to Mount Idaho, but there were people there. People to help Maggie. The critical question was, had Guy been brave enough to stay out alone in the dark in an unfamiliar place with Indians prowling the landscape?

Damn it. What if the man hadn't come alone, and he had a camp full of guns? It made sense. Which way? Mac again scanned the terrain. In that moment, he feared he'd never find her, and his heart chilled.

"Give me something, Maggie."

Some shiny object caught the sun. Inconsequential, Mac would normally call it. Yet hope beyond hope had him moving to it. He dropped from the horse and smiled.

Mac smiled at the silver beauty of one of the nine shiny buttons on the cavalry soldier's jacket. He'd been so slow. The coat had been near her exodus out of the town. He wondered how she'd managed to keep it, hide it from Guy. The ass would be distracted trying to get her out, but carrying with her a whole army coat? He'd like to have seen that.

I'll catch my death, Mac could almost hear her say in her *Goddamn-it-I'm-a-Garth*-tone. Mac squared his shoulders. He knew what to look for. She wouldn't take it for warmth. She wouldn't be thinking like that. He'd found it late, though. Still, the sun was high in the sky. Perfect to glint off those silver buttons.

CHAPTER TWENTY-THREE

R ipped from the safety of the fort with Guy as her captor, Maggie kneeled in a bed of pine needles as he tied her hands together in front. A roar in her ears made her deaf to the movement of Guy's mouth as he tied the knot. Her teeth chattered. Was hell this cold? When her knees gave out, Guy pulled up on the long leash that extended from her prayerful hands. She must have started screaming, because Guy hit her across the mouth.

On her hands and knees, she shook her head. No one had ever, ever hit her. The pain traveled down her neck. She bled over her hands from her nose. No one had ever, ever hit her. The shock lit her brain so that fear came second to the burning skin on her face. She stayed where she was, her head bowed.

If this man hits me again, I will kill him.

Maggie wiped the back of her red spattered hands with the blue wool of a coat she held in her fist. A button scraped her palm. Shiny. And then she remembered grabbing the jacket. She tucked it farther under her body, and then glanced at Guy. He had his back to her, the rope in his hand and his member out, relieving himself on a bush. Maggie ripped off a button and backhand threw it out to the path through the prairie. She was afraid she had waited too long to lay the trail.

They'll see it. They'll see it. The thought was more a mantra than an expectation. She tore more buttons and put them down her blouse. She rubbed more dirt and more blood in to the coat. She wiped her nose with it. When Guy pulled on the leash, she struggled to her feet. She held the coat close to her bosom. He pulled her deeper into the white pine that marched up the mountain at the foot of the prairie.

She thought to lean back against the rope and make him pull her to the top. That would exhaust him. Or he would hit her again, or just shoot her. He had the look of brittle glass, his gaze distracted. He would kill her now.

Guy's arrival, only weeks after her own, meant she hadn't fooled anyone. That she hadn't been clever, or amazing, or even the other side of stupid. She might as well have stayed in the comfort of her own bed and missed the sand in her coffee, the burnt biscuits, and the sun on her skin, the Nez Perce.

She laughed. The noise sounded cracked and shrill. Oh,

Mitchell, neither of them had had an inkling of what was to come. Every moment, every movement of her head, her eyes, now required more strength than she thought she would ever have.

Guy too had eaten sand, developed saddle sores, and evaded Indians. He seemed unhinged in a restless, more intense way. Like an agitated beehive, and hers had been the spoiling hand. He would show no mercy. Maggie didn't know if Randolph and William and Lefcadio would come, if they'd figure it all out, if they had lived. When had she started thinking of William as her savior?

Chaos swirled in her mind, but when she looked ahead at Guy's back, she realized that nothing else could happen but death, and death was the end of chaos. While not welcoming the end of life, her nerves told her it was the end of the throbbing in her heart and body and could be tolerated. Especially if they had died. Most of the soldiers had come back, but not Mac and not William. Had the Nez Perce taken the fort? Her heart felt eviscerated.

As she tried to stay within the length of the rope, Maggie thought of the shock in Guy's eyes when he saw her. When was the last time she had washed her hair? She couldn't remember just now. It didn't matter, either the memory or the dirty hair.

As her wrists burned from the friction of the hemp, she watched him glance around, like a nervous man who couldn't swim crossing a river. When would he step into a deep hole of water and sink in over his head? He didn't rest, and when Maggie fell, the rope yanked Guy's arm and stretched her shoulder muscles. She grabbed it with both hands and pulled. Guy went down on one knee.

"I'm not getting up. Not until we rest, and you give me water."

He didn't speak, hadn't since his first words: "If you don't come with me, I will kill you and I don't care what happens from that. You will be dead." And then whatever he had been saying when he tied the rope.

Guy threw a water container at her.

"How are you going to get me on the train with a rope around my neck?" Maggie asked in between drinks, in a voice that seemed a whisper.

He didn't look at her, didn't smirk or gloat. He just said, "There is a bounty on your head. You've killed William, a man you shot at, at a Way Station. Went crazy, they said." His tone was even, emotionless. His cold heart beat only for revenge. She understood. She'd felt the edges of desperation lick her wounds as well.

At a tug on her rope, Maggie stood and brushed her skirt in front. Guy didn't take the water from her.

"Where are we going? How much longer until we get there?" Her leash pulled in answer.

Guy's stubbly cheeks looked more stretched than she remembered them. His gait was less liquid, his body more frail. She jumped at a fox running across the path in front of Guy. She'd need to calm herself. Nerves didn't make for clear heads.

Don't be silly. If the Indians are out there, you'd be dead by now, she said to herself.

Guy kept going. He bush-wacked as he pulled her up the mountain like a dog trailing behind. She plowed through brush and crushed wildflowers. When she fell on shale, he dragged her for a yard. Her palms became rock indented, her skirt ripped. At the top, they lost the tree line. He already had a camp set up, with pack horses.

From the apex, Maggie could see the sun beginning its second descent to the horizon. Her prospects fell with it. It would be another night alone with her stepfather. Guy could see someone coming from half a mile, if anyone would find her on the summit at all. When darkness came, he again gave her no blanket. She lay on the ground with the jacket as cover. She was too dry in body and mind to weep.

Tied to Guy, on the ground behind him, Maggie spoke toward the stars, her forearm over her forehead. "Why did you come all this way? You possessed Garth. I was gone."

Guy laughed. His body shuddered on a deep inhale and his back seemed to broaden and thicken.

That he'd apparently gone insane jolted her knowledge of him. Guy was not a person who lost his mind. People who lost their minds were people who cared about something. On the other hand, Guy did care about someone: himself. A tickle of satisfaction made Maggie smirk. She hadn't won, but she'd laid a good race. She was not one anyone could take for granted.

Guy didn't light a fire, he didn't speak, he didn't move. Maggie might have thought he was dead, except from time to time, his head turned on its axis like an owl perched in a tree. Guy always talked. He loved to talk. He knew he was good at it, naturally glib. She should be glad he was quiet. Glad he wasn't bluing the air with his opinions, needs, wants. That would be worse, having to listen to his deep, mocking voice. All Maggie could hear was the blood in her ears, and the sounds of animals hunting.

The stars twinkled in the millions. To calm herself, she lay down and began counting them. She would know if Guy moved; she was attached to him. She couldn't keep her mind on numbers. Had she been at forty-five? Her mind darted. She must have dozed, because when she opened her eyes, he was there, standing over her, staring like it was all he could do not to kick her in the spleen and grind her skull into the dirt.

Maggie scrambled to a seated position and hugged her legs to her chest. "What did you think would happen when she died? That I would allow your guardianship? When, even one time, did I give you that idea? I left. I had the freedom to leave. You cannot hold that against me. It doesn't matter what you wanted. It never could have mattered. Don't you see that? How can you not see that? Why are you here? Why didn't you just stay there? I all but gave it to you for my freedom."

Guy's jaw moved. It seemed to grease itself as it worked back and forth. He spat on her. "You. You." His body shook. His eyes closed. "I would not believe that you lived with her. You have learned nothing from her. I kept telling your mother. It's not wise—"

"Wisdom!" The word brought Maggie to her feet. "Where has there ever been any wisdom?"

"You're right. There has never been any wisdom. Your father, your treasured father, he bankrupted your precious Garth. Bankrupted it! There was nothing left. The creditors were about to take the furniture. Your precious father." He spat, nearly hitting her foot.

"Don't speak to me of him. Never speak to me of him. You are not, will never be his equal."

"Thank God for that. You," he sneered, "have never possessed an ounce of her grace or gentleness, or her—" he sputtered, "—goodness. She said 'Don't tell her. Don't ever tell her'. But I will, because you don't deserve that favor. You, who left, not just before she was buried, but before she was dead. No, you don't deserve my silence. She was not your mother. You are your father's daughter, oh yes, that is very clear. But she is not the mother. She could not have children."

Maggie closed her eyes as she wanted to close her ears, and she bowed her head over her tied wrists. She screamed at him to stop, that she didn't believe him.

Guy yanked the rope binding her hands. "No, you will hear this. She wanted me to restore Garth. My hard work. You would have been spending my hard work. She wanted me to restore it for you, so you could have the life your ridiculous father told you, you could have. You cut off my money from me," he yelled.

"I do not believe you. And even if you made money, it was with Garth resources. You didn't do it on your own."

"And that's all, that's all you have to say about any of this? You don't deserve the future she tried to set for you. Do you know why you didn't inherit directly? Because you are as stupid and as silly as your father was."

"Why are you pulling me back? Why come here?"

"I will not be disgraced by you. I will not allow that. You have made the word 'Garth' a joke. You have destroyed your mother's legacy."

"What do you care about our legacy?" Maggie shouted.

"You are so bird-witted."

Maggie scraped her clawed fingers along the soil beneath them and threw dirt and rocks at Guy's ugly mouth. Her fingernails went for his eyes. He slapped her down. "You are not her daughter. Remember that."

He walked away.

What had just happened? Her heavy breath moved grains of earth. She sat up. Guy's back was to her again. She could pick up a rock and bash in his skull. She should. She looked for something big enough. Not her mother's daughter. She would kill him. Oh, she would kill him. A sob tore out of her. She hardly knew where she was anymore.

The full moon was bright, but not bright enough in the dense forest to pick up her trail. If Mac didn't have the sun, then he'd make his own light. He hacked a greenwood stick from a tree and ripped his shirt in sections. He wove the pieces into a knot around the head of the stick, interweaving slices of pitchy bark into the fabric. He made as many torches as he could from the clothes he had to spare.

The buttons had gotten him to the edge of the forest. Now all he had to do was look for the large imprints of humans. Torch in hand, he saw the path of broken nature. The good thing about obstinate females, they never give up. They get teary, and desperate, but they never give up. Guy would be lucky if she didn't have her knife in him by the end of the night.

Mac should have put the man out of his misery the first time.

It would have saved them all this trouble. Mac had sensed the dark soul in Guy, but something had stayed his hand. Usually quick to know his enemies, Mac thought about his hesitation. It must have been his brain still asleep from his death. That wasn't enough explanation. There was another instinct that Mac couldn't place.

The thought was gone when Mac saw the places where Maggie had fallen. He put the light closer to the earth where she had been dragged. This man would not live through the night. He paused to listen to see if Maggie's movements could be heard.

No. He was still too far away. He swayed in his boots. He shook his head to try and clear it. His body cried for food, his leg muscles bunched in protest from the lack of rest. Guy was not a big man. That's all he would have in his favor. That and Guy had also climbed this mountain.

Mac took a long step. The shale gave way under his weight. He slipped eight feet back down the mountain. Scabbed wounds on his legs reopened. His elbow hit a rock. "Jesus, Mary, and Joseph!" He gritted his teeth and held his elbow until the pain subsided. Whatever had held his hand before, he vowed, that power wouldn't stay his hand again.

He rose and then heard the sound of a woman's voice, yelling. By God, she still had some life left in her. The sound of her voice gave his legs energy. Miracle though it was, he would get to her. He would fight the demon as he had been sent here to do. Whether he was here or in another time, he still was bound by his oath. The Morrigan would expect no less from him.

———

When a stone hit her, Maggie flattened to the ground, her hands over her head. The words, "Jesus, for the love of God, Maggie!" filtered through her fingers to her ears, a voice so low she wondered if she'd heard it at all.

The voice and its attached man elbow-walked toward her position.

"Mac!"

He put his finger over his lips before he sawed on her ropes with his knife.

Dizzy with relief, she pushed up next to the length of his body. She wanted to feel the substance of him. "You're alive," she squeaked.

"Shh." He held the rope, trying to keep it from tugging on Guy's waist. Mac kept his gaze on Guy. Maggie followed his glance to the back of Guy, his filthy clothes once so brilliantly clean, his mass of hair, his thin skeleton.

"When I cut this, get out of the way, into the forest. Run and keep running. Don't wait, don't look back. And for God's sake, don't help."

She directed her gaze back to Mac and held in view the dearness of his dark hair, the curve of his nose and lips, the steel of his gaze. More than her life, she wanted to touch him—to stroke his forehead, the curve of his neck, and the folds of his ear.

Maggie's glance bounced back to Guy, the shambles of his

persona. And then Guy's head began to turn. She saw the movement as a slow fluid motion, feeling in advance his sight on them like the razor eyes of a predator. The gun in his hand circled, a part of the action, as his line of sight met with hers. Her rope mostly frayed, but not complete, the bottom of her vision saw Mac rise to a crouch as he flipped the blade of his knife to be held in his fingers. With his blade in his hand, he was ready to throw. She sprang in front of Mac's knife arm, blocking his body with her own.

"Stop. It's yours," she yelled as she stood, and then she shut her eyes and waited for Guy to shoot. She didn't feel the invasion of hot lead. Maggie only heard Mac swear and then say, "Not again, woman."

On her feet like a gladiator, she faced Guy and his gun. Only she hadn't in mind to fight. Her hands were up, palms out. "It's yours, Guy, take it, take Garth. You deserve it. You deserve it. I want you to have it, free from my ownership. I don't want it. You deserve it. I don't want it. Do you hear me? *I don't want it.*" Maggie's voice choked.

She struggled to take breath. She didn't know she had those words in her. He wouldn't believe her. She had to make him believe her. She had to push out more words through her narrowed throat.

"You... you helped her live. You were the one; you helped her die. She loved you. I see that now." She had to stop. She had to wait until she could speak again, but she had to fill the space. She had to get it into Guy's head. "I'll wire Mitchell, no, your lawyer, to draw up the papers. I promise you that. I promise you. I will. I'm not going back. I don't want to go back. I'm staying here."

She floundered. "Tell people. Tell them I've married a man named James MacArthur, and we have settled here. Tell them." She grasped for words, for the power to sway him.

"Tell them Mother didn't really like him much, but that I was so alone when she died, that I ran away with him, and you came and have seen that I am all right. That will work, because... because, I didn't know it until now, but it is all true. Tell them that." She panted as she waited for any sign that Guy was with her. His gun lowered by inches, his face softened by degrees.

"You deserve it more than I do." Her heart pushed the words at him.

When he didn't move right away, she stared at McMillan as she finished. "It's not Randolph." Then she didn't want Guy to think her crazy. That would make him wary of all she had said.

"He's a different person. Why not? Look at you."

Was she breathing? She couldn't tell. The two men, one beside her and one in front were like wooden, painted men, facing down each other in a child's nightmare. She had no other moves, no other words to make Guy believe her. And then she heard Mac's knife hit the ground.

He had made them defenseless. He knew that was the next step. She had seen in his glance that Mac was here to kill Guy. His understanding, his willingness to stand without his weapon next to her, opened herself to him, as one with him. She moved closer, put her arm through his and leaned on his body. She felt the warmth of his side, the hardness of his arm muscles, and smelled the freshness of the woods in his scent.

Guy became less to her than he'd ever been. Garth became her past, not her future. Her mind steadied, her shoulders relaxed. The curves of her face lifted. Guy's gun arm dropped, and she exhaled.

CHAPTER TWENTY-FOUR

Maggie wiped her hands on a towel after putting the last breakfast dish on the shelf, precious dish, precious shelf. With her return, she'd felt the Johnson House wrap around her with solid walls that she swore she would never, ever leave again. That wasn't why she was inside, though, while Guy, William, and Lefcadio saddled their horses for the trip back to Utah. They had not been guests, she said to herself, though the word "family" with Guy included in it seemed foreign to her thoughts.

Still, she was grateful her dim view of Guy had brightened, that things had worked out well enough... except... Oh, never mind, he was leaving...and taking William and Lefcadio with him. The Johnson home would be quiet, like winter after a long summer. She wouldn't—couldn't watch them all leave. Maggie had said her good-byes, but the window drew her.

She was halfway across the room when the door flung open, Mac at the jamb. His hair blew about his face in a midsummer breeze and framed his blue eyes. His predatory stare made her step back. Her body quickened. An effervescent feeling rose up her spine and out her mouth in a giggle that startled her. He closed the door and advanced, possessing the floor, the room. Mac penetrated the air with his needs and wants, and Maggie couldn't breathe; inhaling his air seemed impossible. She took another step backwards as he stalked forward.

Her hip hit the table. She arched around it. Still he advanced. A moan escaped as she retreated until her back hit a wall. She couldn't look away from his blue eyes that promised everything she had ever wanted, had ever asked for, and when he was close enough that she could hear the tick of his heart, feel his breath on her face, he kissed her. His lips felt warm, her heart opening.

With Mac's hands in her hair, holding her head, he kissed the length of her neck, her ear, and then again, her lips. He penetrated her parted mouth with his tongue. It tickled. She played with him, wrestled, tongues curving, joining. "Oh, my God," she whispered when he paused, and he leaned his forehead against hers.

Her arms wrapped around his well-muscled chest, a chest she had first seen as he stripped off the bloody shirt and she had looked for wounds. His chest that she had had to touch as they lay side by side in the wagon at dawn, his upper body that had haunted her thoughts like an unfinished rhyme. She held him against her. The feel of his body was so delicious that Maggie pulled at the collar of his shirt. She wanted him again, stripped and in between white sheets that smelled of rain. He pushed back from her, and she cried out at the cool air between them. His arm under her knees, Mac picked her up. Without letting her face get far away, he smiled a mocking, lusty smile that made her laugh, so good to laugh.

He placed her on the bed, but she sprang up to begin unbuttoning his shirt. With clumsy fingers, she tore at the buttons and heard them hitting the floor. She giggled. The happiness in her could not be contained, and she laughed so that she would not burst. When he was naked, Mac lay next to her on the bed. She rained his body with light kisses until he moved her under him. She shifted as he pushed the yards of her floral cotton skirt up to her thighs. Maggie opened her legs for him. He pushed through her maidenhead and up into the place that had been waiting for him.

"Ahhh." It hurt.

Mac pulled out at her cry, like he had impaled her with his sword instead. "It's pain you feel?"

"It's not supposed to, is it?" Oh, God, was it? Her mother had never said so. She always seemed so satisfied with having men near her.

"I haven't...I mean, I've seen, but... I've heard women cry out, but it was forced upon them. I am not forcing you. The blood of a woman giving herself for the first time. I should have thought. Blood does not flow without injury."

His erection now at half-mast, Maggie moved to kneeling on the bed. She still wanted to touch him on that projection that her body seemed to know would satisfy the pulse that still tickled where the pain had been. She leaned for him, her arms out. "It will get better."

He kissed her, his member poking in the space between her legs, rising again. She pressed her thighs together to capture it. He entered more slowly this time, moving against the entrance and pushing deeper according to the sound of pleasure from her gasps. She opened her legs wide for him, and then, with all pain gone and only bliss in the space that he had taken, she crossed her legs over his back and rode him as a woman rides a man. Mac rocked and moved in and out of her. Maggie pushed her hips to receive him again and again, and then she exploded into waves of sensation that had her crying out in release.

She listened to his heavy breathing as he balanced his weight on top of her. Her eyes were closed. Her legs bent at the knees beside his hips. Mac's teeth nibbled at the top of her shoulder and then he rested his head in the curve of her neck, inhaling and exhaling against her breast. His manhood still throbbed inside her, and she tightened around it, never wanting to let him go. That wasn't painful at all.

For a long while he didn't stir, Maggie's arm lightly draped around his shoulder. She wondered how long before they could do it again.

Hours later, Mac said, while snuggled next to her and playing with her nipple, "I'm starving. I've only eaten you since breakfast."

"There's bread, cheese, some sausage. I hid a bottle of whiskey from Lefcadio." Maggie began to rise.

"No, stay there."

Her gaze raked over Mac's naked body as he rose from the bed and left the room. "I'm going to miss them all," Maggie called to him. "You will, too."

"Don't know. There's only one bed. It's possible. Maybe later, much later," he called back.

Maggie settled into that one bed in a cat-got-the-cream sort of way. The walls in the Johnson homestead seemed wallpapered in gold velum, so satisfied was she, and Garth, the legal documents she'd signed, didn't chafe her mind at all. No, not at all. The transfer of it lifted a weight from her that she didn't realize she carried. Garth hadn't been what she wanted. It really hadn't been hers all along. Maybe she had known that. She listened to the sounds of Mac's movements and waited without patience for the sounds of his steps back to her.

"Maggie?"

"Yes, darling?"

Mac didn't respond immediately. He had arrived at the door with a plate of food, a bottle under his arm and two glasses. Stopping there and leaning against the jamb, he studied her for a brief time. She expected him to say how beautiful she was, or some other after-bedroom talk, whatever men who loved women say after bedding them numerous times in a few hours of the morning.

"Do you think that I am James MacArthur?"

"Oh, for God's sake." Maggie's hand flew to her mouth. "No, I meant...it's just that...what does it matter?" She knew it was going to go against her. He had surprised her with the question, damn him. Couldn't he just let the thing go? "I haven't been thinking about it. Who's had time?" She didn't like the rising pique in her voice. Maggie didn't want this discussion, not now, maybe not ever. *How can he do this to me right now?* "Can't we talk about this some other day?"

Mac wouldn't look at her now. He put the plate on the bed and the glasses on the floor as he poured two drinks. He gave her one and then walked away with the other and sat on a chair.

"No."

"It's impossible." Oh Lord, another mistake. She needed to handle this better. *Lie to him.* She rubbed her forehead with her fingers and took a long drink. She was a compulsive truth-teller, she knew that, and she knew she was sunk. Oh, to hell with it. "What would you think if things were reversed, and I told you the same thing?" she snapped. "Oh no, before you open your mouth—" She pointed at him with her glass in her hand. "—you think about it. Give it long thought."

"Maybe it's impossible."

"No." Maggie rose from the bed. She spilled whiskey over her naked body. "You can't say that because you don't mean it. It shouldn't matter, though. You are who you are. I love all of you, that is." Her mouth shut. Neither of them had spoken of love. The word had never been said. He had never said he loved her. She felt queasy. She dropped, sitting onto the bed, onto the plate.

Damn it. She drank the liquor down.

"More?"

"No." The drink had hit her stomach like a fireball. Her eyes watered.

Mac hit the cork into the bottle with the palm of his hand. "I'm sorry to upset you, but for me much would be lost in our love without the belief that I am who I say I am. You loving me."

"How can that be?" She was going to lose it all, her home, her love. Again. "I signed away everything to be here with you. That has to matter. Doesn't it? Doesn't it?"

Mac walked across the room to her. She wrapped herself in a sheet as he neared. He sighed and moving the bread and cheese back onto the plate and the plate onto the floor, he sat next to her on the bed. "It does. Of course it does."

"I can see that. Damn you for bringing it up. It has all been so lovely. Now look at us, sitting next to each other like love has been dashed." Damn him, damn the damn book. *Oh my God,* she thought, *not that, too.* Must she leave all the hopes and dreams of her father behind?

"Everything matters."

"No!" She stood, took a few steps forward, and tugged on the sheet wrapping her body, which Mac still sat on. "What matters is you and I, right here, right now. Will you leave me if I say no?"

Mac was looking down and swirling the liquid in his glass. "No, of course not. I was hoping, of course, because it won't be the same...for me."

Maggie wanted William and Lefcadio back. She wanted to fall to her knees and beg and cry. Maybe she should go out and saddle her own horse. She could still catch up to the men.

"Don't start making plans."

"I'm not."

He shook his head. "Pfft. You are. You can't keep leaving hard things behind. Maybe now wasn't the time, but we are not going to bury this. I thought we could just start a conversation."

"You will have it there between us as salt in a wound."

"Sand in an oyster, for a pearl."

Maggie cried. She wanted her happiness back. Part of her itched to shrug off the arm he had put across her shoulder, but she liked the steady pressure there as she let tears flow. She was tired of feeling alone. Mac pulled her closer to him, and with her head against his chest, he rested his chin on the top of her head.

He'd always felt this familiar, from the beginning.

Nearer to him, the comfort of him eased her mind into thoughts of Mac in retrospect. As in extremis, when a life passes through the mind's eye, she could see details of all that Mac had been since her first meeting with him. She recognized the moods of his face, the kindness centered in his eyes, back, all the way back to when he opened his eyes in the thunder and in the rain.

Maggie gasped. In this moment of clarity, she remembered his open eyes. She had lifted her head as the lightning had rent the sky. In the brief brightness, she had seen his eyes, the sightless, dull, eyes, and from them the stare of a dead man. In her first instinct, she had known the body to be lifeless, had tried to throw herself off the corpse.

She took the living Mac's face between her hands and stared into his blue irises, the sea-colored eyes so full of vitality that she had seen in the next lightning flash. Words she had read in the Cincinnati Post one summer's day on a hot porch on a swing in Kentucky rose to the surface of her awareness. 'My darling Randolph has the rich brown eyes of his mother.'

"My God." She released Mac's should-be-dead face. She paced and then circled him from all sides.

"Am I a horse?"

She didn't believe him, but did, but didn't. It couldn't be, but it was. Joy bubbled up, overflowed. She threw herself at him. She laughed, cried, held him to her as close as two bodies could be pressed together.

He kissed her back. "It doesn't matter," he said. "I was a fool."

"I believe you." She kissed his nose. "I believe you." His mouth. "I believe you."

He captured her head and kissed her with slow, hot kisses that excited her. With his hands around her, holding her, and as his lips traveled down the length of her throat, he inched her toward the bed. The sheet dropped, and Maggie stepped on it, bit by bit, on her way backwards. Her nipples tingled against the hair on his chest. Even as she moved, she felt the place between her legs pulsing, opening for him, for the man she had been promised.

Back on the bed once more, she licked and tasted the salt on his skin and on his hard erection. She kissed his mouth as he rolled her under him. Maggie pushed up toward him as his tongue teased her breasts.

"Inside me, please," she said on a gasp. He spread her, and then his fingers stroked her thighs, the nub between her legs. He nearly brought her and then stopped as her head thrashed back and forth on the pillow. "Now," she called.

Divine pressure pushed into her as James MacArthur, with all the awakened passion of his nature. When Mac pushed inside her, she barely thought, *and he is mine... all of him* before the pulse of his hips brought them both to fulfillment.

Lying entwined with her, Mac said, "It doesn't mat—"

Maggie put a finger over his swollen lips, and then she kissed them and washed them with her tongue. "Damn it. I believe you," her lips said against his.

"You don't have to say—"

"I-believe-you." Maggie laughed as she rolled away from him. "Now the shoe is on the other foot. Are you ever going to believe me?" She rolled to her side, head on her arm, and circled his nipple with her finger.

Mac lightly slapped the curve of her bottom and pulled her to him.

She wiggled her hips against him. "You were right, you know. Even a small thorn causes festering."

Mac said in Gaelic, "You must live with a person to know a person. If you want to know me come and live with me."

"Now you're showing off."

"I shouldn't have said anything, Maggie. It was just in me that I couldn't bear you making love to McMillan."

Maggie laid her head on his shoulder. "I'm not. I will call you James instead of Mac. I like it better. Now for you to believe me, let me tell you—"

"You don't have to explain—"

"I will have you know the truth of it, and how it came to me. Lefcadio saw it first, but he has an awareness of people that is uncanny. I live too much within myself to see much beyond the outline of others, but just then, when it was all falling apart, I saw things...you, clearly. All of it. I saw them, the dead eyes of Randolph's body in the lightening. I... I...didn't... I wasn't aware of it until just now. The open eyes were dead eyes. They were dead, James, and his eyes were brown. I read that in a newspaper. Once that came to me, the rest flooded on through."

"Before...before you believed, you gave Garth away for Randolph?"

"No, never. I gave it away for the man sawing on the ropes that bound me to Garth. That man became more precious to me than anything else in the world." Maggie expected at least a kiss for her pronouncement, but Mac gazed at the ceiling. She love-bit his ear. It occurred to her that *he* still hadn't said he loved her. "You arrived, you saved me. You got me into your bed. Will you now move on to the next lass in distress? The present quest is finished, the Holy Grail in hand, back to the land from whence you came?" When he was still quiet, Maggie made to stand up.

Mac grabbed her and wrapped himself around her so they were neatly one. Even so, she was afraid, deep down. He might leave, if he didn't love her.

"I thought I was here to rescue a fair damsel—" he said to the face so close to his on the pillow.

"I beg your pardon. I saved your life—"

"I think, in fact, we were even—"

"And twice after—"

"I *thought* I was rescuing you. I thought I was here to see you to safety, but as it turns out you were doing most of the saving." He looked down at her face looking up at his. "You are a smug lass." Mac laughed and kissed her forehead. "Before I died in England long ago, the runes were thrown. The crow, the Morrigan, was my fate. She did have a hand in this. Moira has never been wrong."

Maggie stirred. The story was interesting, but was it a way to avoid saying the words she needed to hear?

"But...but the Morrigan did not speed me through time to save you, as I thought. I am here for you to rescue me. The Morrigan's prize for all my endeavors is you...the woman I have always wanted, that I will always love."

Maggie took in his blue eyes. It was going to be all right, just as her father had said. She had a man of courage and loyalty, a knight that would love her forever. They would build something together here.

"I never thought that I would ask this of any woman, that my member would work at all, much less as well as it does. Realize that I never, ever thought that I would ask it of the greatest love of my life. Would you do me the honor of becoming my wife?"

Maggie's whole body felt the smile at her face. "I will, provided you make love to me with that-which-works-so-exceptionally-well at least twice a day. I want to ride you on top this time."

Mac rolled over and Maggie with him. She slid his honed sword into her well-oiled sheath. On top of him, she rotated her hips. When he groaned, her power over him delighted her. Her hips circled some more and then stopped. Mac's eyes opened, and he narrowed them.

He's realizing that I am in control, she thought, while gloating back.

She arched her eyebrows. In a flash, Mac flipped her onto her back and reentered her. He moved deeply in and out, and then she couldn't hold his gaze any longer. The joy was swelling, growing, and she gave into it, let it overtake her. Her legs opened wider to let him press deeper, down into her soul. Wanting him within her at every stroke, she pushed up, and then up, and then up, until they both exploded in lightning ecstasy.

Mac dropped on her. She took his weight. She felt the light sheen of sweat between them. Their connection still pulsed.

"I love you," he said.

"I love you too, Mac." She said she'd call him James, but in that moment, she knew he would always be Mac to her. When he slipped out of her, she already wanted him back.

"Hungry?"

"Starving."

"Maybe this time we should eat."

Mac didn't move, and she didn't want to, not until the last glow of feeling.

"I also think we have a cow that needs milking." Mac rolled from the bed. He picked up the plate.

Maggie sat up. "Glad we got all that settled, so we can eat. God, I'm ravenous. Is this all there is?"

"I'll fry some eggs." Mac slipped on his pants. He winked at her and then bent over to kiss her cheek and then her neck. He shoved one arm into his sleeve when there was a knock at the door.

"Dear Lord, who could that, be?" Maggie gathered the sheet to her again.

More knocking, and louder.

"You don't suppose they've all had to return? Although I think Lefcadio would walk in." *Knock, knock, knock.*

Maggie returned Mac's look. She heard the door open and then footsteps. "My dress, quick," she whispered to Mac.

"*Randolph*! Randolph, are you here? It's your mother. I've come all this way. Are you here? Is she with you? They said that you live here —" Her tone lowered. "—in this God-awful place."

Maggie held her dress as a shield. "Go out there. Go! Before she comes in! You have to. No, button your shirt and stop her from coming back." Maggie pushed him. "Now!"

———

Mac looked forward and then back and then forward again. He took the fateful steps out the door. He swore that he could hear from behind him the Morrigan, along with his fiancée, laughing, the sound of a crow's cackle and a woman's sheer pleasure.

Maggie hadn't seen Garth in five years. She had to admit it had prospered under Guy's hard work, and William's. She wandered the stables and remembered that night when her world had broken apart and then came back together better than before. In the courtyard, she couldn't help but look up at her mother's bedroom window. Tomorrow she was going to visit the grave she'd never seen.

Today was all about the wedding. She and Molly were doing whatever needed to be done, cleaning, cooking, flower arranging. Maggie was excited for William. She hadn't known Melanie, except as a girl, but she came from a good family. Maggie would form an opinion tonight at dinner, whether the woman was good enough for him.

She had tucked into the suitcase a picture of the Johnson Homestead, now MacArthur Ranch spelled out high above the entrance gate. The original house had been kept as the bedroom. Maggie hadn't been able to bear to part with it. The house now had a parlor with a crystal chandelier and five other bedrooms, not entirely due to the ranching business, but because once the first child came,

Grandmother McMillan came for long stays, and she didn't like living rustic.

Mac was there now, with The Hog King and his wife at the McMillan family home. With him were Mac and Maggie's children, two boys and a girl. His "mother" had nearly knocked down their door that first visit in Grangeville when she'd come after Randolph. Then, after Mac's lengthy story, she had cried, and then she did what most people did when they knew, she believed what she wanted to believe and didn't think about the rest. She knew her son had needed to get away.

She liked this new young man who looked exactly like her son, and she wasn't going to let him go. She stayed that first time long enough to see them married and then returned for a year when Lucas arrived.

This was the first time Mac had returned to Cincinnati. The Hog King's wife told him she'd set the stage by telling everyone he'd been knocked over the head five years ago and couldn't remember anyone or anything. Mac had sighed and given in.

Upon returning to Cincinnati, Lefcadio had written a suitably vague story about the conversion and/or death of Randolph McMillian.

Maggie opened the door of her mother's bedroom. Guy had kept it exactly the same, down to full perfume bottles, even though the original scent must have evaporated years ago. Maggie opened one and smelled her mother, magnolias. The tree out the window was even larger. She smiled at it and at her mother's portrait. She let the atmosphere of the room envelop her.

One thing that was still an ache in Maggie's heart was Guy's words about this woman not being her mother. The past five years, the knowledge hurt the memories she had. In this room, though, surrounded by the items attached to those memories, Maggie knew that her mother had loved her, had loved her father. Grace had had a big enough heart for everyone.

Maggie placed a Nez Perce necklace on her mother's bedside table. She hoped she had proven herself to that Indian's expectations, and to her mother's. She closed the door as she left. She heard her husband and children arriving, the children pounding up the main staircase of Garth House. She wondered how the visit had gone in Cincinnati. In the hallway, she caught the boys as they ran up to her, boys who were the spitting image of a picture of James MacArthur in her father's favorite book. The Morrigan had seen to the details.

THE END

———

Don't miss out on your next favorite book!

Join the Satin Romance mailing list
www.satinromance.com/mail.html

THANK YOU FOR READING

Did you enjoy this book?

We invite you to leave a review at your favorite book site, such as Goodreads, Amazon, Barnes & Noble, etc.

DID YOU KNOW THAT LEAVING A REVIEW...

- Helps other readers find books they may enjoy.
- Gives you a chance to let your voice be heard.
- Gives authors recognition for their hard work.
- Doesn't have to be long. A sentence or two about why you liked the book will do.

FLIPPING RICH BASTARDS

Lady Eleanor Albright has left her, 'brothel-loving, girl-seducing, entitlement-inflated husband with whom she can't believe she ever had sex,' and is—again— living with her Irish mother, Lady Alannah Albright. With her daughter's marital woes unacceptable, Lady Alannah schemes to end Eleanor's "problems" one of which is her daughter's attachment to a man seven years her junior, a barrister, Lord Henry Faraday. To add insult to injury, Henry has included Eleanor, as an expert chemist (and purveyor of women's creams), into the investigation of the death of the sanctimonious Baron of Tweedmouth. "She'll be up to her elbows in the contents of his stomach."

————

Judged two first places, a third and fourth in The Mystery Writers of America Helen McCloy Scholarship for Mystery Writers

————

CHAPTER ONE

The baby doesn't understand English and the Devil knows Latin.
—Monsignor Roland Knox

Lady Eleanor Albright shifted on the skinny cross-end of a polished shooting stick that was folded open. A beautiful day in the Cotswold ruined. She turned her head from the shot red grouse that rained from a deep blue sky as if Maxim heavy machine guns were the weaponry of choice instead of breech-loading shotguns. Again, she adjusted her skinny behind on the damnable seat. Trying to ignore the pain from a blossoming bruise of the derriere, she pulled at her corset. To breathe some air in this heat!

Irritation picked at her last happy thought as downwind she heard her brothel-loving, twelve-year-old-girl-seducing, entitlement-inflated, estranged husband, with whom she couldn't believe she'd ever had sex, laugh. A desire to rip a gun from any nearby loader and shoot the man was making her nauseous. She hadn't really processed that Lord Flipping Albright would be here.

"Dear Lord, and I bloody insisted on coming."

She sat behind the long line of gentlemen standing in their crescent-shaped shooting-butts. Why the hunters call the place they perch themselves "shooting butts" she had yet to understand. Maybe because they are shooting, and because she could see their butts—some were larger than others.

Eleanor's blistered thoughts also wondered why only the birds were being killed and not the beaters. The beaters were the men out in front of the guns who wandered about and hit at the brush to get the birds to fly. Which was even more insane than attending the shoot. Granted, the beaters resemble the king, queen and jack in a deck of cards, and they are much brighter and much, much bigger than the birds. Still, with some of these shooters, regardless of the red tunics, size mattered.

Just in front of her, size seemed to matter to the host of the event. Lord Haversack. He was shooting—*bang, bang, bang, bang, bang*—and then swearing like a man possessed. He needed really big fowl.

Possessed, that's what I must have been when I decided to get out of a soft bed in the middle of the night to scramble through a barley field in a long skirt. She picked at her blouse. Her undergarments were sticking to her like a depilatory. She pulled at her corset again. Damn thing. It was like being in the clutches of a drowning man. She fanned down her neck. Who would have thought October to be so hot? She wanted to raise her arms and let perspiration dry in the wind.

Her heart ached for the birds. They seemed forsaken. Oh, dear girl, ridiculous "forsaken," maybe defenseless. Whatever they were, she felt one with them.

She poked cotton wool farther down her ears and tried not to flinch at the incessant sound of exploding powder across the golden stubble of the area. Her narrow shoulders seemed permanently lodged against her ears. She felt like an egg-bound hen. All this because she had left her husband and was back living with her mother. Mutiny. Damn it.

The dogs piled limp-headed birds at their masters' feet.

"Just keep remembering who you are not sitting next to at the lodge, your mother-in-law…your mother…and Lady Pillock," Eleanor said to herself, again.

She pictured Lady Pillock striding room to room, searching for any immobile person with two ears. Lady P had never been much of a philosopher even on her sober days. The woman was upheld most evenings by the stays in her full dresses. She always woke early, probably from her snoring. Lady Pillock was a hard female to avoid. She had just moved to Minister Lovell. She attended every party, was never ill, and her weight was in relation to how much she drank. Tons. The problem was, Eleanor did feel sorry for the woman and was an easy target for conversation.

Eleanor blew her nose and sighed. Her picture of Lady Pillock, wrapped in massive yards of seemingly armor-plated fabric, moving down the hallways like a river barge blasting a foghorn, made Eleanor smile, but it wasn't enough. The air smelled bloody and smoky. As Eleanor watched clouds of birds rise like a fog, only to fall back to the ground again dead, she wished for a dram of what kept Lady P afloat.

She glanced next to her at Lord Louis Montfire and at the flask of whiskey he had in his hand. The Baron of Tweedmouth's son had propped himself and his stick against a young tree, for support. A veteran of the carnage no doubt, he had brought refreshments.

She noticed that Louis looked pale and vague. He held his handkerchief to his nose and mouth. Now and then he wiped his eyes. A gentle soul, like a plump cherub, Louis Monfire tended to be a little soft around the edges. With birds dying everywhere, he was here, no doubt, in an endless attempt to please his father. What was it like to be the sweet son of a think-from-the-crotch type of father? Eleanor couldn't imagine. Louis just kept covering his eyes and wiping his nose and leaning against the skinny tree.

She patted his shoulder, and then her nose seized. She sneezed and sneezed. Damn, what a world. They were both miserable, but here they were. It was like an Irishman's raise, a foot forward, two back.

Louis handed her a fresh handkerchief. "I bring loads to these things."

Lavender scented, she noted. "You here for your father?"

"Absolutely, and I believe it is more peaceful here than at home. Here, I have the beautiful countryside. There, I have a house that's a stage for a cast of bad actors. King Lear and his wife. You?"

"I have Lady Pillock. I'm too kind to shake her, and she knows it. Talk about a performer."

He smiled—a little.

It was the most she had gotten out of him all morning. He was usually such fun. Talking, talking, talking like a female, a good-natured one. He was a hugger and a hand-patter, and his hazel eyes always shone in instant sympathy. He was everyone's best friend. Today, though, he seemed leaky, like something had let the air out of his soft body.

His pallor worried her. She always had concerns for Louis.

Eleanor glanced at her still-legal husband. She realized Louis had a million more reasons to do in his father. She placed her hand on Louis's shoulder again. With the other hand, she dashed a tear from a corner of her eye. "You hate this sort of thing." Eleanor waved out to the dying birds.

"I used to shoot, you know. I'd just shoot into the air, pretending, until I hit one. Now I watch. In a few more years maybe I can just show up for the wine at the luncheon."

"How is your Father anyway?"

"Noisy."

"The asthma not any better?" Or any worse, she thought to herself.

"I don't ask." He turned toward her. "Why are you here?"

"I couldn't listen to one ounce more advice on being a good wife. He isn't a good husband. I needed some air." As the man she had promised to love and obey waited for more birds, she could hear him laugh.

"He doesn't have a care in the world. Why do I feel so guilty, like I could have done more...or less? I'm so angry at the world that I'm snapping at everyone. It's safer for them all if I'm here. I forgot he'd be here, and now this." She waved her arm at the scene again. "They kill so many. It's like they feel entitled to, to everything. I should have brought seed or something to feed the ones who live."

Louis patted the back of her hand as she gazed again at the exponentially increasing number of dead birds. She tossed Louis a we're-in-hell look, and then averted her eyes to the plump hills. Lines of beech trees quilted the fields in a patchwork. Red grouse had escaped to the branches. Probably the ones Haversack had been shooting at. Amen.

The beaters in their colorful, medieval tunics flushed another round of panting birds. The gracious host once again shot like a madman. His loader sweated at his side. There was a yell from the field, and then more yelling. Eleanor stood, letting her shooting stick fall to earth. She shaded her eyes. The butts were emptying; all the gentlemen had rushed out, all but the maniac shooter. At least Haversack had gone quiet. Her sanity felt better already.

With Louis beside her, Eleanor hurried forward. A beater was yelling. Someone was down, a beater in a purple tunic. She thought she knew the fair hair. Early that morning, he'd helped her over a ditch.

She walked faster, concentrating on missing any ankle-turning holes in the ground. Anger pushed her steps. Stupid. No one should walk in front of half of these lords especially with said lords' guns loaded and half-cocked.

Louis got to the man first.

"Just a grazing," he called out. "He's breathing."

Just a grazing, as in what a great shot to have just missed?

At the information, the lords about-faced in one movement, except Louis who took out his flask and another of his endless supply of handkerchiefs. He wet the cloth and pressed it against the man's blonde hair. Patting either side of the beater's jaw with the flat of his hand, Louis called, "Hello...hello?" Louis glanced up and down the body for another possible pooling of blood.

Eleanor knelt just as the beater's eyes opened.

"Good man," Louis said as he helped the man sit up, and then he gave him a drink from his flask.

Eleanor had been wondering about the flask. Louis never drank hard alcohol and didn't like beer because it bloated him, but he had been sipping from the flask all morning.

Louis stayed with the man. "Scotch is just the thing," he said as he offered what was left in his flask to the beater.

"Jesus," the man kept saying as he scrutinized the field of shooters.

Louis and Eleanor helped the beater stand and walked with him to a wagon. He had been kind to her, and, well she stuffed some silver into the man's hand.

Louis left the man in the charge of the other beaters. As Eleanor ambled away with Louis, she said to him, "I'm glad he is well. How do you get people to be beaters? It seems so dangerous."

"It's something men do."

Eleanor attempted a deep breath. "I've been telling myself that a little fresh air is good for me. All this fresh air has done is clog up my sinuses."

"We should trade," Louis said. "I need your mother to say, 'Stay at the lodge, darling, and let's have a good chat,' and you need my father to say, 'Go out and make your mark.'"

She smiled at his observation. "Maybe it's more interesting if you shoot? Not so damn many, but one for dinner."

"It's decent, until you hit something."

Eleanor used her finger and thumb to make the shape of a gun, and then she aimed it at the backside of her husband. "Bam, bam." She blew pretend smoke from the end of her finger. "See, that could be fun, and I wouldn't mind hitting him." She continued to stare at him. "Not at all."

Louis laughed and then coughed and coughed.

She laughed and then sneezed.

"You are angry." He handed her a fistful of handkerchiefs.

"Livid with an added drop or more of bitters." She took the proffered linens.

"It's good to have you and your finger here." He laughed again. Now he was sounding more like himself. She also felt her mind lighten. Maybe this had been a good idea.

Louis and Eleanor ambled toward the rest of the shooters who were slapping each other on their backs and drinking whiskey from their silver flasks. The gentleman hunters were talking of traveling out of the area to the next shoot, and of joining King Edward at Sandringham. They talked about Sandringham, and how three hundred thousand pounds had been spent on it, thereby making it into a first class venue. The King had been talking of introducing Virginia quail and red grouse.

"Shooting may be the opposite of a hen party, but both have plenty of bloodshed," she said to Louis as he continued to walk beside her. "Is it necessary, do you think, that they all shoot like maniacs?"

"According to the Great Lord Ripton, 'Aim high, keep the gun moving, never check.' At least that's the advice I've been given"

She shook her head. "No wonder Haversack is out of control."

"He's not the only one. He's just the most obvious. He shoots his foot every time; the others can at least miss their feet. There are some who are very good shots."

"Three thousand five hundred and eighty," a man called from the line of dead birds.

"Yes, I suppose there must be," she said.

Eleanor left Louis to the men and walked to the luncheon tents. She thought of the very large glass of wine she was going to drink. To toast the health of the beater, and to Louis—a kind, suffering man. She couldn't celebrate all that in just one glass.

Louis had joined the backslapping of the men. He seemed to enjoy that part. The other men liked him like they liked their favorite dogs. Better than their wives.

Eleanor wandered to the Windrush Creek to freshen a bit. She brushed hard at the straw imbedded in the fabric of her new skirt. The yellowed bits annoyed her with their tenacity. The great outdoors she thought with irritation, and then she dipped Louis's handkerchief into the stream and dabbed at her neck and face.

She always left the house looking impeccable; somehow, she never returned that way. Louis on the other hand was always turned out. His thinning black hair always in place, his long hands always manicured. She must get some pointers.

The water felt good on her neck. Louis's smell of lavender was soothing. The third-day-of-October's bright sun had probably reddened her cheeks. Then, no one would notice if she had three large glasses of wine. Her Irish ancestors were right. Drink helped. Time to forget her husband and his fetishes; forget nearly dead beaters, and dead birds, and smoke, and blood.

As she was sweeping escaped locks of reddish-brown hair back into pins, she heard Lady Pillock's booming voice. Oh God, the women were arriving—like beautiful, feathered parrots disgorging from their opened cages. The sound was increasing.

Women are noisy.

The fish were rising. She wished she had her pole. Now that's a sport. It did involve dead fish though. Maybe she could learn to shoot. A brace of birds, not a mob of the things. Not enough to wipe out the species for all eternity.

With that thought, Eleanor strolled through the servants who moved about the picnic area like insects while they finished unpacking the luncheon and arranging the tables in the tent with linen and silver. She bribed three full champagne glasses from the busy butler with a winning smile and felt good that she had done it. The first of the wine was going to Louis who still looked ghastly. If Louis was coming down with something, he should be in bed.

"Three? You are a darling," he said. He took two, one for himself and one for Lord Charles Wallingford, and then kissed her on the cheek. She rolled her eyes. Of course she should have anticipated Charles would be with him. His fondness for Charles was legendary. She paused to take her own deep drink, one meant to wet the beater's head, and then she looked for another waiter. Stocked, again with two glasses, she walked toward the long line of carriages, and wondered who had injured the beater. As Louis had said, most of the shooters could at least manage to miss their extremities. Still, she could think of at least one who would be challenged to even hit the slow moving Pillock woman, and she was an ample target. With some shooters, the field was dangerous for everyone but the birds.

ABOUT THE AUTHOR

Julie Murphy has a B.A. in Communications from the University of Idaho and a M.A in Writing Popular Fiction from Seton Hill University.

After college, she worked in Nagasaki, Japan for two years for Kwassui Tandai, a women's high school and junior college. She taught English as a foreign language, learned about the H-bomb, the Japanese, and about sushi. She met her husband there, an Irish national and at the time a sea-going engineer with British Petroleum.

After her marriage, she lived in Ireland and went to sea with him on BP oil tankers. Her first four-month voyage started in Rotterdam, crossed the equator, through the Panama Canal to Australia.

After returning to America, she substitute taught, completed a Certificate of Completion in short story writing with the Long-RidgeWritersGroup, and raised three daughters.

Her thesis, *Flipping Rich Bastards, an Eleanor Albright Mystery* received a First, Third, and Fourth from the five judges associated with the Helen McCloy Mystery Writers of America Scholarship for Mystery Writing. She also has a YA dystopian published, *As If Something Happened*.

In writing *Western Knight,* she has mined her background of having lived in and around England, Ireland, Cincinnati, and Idaho for the last twenty years.

Connect with Julie:

Juliegmurphy@gmail.com
juliegmurphy.wpcomstaging.com

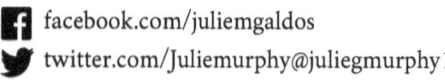 facebook.com/juliemgaldos
twitter.com/Juliemurphy@juliegmurphy1